MW00628925

Altar of the Cross

Cece Whittaker

Unam sanctam catholicam.
https://www.cecewhittakerstories.com

Another Great Cover Design by
Jennifer Givner, AcapellaBookCoverDesign.com

Written and Printed in the United States.
U.S. Library of Congress

ISBN: 978-0-9767921-1-6
Christus Vincit.

A Prayer for Priests

O Jesus, Eternal Priest, keep Thy priests within the shelter of Thy Sacred Heart, where none may touch them.

Keep unstained their anointed hands, which daily touch Thy Sacred Body.
Keep unsullied their lips, daily purpled with Thy Precious Blood.

Keep pure and unworldly their hearts, seal with the sublime mark of the priesthood.
Let Thy Holy Love surround them from the world's contagion.

Bless their labors with abundant fruit, and may the souls to whom they minister be their joy and consolation here and their everlasting crown hereafter.

Mary, Queen of Clergy, pray for us: obtain for us numerous and holy priests. Amen.

Dedication

To all the Holy Souls
who seek our salvation,
and
Praise to the Divine Heart
that wrought our salvation;
to It be Glory & Honor
forever.

Chapter One

Just inside the rear entrance to Philadelphia's Sacred Heart Roman Catholic Church, mercifully shielded from the icy wind that had just shoved them through the door with greater urgency than they expected, huddled Nunzio, Carlo, Frankie, and Pete, four of the church's most dedicated altar boys. The boiler had kicked on only minutes before their arrival, and it was churning up heat rapidly through the radiators situated along the walls. That winter of 1957, the brand-new heating system was the pride of the neighborhood, purchased with funds collected from the proceeds of countless bake sales and bingos and installed by two of the church's own parishioners.

Nunzio DiAngelis, eight years old and the oldest of the four by two months, dropped his coat onto the bench and bent down to tie his shoe. "I bet it's zero degrees out there," he said, trying to hold his ungloved hands close to the radiator as he worked.

"It can't be zero or it would be snowing," said Frankie Ciacci, the practical thinker of the group.

"It could snow if it was 32," Carlo diFrancisco pointed out, following Nunzio's example and trying to find a direct heat source. He wore navy blue gloves crocheted by his mother Viviana, that bore his name written in laundry marker on a tag sewn inside.

"Never gonna snow," said Pete Costello, blowing on his bare hands. "My pop says it never snows in the city."

"It snowed last year," corrected Carlo.

Pete stared at him. "You always got the answers, don't you?"

Carlo stared back. "Yep," he said.

"You guys ain't getting the doughnuts after Mass if they catch you fighting," Nunzio pointed out.

"I ain't fightin'," Pete said. "Just sayin' Carlo always gotta be right."

"Well," said Frankie, "it did snow last year. And we were here, in the city. Know what I mean?"

Nunzio smiled with his back to Pete. Of course Pete was right. Carlo did insist on having the correct information, but nobody really minded. Except maybe Pete.

On that frigid day in November of '57, they were there to serve 6:30am Mass for Father Kelly or Monsignor French, they never knew which priest would celebrate that day until they arrived. Nunzio didn't care which priest they had. Both had advantages. With Father Kelly, there was always an extra doughnut after Mass to divide up. The other boys didn't know why, but Nunzio did. A few months earlier, when the others were still changing out of their cassocks, Nunzio had looked for a hanger to hang his surplice on. Seeing none on the usual hooks, he looked in the next room where the priests were placing the doughnuts on a plate for the boys.

"You're sacrificing again, I see, Father Kelly," Monsignor said. "You put me to shame!"

Father Kelly shook his head. "These boys will probably get nothing more than this for their breakfast," he said. "And I've heard them. They're good, they divide the fifth one evenly between them. Let them enjoy it."

Nunzio had backed out of the room unseen, a funny feeling in his chest, somewhere between the feeling of the playground swings going way up high, and the hollow pangs of hunger. He had leaned against the wall, holding his surplice in his hand up to his chest, imagining how it would feel if he were asked to give up his fresh-from-the-bakery jelly and powdered sugar doughnut.

Before he made a move, the thin, saintly Father Kelly had walked by carrying the plate of goodies, tapping him on the shoulder, smiling. "Look what I've got!" he said in a jolly, rollicking manner. Nunzio followed behind, contemplating the holy priest's secret sacrifice, touched by the generosity yet conflicted by the urge to do the same.

Monsignor French, on the other hand, always had stories to tell about his life. True, sometimes the boys had heard one or two of them before, but that didn't bother them as the tales always seemed different enough from the previous telling to be very entertaining still. Nunzio, and probably Carlo, too, for that matter, knew that they couldn't possibly be true. For one thing, you can't go from being a pirate to a Monsignor. Even a first grader would know that. At least he didn't *think* you could. But the stories always seemed to lead Monsignor right to the door "of the blessed seminary" as he called it. Nunzio wondered about that, too, but not very much.

The older and moderately rounder Monsignor had spent years with men overseas during the wars, and he knew the power of pain inside a young man's head. He knew how it could lead to greater pain and a confusion between the recognition of good and evil. Many years before becoming Pastor of Sacred Heart Church, he had accepted his mission to keep a watchful eye on the young and vulnerable.

The city of Philadelphia was welcoming and buzzing with life, but he knew, just as Father Kelly had recognized, that the children there were not all well-fed and clothed, and some sadly, were not even particularly welcome in their own homes. In his ministry to the young fellows who assisted in his church, he was at least able to offer the humblest departure of a fresh doughnut every morning that they served at Mass and an offering from his never-ending supply of adventure stories.

Nunzio left his reminiscing behind and joined the other three boys as they retrieved the candles from their stands in the sanctuary and formed up at the back of the church, standing in a well-ordered cluster. There they were joined by Father Kelly, and Pete smiled and elbowed Frankie. Extra doughnuts today.

The church was still filling up, and the Sisters in their rich brown habits were gently and soundlessly entering the pews, genuflecting so lightly, Nunzio imagined them to be floating just slightly above the shiny marble floor. There were twelve attending and they filled two pews, one behind the other. Once they were settled, one of them popped back up to help a mother who was struggling to get her baby carriage out of the aisle.

Nunzio thought of his brother Louie at home, getting ready for school. His older brother did not serve at Sacred Heart and never had. He couldn't imagine not serving at Mass himself. On that day, he was to carry the incense and he was very good at it. Father Kelly often gave that job to him. Even before they processed from the back of the church, its perfume began to rise in hazy wisps, filling the church with its scent.

Once the last of the straggling parishioners were seated, Father Kelly nodded at the organist to begin. The deep, rich blends of sound traveling through the pipes up on the walls encircled the House of God with richly flowing prayer in motion as the little procession moved forward toward the sanctuary.

Nunzio, as he was at every Mass, was completely transported.

After Mass, Frankie and Pete went one way, and Carlo and Nunzio went the other.

"I'm supposed to stop for milk," Carlo said. "You wanna wait?"

"Sure, I'm in no rush," Nunzio said.

As Carlo went in for the milk at the corner store, Nunzio glanced up surprised to see the wagon that the old Clydesdale pulled already set up for the holidays.

"Look at that," he said as Carlo came out of the store. "Setting up for chestnuts already."

"It's Thanksgiving in a week," Carlo said.

"Really?"

Carlo laughed. "Yeah. You sleepin' through the month?"

Nunzio and Carlo had been friends for a long time, and Carlo's answer to everything Nunzio didn't know had to do with sleeping. "you sleepin' in class?" or "you spend your life sleepin'?" But Nunzio didn't mind. In Carlo, he had his own neighborhood reporter, who seemed to always know whatever was going on, or even what was *going to* go on.

So Thanksgiving was coming up. Wow. "I wonder if we're going to Grandma's or if she's coming over," Nunzio said.

"They're coming over at my house," Carlo said.

"They always come over at your house," Nunzio said.

"I wish *you* could," Carlo said thoughtfully.

"Hey, *we* do Thanksgiving at my house."

"I know, but it would be fun if we did it at the same house."

"I don't think it works that way," Nunzio said.

"They oughta have a Thanksgiving for kids, and a Thanksgiving for adults. That way everybody would have a good time," Carlo said.

"Depends on whose coming. Like Pete and Frankie and us, but not Louie."

"No, not your brother. He's not a kid anyway."

"He's not an adult."

"Well he acts like one."

"Yeah, you're right. He's in eighth grade but he acts like he's a grownup."

"Well, he ain't coming to the kid Thanksgiving, that's for sure," Carlo proclaimed.

"Hey Carlo, ain't nobody coming to the kid Thanksgiving!" Nunzio laughed.

They had reached their corner where a pretty girl wearing very red lipstick stood waiting for the bus. "Hi Nunzio!" she called sweetly. "Say hello to Louie for me!"

Nunzio rolled his eyes and shook his head at Carlo who laughed out loud.

"See ya at school, Nunz," he said.

"See ya, Carlo."

When Nunzio reached the house, he had to rush into his bedroom to get his school things and then to the kitchen to pack his lunch.

"Don't make a mess. I just cleaned up in there," his mother called from the hall.

Louie was going out the door, and Mrs. DiAngelis was checking his backpack.

"Leave it alone, ma," Louie said. "I got everything."

"Do you have your lunch money? I don't want you going to school all day without lunch."

"I got it, I got it. See ya," he said and slammed past her as she reached out for a kiss.

She watched him walk past the three rowhomes and turn the corner. What a handsome kid, she thought, and never a problem. Not like Nunzio in there, whose battery never seemed to run down. "Don't make a mess in there!" she yelled again.

Nunzio wrapped up his sandwich in wax paper and into the old lunch pail Louie had used for years. "Can I take an apple?" he called.

"Well," his mother said. "How many do we have?"

"Four."

"All right."

Nunzio's mother padded down the hallway, still wearing her bedroom slippers and stood in the kitchen doorway, watching Nunzio pack his lunch. "Wipe the counter, Nunzio," she instructed, taking a drag on her cigarette.

"Where's Pop?" Nunzio asked as he re-wiped the already spotless counter.

"At the shop," Mrs. DiAngelis answered impatiently. "Where he always is this time of day. Why, are you taking a survey?"

Nunzio smiled. "No," he said. "Okay, bye Mom." He gave her a kiss on the cheek. He was just slightly taller than her, at five foot three inches, a fact which for some reason made him happy.

"All right, all right," she said as he rushed down the hall and out the door.

At the corner, where Nunzio's father, Nick DiAngelis, shared a four-chair barber shop with his buddy Morris Schultz, Nunzio paused and peered in through the thick glass window. He could see his father, a thin, quiet man with thick dark hair combed straight back, cleaning the combs, and laying them on a towel next to the sink. Nunzio tapped on the window and Nick turned, waved and smiled.

Just then, Mr. Schultz's car drove up, pulled into the space in front of the shop, and puffed and shuddered and let out a final lengthy hiss before coming to a stop. "Hi Mr. Schultz!" Nunzio called, stepping away from the window and moving down the block.

"You're a good kid, Nunz!" the man called behind him.

Just before reaching the Sacred Heart grade school, Nunzio caught sight of Louie behind a tree huddled up with the girl he'd seen earlier at the bus stop. They were hugging and kissing like they thought they were in the movies.

It's freezing cold out here, Nunzio thought, and there they are standing around necking. Brother!

"Nunzio, come on! We're gonna be late!" Carlo called from the open door to the school. Nunzio could see the telltale brown veils of the habits their teaching Sisters wore growing closer through the glass of the wide windows. Tardiness was not a welcome trait, even in an altar boy who had served Mass that morning. He raced toward the door. "I'm comin'!" he cried.

Chapter Two

All in all, Nunzio couldn't complain, he thought. He had aced his spelling test, got a 96 on the math test and instead of saying "needs a little improvement" when he read out loud that day, Sister had said, "Sounds very good." He didn't like to compare himself to Carlo, who was naturally smart, but he didn't mind doing the same where Frankie and Pete were concerned. Frankie was good with figures but spelling? Nunzio knew first graders who could do better. He was at a disadvantage though, Nunzio had to admit. His parents didn't speak English at home. Maybe if they did, they could help him out a little, Nunzio thought. And Pete, well, he was still trying to figure things out, as his pop would say.

Nunzio had long dreamed of becoming a general in the United States Army. Fueled by his admiration of the World War II Generals in Europe and the South Pacific, his plans included getting high marks throughout grade school, and then ROTC in high school. He wondered if the other guys would join up. He wondered how smart you had to be to make General.

He walked home alone that day because Carlo's parents were taking him to get new shoes. It was only a few blocks between the school and his home, but he took his time. He loved the city, and truth be told, being on his own, he had some time to listen to what he had come to believe was the voice of his Guardian Angel. On good days, he felt his angel's praise, not so much in words; but more like a warm, protected kind of feeling. Those days where he hadn't done his best, or even gave in to self-pity or anger, he was sure his celestial companion was frowning at him.

On that day, he gazed happily ahead. He went through things in his mind. Sure, he could have gotten jealous about Carlo's new shoes, or even Carlo's mother. Carlo's mother loved everyone, but she especially loved Carlo. Nunzio had seen plenty of mothers at the school or on Sundays at Mass. They were pretty, wore nice jewelry, and nice to everyone in sight. But then he'd see those same women swap their smiles for scowls just as soon as they got out of sight, smacking one kid and yelling at another. Those women's smiles were just for show, Nunzio had learned, but Carlo's mother's was genuine. And she smiled all the time! He wondered if that little thing could be the difference between Carlo's family and all the other kids' folks. Carlo never really needed stuff, not the way Nunzio, Frankie and Pete did.

Take today, he told his angel, kicking a stone with his scuffed hand-me-down oxfords, how 'bout him going to get new shoes when the old ones were still fine and wearable? What is he going to do with two pairs of shoes? You can only wear one at a time. Just then, he was distracted by a crow fluttering down onto the sidewalk in front of him, the bird's large body seeming to bounce while his feet stayed on the ground. "Them birds got good shocks," Frankie would say, who considered himself knowledgeable in the automotive area. "See how they make that soft landing? It's easy on the body."

Studying the bird's seemingly disapproving eyes, Nunzio was sure that these creatures talked to each other in the manner that his mother and the neighbor ladies often did, calling across the way from one upper window to another. "You got any starch? I'm out!" or "Come on over for coffee, I just made a pot!" He figured the birds probably said stuff like, "Hey, that's my worm, go get your own," or "Where's your old man? I haven't seen him in a while."

He wanted to laugh at the idea, but the thought had brought a kind of internal struggle of Nunzio's to the surface. He had heard those comments coming from his mother aimed at their neighbor. It had turned out that after six years of marriage, the husband had simply gone away. He hadn't taken his wife or their children. He just left. Nobody knew where. Or if they did, they didn't say. But before all of that happened, Nunzio and Louie would lean against the window in the front room and hear some wild fights going on in the house across the street. Their concern over that situation was just about the only thing the two brothers had in common.

"I hope it ain't catching," Louie had said, retreating from the angry voices.

"Yeah," Nunzio had agreed, following his brother.

One time, Louie had stayed to get the full story. Later, he told Nunzio that the woman had accused the man of running around with someone, and the man had said "I gotta run around with somebody if I wanna get anything!" Louie had laughed when he made his report, but after he left, Nunzio sat wondering what it meant.

What made Nunzio uneasy was the fact that he had caught an argument between his own parents the previous week. It hadn't been violent or even particularly loud, but his father seemed to be accusing his mother of something. And she was kind of laughing and only partly denying it. His ordinarily mild and quiet father had slammed something down on the kitchen counter. Nunzio thought it might have been his fist. But then, the argument had dissipated, and his pop had simply gone out to get the newspaper.

Nunzio's thoughts brightened as he passed the house where two old widowers lived. That particular house was interesting not because of its inhabitants, who were certainly remarkable themselves, but because in as long as he could remember, the two old men had been working on creating a garage. In the modern houses, Nunzio knew that there were those baffling places to put a car, but in the city, it was pretty rare. In fact, having a car itself was pretty rare. You had to own one of those mansions up on Stables Creek to have a garage, and not even all of them had one, according to Frankie. There was barely enough room for the people where Nunzio lived. But those two old fellows, both having lost their wives years before, had decided to share a house and the perpetual project of building a garage into their rowhome.

"Hello, Mr. Finn," Nunzio called out. The old man was sitting on a wooden stool that had been painted red, his coat pulled snugly around him, a pipe in his mouth and a cup of coffee in his hand. The vinyl-backed kitchen chair next to him was empty.

"Hello, young Nunzio!" called Finn in his thin, raspy voice, followed by a couple of short hollow coughs. "A little chilly out today, huh?"

"Yes, sir," said Nunzio. He looked at the men's building project as he passed by. No matter how hard he tried, he could not find anything changed since the last time he'd seen it. It reminded him of the workbook pages they sometimes had in earlier grades where their task was to find the differences between the two pictures. He had always exercised method in those cases, and if there had been any differences, he had identified them. But the garage project, according to his best analysis, was still pretty much the same rugged hole in the wall it had been during all the previous months.

When Nunzio reached his block, he turned the corner and looked in the window of his pop's barber shop. Mr. Schultz was cutting a man's hair who hardly had any to begin with. Nick giggled unintentionally. His pop waved to him from the sink, wagging a finger at him jokingly for giggling at the bald haircut. Nunzio waved back and smiled.

That night they had franks and beans, one of Nunzio's favorites. His mother was pretty good with the traditional Italian dishes, but when it came to American food, "*Medigán*" as they called it, she was lost. She could manage the business of cooking up the franks, though, and when Nunzio got his portion of baked beans, he added the catsup and mustard that Pete talked about once, and a little sugar on the sly, and they were delicious.

"I see you're making a mess of my cookin' again," his mother commented.

"I'm going to eat it all, though," Nunzio said.

"That's disgusting," said Louie.

"Leave the kid alone, Louie," said Nick. "He knows how he likes it. If your mother can't fix it that way, he can do it himself."

"I *can* fix it that way," Mrs. DiAngelis argued, "but I don't find it appealing."

"Yeah, well *he* does, all right?" said Nick, showing rare outward discord.

The discussion was beginning to make Nunzio very nervous. Even Louie backed off. For a moment, it even seemed as if Mrs. DiAngelis was about to launch into an argument. But instead she said nothing, and shook her head, deciding it wasn't worth the effort. In the meantime, Nunzio had finished off his baked beans.

"Have some more if you like," Nick said, motioning to the serving bowl. "There's plenty."

"Thanks, Pop," said Nunzio with a smile.

His mother murmured an expletive, but he knew the tension was over.

Later that night, after he'd finished his homework, and put away his Army men, he opened his bedroom door to the sound of arguing. It was louder than it had been before, and his father's voice sounded pained, the way he remembered Pete's voice sounding when he thought their family was moving. Nunzio didn't want to hear, but he wanted to know what was going on. Again he felt that dichotomy of hope and fear tangling together in his chest.

Louie poked his head out the door. "Again?" he said, feigning impatience.

"You heard it last night?" Nunzio asked.

"Who didn't in the whole neighborhood?" he asked sarcastically. Nunzio was quite certain no one outside the house had heard his parents arguing that night. But tonight, that's a different story, he feared.

"You don't have to deny it," Nick said forcefully. "There's no reason to bother denying it."

"All right, I won't!" Nunzio's mother said. "I won't deny nothin'! Now what are ya gonna do?"

"Is this what you want?" Nick continued. "You wanna tear us apart, tear the family apart?"

"What family! We're barely scraping by on what you make at that shop. We've got nothin' to eat—"

Well that wasn't true, Nunzio knew. He'd just had his favorite food. His mother must have forgotten.

"I can't make any money if you're gonna keep spending it on dresses and makeup and beauty parlors!" Nick's voice went low. "Why don't you get *him* to pay for that stuff if he's got so much?" he growled.

"You say that to his face, Nick DiAngelis!" his mother screamed. "Go ahead! I dare ya!"

"You go ahead and leave if you want to, go shack up with him, see how many of your friends you hold onto from this neighborhood!" Nick yelled.

Louie slapped his forehead. "Well I *know* they all heard that!" he said.

"What are they talking about?" Nunzio said. "Who is pop talking about?"

"Ma's gangster. You know, the guy who drops her off—oh well, you wouldn't know. You're still at school."

"*Gangster?* What? What gangster? You mean like Bobby the Skunk and those guys?"

"Yeah, but he ain't one of them. He's a *boss*, you know, their capo."

Nunzio sank down against the wall. "Ma's cheatin' on pop? With a mob boss?"

"Yeah," Louie said, matter-of-factly, as if he were saying he'd just taken out the trash. "And he's got some bucks, too."

Nunzio stared at Louie. If the guy was a mob boss, of *course* he had some bucks. At that brutally painful moment, as he stood barely supporting his own weight in his bedroom in their cozy rowhome in South Philadelphia, the light inside his heart flickered on. One brief flash revealing the certainty of too many long-tortured wonderings plastered him against the wall of reality, showing all of the dirt and grit, all the truth that Nunzio's eight-year-old heart had determined never to see. Number one, his brother was an idiot, number two, his mother was a floozy, and number three, their family was not going to survive. Deep inside, he had felt the fear, the clamoring for light that the dark forces would always crave, seeking to convert, to make more dark. But he had kept it down, weighted down by the hope, trying to outrun the eventuality.

At that moment, he knew he had lost. His breath came hard as he slammed the door to his bedroom and crushed himself against the wall, wanting to destroy the feeling welling in his chest, calling for tears and release of his impossible heartache. But eight years old is too young to command the forces of evil, and tears shot from his eyes onto his chin and down his shirt like defense rounds, protecting against the onslaught of the enemy.

It was a short-lived battle. Someone was coming up the stairs. The yelling downstairs must have stopped, interrupted by his own emotional display, but now he would have to answer for his behavior. He hoped it wasn't his mother. He couldn't face her, look at her, see her the same way.

The door opened. "Son?" It was Nick.

Nunzio lowered his head, trying to play down his emotional state. "Yeah, Pop?"

"Nunz, I'm sorry you had to hear that. Your mother and I were just discussing a problem."

"That's okay, Pop."

"I don't want you to worry about it."

"Okay."

"Look," Nick said gently, "it ain't your mess. It's your mother's and mine. I know you're a smart kid. But don't get any ideas this has to do with you. It's got nothin' to do with you, all right?" Nick lowered his head so he could look into his son's eyes. "All right?" he repeated.

"Yeah, Pop." Nunzio reached out his hand, wanting to be more grown up than he was.

Nick instantly grabbed his son and kissed him on his tear-stained cheek. "It ain't got nothin' to do with you. You just keep bein' a good kid, okay? Everything'll be all right. Don't worry."

The house was quiet after that. Maybe Mrs. DiAngelis was thinking better of her brash behavior and decided to think things over, because there was no further arguing that night. After an hour or so, Nunzio noticed that the next-door neighbor's window, having been open a few inches, was quietly closed. He sighed, knowing that if that woman had caught it all, the story would be fully circulated throughout the neighborhood before he even got to church the next day.

The facts had come to light, Nunzio thought, but were they really true? If Pop said everything would be all right, maybe it would be. Maybe they were just, what did Pete call it? Blowing off steam. Topping off the radiator, as Frankie called it.

Nunzio got dressed for bed, brushed his teeth, and knelt down by his bed to say his Act of Contrition. He wondered if Louie ever said it anymore. That got him wondering if his mother ever did. If she did what she said she did, she would have to go to Confession, he thought. He wondered if that was why she always said she and Louie would go to a different Mass than he and his father. Maybe neither one went to Communion.

But his brain was way too tired to try to unravel any additional mysteries, and after his prayers, he got into his bed, contemplating the morning to come and Father Kelly's fresh bakery doughnuts.

Chapter Three

Next morning, it was as if nothing that had gone on the night before had really happened. The great tidal wave of emotion Nunzio had felt only eight hours before seemed to have rolled through the house and out the front door. Louie was the same miserable grouch, Nick had left for work early, and Nunzio's mother was smoking and painting her fingernails.

Grabbing his coat, Nunzio shot out the door, spotting Carlo down the walk. Carlo saw him and the race was on, both running as fast as they could to the corner where they met up each morning before Mass.

Nunzio had learned that raising his feet just a little higher would increase the reach of each stride and increase his speed. But Carlo was a little faster, so even without Nunzio's secret method, he would come close to the same speed. It was another ice-cold morning, and the wind bit against their young faces, but neither one felt it. It was a short race that neither boy won; they reached their corner at the exact same time.

"Hey, them new shoes are sharp!" Nunzio said, nodding and catching his breath. "I bet they cost a few bucks."

"I don't know," Carlo puffed. "Pop says you gotta watch out for your feet. I don't know what that means."

Nunzio laughed. "He's a neat guy, your pop."

"Yeah," Carlo said noncommittally. But Nunzio knew he loved his dad, same as Nunzio loved his own.

By that time, they had come to Nick and Mr. Schultz's shop.

"Hey look," Carlo said, "you're dad's cutting Bobby the Skunk!"

"That ain't Bobby the Skunk, that's Big Rio. They look a lot alike."

"Who's Big Rio?"

"Just another one of them guys, you know."

"Who's he with?"

"Jeeze, Carlo! You don't ask that!"

Carlo looked embarrassed. "Sorry," he said, looking away.

"It ain't nothin' to me, Carlo. But I'm just sayin', you can't ask that."

"Okay," Carlo said brightening.

"Not that it matters, but they're both with the Genovese."

Carlo whistled. "No kidding!"

"Yeah, but you didn't hear it from me."

"Who me? I don't know nothin'!" Carlo said, mimicking his father.

They both laughed.

Through the window of his barber shop Nick saw his younger son passing by, carefree in conversation with his buddy. He studied the pair as they headed up the block to the church. It was a blessing how the young could throw things off, he thought. He probably doesn't even remember what happened last night.

Just then Schultz interrupted his thoughts with a request for a receipt book. "He's a good-looking kid, Nick," Schultz said. "Studies hard, too."

"He's an altar boy, you know," Nick said, lighting a cigarette. "Did I tell you that? He serves Mass every morning."

"Yeah, I think you told me," Schultz said. "About a thousand times."

Nick snickered as he took a drag and turned to watch the boys as they continued down the block. I wish there was a way to make things easier on him, he thought. Louie don't care about nothin', but Nunzio, he's a good kid. It's gonna be hard on him. Maybe I oughta give consideration to sending him to that school, get him away from all the arguing.

That morning, Father Kelly gave the boys each a special holy card. "This is the Sacred Heart," he said, "and it has special meaning. If you turn it over, you'll see there are twelve promises that Jesus made to those who honor Him."

Frankie stared hard at the words. After Father Kelly had gone to the kitchen to get the doughnuts, he looked up at Nunzio. "How 'bout you read 'em out loud?" he said.

Nunzio began reading as Frankie sat listening and nodding. When he got to Promise 10, he stopped.

"Is that it?" Frankie said.

"No, hold on a sec," Nunzio said, his mind was working, conjuring up images.

"I'll read it," said Pete.

"No, that's okay," said Frankie.

"It says 'I will give to priests the gift of touching the most hardened hearts,'" Pete read.

"Okay," said Frankie. "Is that it?"

"What about that?" Nunzio asked Carlo.

"I like that one," Carlo said. "But I really like the one about blessing every place where there's a pi'ture of Him."

"I mean about the priest," Nunzio said. "The power of the priest."

Pete had begun to read the last promises to Frankie, who sat nodding and listening as if he were taking Confession.

"Yeah," said Carlo. "Yeah." Carlo had never said a word to his parents or to Nunzio, but his young heart had already been set on becoming a priest. His admiration for Father Kelly and Monsignor French were akin to what some boys felt for Firemen or Police Officers. He wondered if Nunzio had ever thought of becoming a priest.

By then, Father Kelly was back with the doughnuts. "They're all jelly today!" he called out to the boys' delight. There were four on the plate, and as usual when Father Kelly brought them, there was a fifth one cut into fours, its confectioner's sugar dotting the jelly seeping out slightly along the edges.

Father Kelly took great pleasure in watching his hungry altar boys gobble down the doughnuts before he took the plate back to the kitchen.

"Thanks, Father," Pete called after him.

All the other boys chimed in afterwards, as Father turned to give his customary wave that, to Nunzio, always looked more like a blessing.

"Race ya!" Carlo said, buttoning up his coat.

"Get ready to lose!" Nunzio called as he ran out the door, still putting on his coat.

"No fair!" called Carlo.

Seven minutes later, Nunzio headed to the kitchen to make his lunch.

"One sandwich!" his mother called. "Your brother's gotta eat, too!"

"Okay," Nunzio said. She had not said he couldn't spread the peanut butter thick, which signified the value of a truly good peanut butter and jelly sandwich. Besides, he had firsthand knowledge that Louie routinely tossed his own sandwich in the trashcan by the church. Peter Costello could attest to that fact as well. He came from the opposite side of the main road to get to Sacred Heart. If he timed it just right, Pete could get to Louie's regular sandwich discard point and grab the fully wrapped sandwich right after Louie pitched it without anybody seeing him do it. Of course his stealthy subterfuge was wasted by his revelation of the act after the fact, but Nunzio was happy for him. "Hey, if you're hungry, it's good food," he would respond. Louie did not make his own sandwiches. His mother packed his whole lunch, usually well before Nunzio got to the kitchen.

On that particular morning, though, the peanut butter, jelly, and bread were sitting out but untouched. Seeing his chance, Nunzio crafted an enormously thick sandwich and quickly wrapped it up in waxed paper, grabbed an apple, a handful of fig newtons, and his thermos bottle of milk and stashed it all in his bookbag.

"See ya, Ma," he yelled as he hurried out the door.

"Where's he going in such a hurry?" Louie asked, coming down the stairs.

His mother shrugged and tapped her cigarette. "Who knows, who cares?"

After school, Carlo and Nunzio stopped by the drug store window to see what Dickinson's put on the new candy rack. It seemed like they had new things every week, from square candy bars to new flavors of two-color lollipops, like root beer and strawberry crème.

"Same as last week," Carlo said, mildly disappointed.

"You couldn't have gotten anything anyway," Nunzio pointed out.

"Yeah," Carlo said. "But it's nice to have something to save for."

Nunzio considered that. "Yeah, I guess so," he said.

"We're going to Melrose tonight," Carlo said brightly as they turned to walk toward home.

"How come?"

"I don't know. Pop says Ma works too hard. So he said plan on going out tonight, Matilda."

"Your ma ain't called 'Matilda.'"

Carlo chuckled. "I know. He's always giving everybody different names."

"You walkin'? Passyunk Avenue's right over there near your house."

"I don't know. Probably."

When they passed the house with the perpetual garage project, Mr. Tucker was sitting out front, smoking cigarettes. He wore a heavy coat and his close-fitting hat with ear flaps nearly masked his face completely. The boys subconsciously slowed down in order to inspect the hole in the building's lower wall. Mr. Tucker looked up and grunted.

"Hi, Mr. Tucker," Nunzio called out.

"Hello, boy," he said. "You stay in school boy, you hear? 'Til you're good and finished."

"Yes, Sir, Mr. Tucker," Nunzio said.

Once they'd cleared the old man's house, Carlo snickered.

"What?" Nunzio asked.

"What if old Mr. Tucker and old Mr. Finn are the same fella? And they just change chairs and put on disguises every day?"

Nunzio smiled. "And change from cigars to cigarettes!" he added.

"Yeah!"

"That could be true," Nunzio said. "I don't think I've ever seen them two together."

"Me neither," giggled Carlo.

They came to a stop at their corner. "What are you gonna have at Melrose?" Nunzio asked.

"They'll probably order for me, like they always do," Carlo said somewhat forlornly. "And it's usually the turkey dinner or the fried chicken dinner."

"That sounds good," Nunzio said, his eyes wide, imagining a whole plate brought just to him with fried chicken and cranberry sauce and mashed potatoes. He stopped imagining.

"I guess so. Well, see you, Nunz."

"See ya, Carlo."

After they parted, Nunzio thought about the family dinner out that his buddy was going to have that evening. He wondered what that would be like. It wasn't hard to imagine Carlo and his parents at the diner, sitting across from each other, his mother smiling and his father telling jokes.

Pop tells me jokes, he thought, but he don't say nothin' funny to ma, not ever. Not Louie neither. I wonder why. Maybe just he and me can go there sometime. We could each get the fried chicken platter.

As he entered the house, he was immediately startled by the quietness. His mother always had the radio going, always. But today, he could smell cigarettes, but there was a weird, uncomfortable kind of silence. He stopped just inside, trying to decide whether to go to the kitchen and drop off his thermos bottle, or sneak upstairs undetected. It turned out that he didn't have to make that decision.

"Nunzio," called his mother in an oddly slick voice. "Come in here. I'd like you to meet someone."

He didn't know why, but Nunzio was suddenly consumed with the feeling that he did not wish to meet his mother's someone. He put down his book bag, then picked it back up again, and took his time wiping his shoes on the mat.

"Nunzio!" his mother called, slightly less ladylike.

"Comin', Ma," he said.

When he entered the living room, there next to his mother on their war-torn couch sat a very large man, both very tall and very heavy. In his fine suit and spanking clean, shining black-as-night shoes, he made the modest DiAngelis living room look, in Nunzio's embarrassed estimation, like a dump.

"How do you do, young fellow?" the giant said, standing up to shake Nunzio's hand.

"Hi," Nunzio said, thoroughly intimidated.

"Go on, shake his hand, Nunzio. This is Mr. Saco. Him and me'll be gettin' married. How 'bout that?"

As Mr. Saco reached out to shake Nunzio's hand, Nunzio was instantly repulsed. They say the young have strong, naturally perceptive powers, and can intuitively tell if a person is a good person or a bad person. At that moment, Nunzio had no doubt that the giant Mr. Saco was a bad man.

"Where's Pop?" was all he could think of to say.

The giant laughed, a darkly merry laugh that came shooting out of a huge and gold decorated mouth.

"Your father's at the shop," snapped his mother. "Where else would he be?"

It was then that Nunzio noticed Louie sitting in the easy chair on the other side of the room. And Louie was smoking a cigarette! And neither his mother nor the giant seemed to be disturbed by that deep infringement of the rules. What was going on?

His mother was on her feet, apologizing and half-laughing, half-scowling. "I'm sorry, Eddie—"

"Give the kid a chance to get used to the idea," Eddie Saco said absently. "Where's my hat? Let's go. I'm hungry."

They left without another word. Louie put out his cigarette as if he'd been smoking all his life and followed them out the door. It was then that Nunzio realized he'd been holding his breath. He let it out, and unexpectedly tears sprang to his eyes as he tried to control his rising feeling of helplessness. Ma's marrying someone other than Pop? How can she marry someone else if she's already married? And that man, he's the one? He's like a monster in a bad dream. And Louie--Louie is smoking?

He wanted to run somewhere, like he would if someone were chasing him. Run home, where it was safe. But I'm already home, he told himself as he stood there, still holding his bookbag. So where do I go? He thought about going to see his pop, but he was probably at his busiest, it being afternoon when everybody came in for haircuts. Did Pop know, he wondered. His mind was filling up with so many questions and worries that again he felt the desperate need to run somewhere to leave it off. He dropped his bookbag, and turned around, and ran all the way to Sacred Heart Church.

Chapter Four

The train rattled and wobbled back and forth, as the grey day opened beyond Thirtieth Street Station in Philadelphia into simply more grey fog. Nunzio sat staring out the window, wondering if he would see anything familiar as he made his long journey to a place called Virginia. He wondered how everything had happened so fast, how his life had suddenly taken a completely unexpected turn. Things seemed to move so fast that it was all he could do to keep pace with what he had to do to prepare for his new circumstances.

He leaned back against the seat and stared at the light green ceiling of the train and its two thin strips of light lining the length of the coach. As he cast his mind back to only a short while before, he remembered the horror of his first unexpectedly scary meeting with his mother's "boyfriend," as everyone was calling him. Boyfriend seemed like the wrong word. Eddie Saco was a lot of things, but definitely not a boy, and the word "friend" didn't even enter into it.

On that night, after meeting Eddie, when Nunzio had run to the church, he had found Monsignor and Father setting up for vespers that evening. Immediately they knew something was wrong and set aside what they were working on to listen to his tale of trauma. As he told them about the meeting, he thought he saw anger in Monsignor French's eyes. It didn't trouble him because he knew the Monsignor was not angry at him. He wasn't even sure that he was angry. In fact, something about his response seemed protective. Nunzio felt a kind of reinforcement that he had not realized he needed.

Monsignor French left shortly afterward, but Father Kelly continued to listen, nodding a lot, and smiling where he thought it might help. His strong but gentle resolve was almost tangible. Between his support and Monsignor's validation, Nunzio was able to calm down.

"No matter how tough things get, Nunzio," Father Kelly told him, "Jesus will never leave your side. Monsignor and I, and your friends, we can't always be there for you, but Jesus is always there. He is always at your side. Don't ever forget that."

"I wish I could see Him, though," Nunzio had said in a small voice.

Father Kelly nodded.

Monsignor had returned then, not as angry, but clearly resolute. "I think things'll get better for you, Nunzio. Here, take this and have a nice dinner with your pop." He handed him a covered dish. Nunzio knew it must have been prepared for the priests' dinner, and he hesitated, but Monsignor insisted. "Oh you have to take it," he said with a twinkle in his eye. "It was prepared just for you by the angels."

Nunzio had smiled slightly and accepted the dish. His walk home was slow, even though it was getting dark. The food he carried was warm, so the wind didn't have the same bite, and he was in no hurry to go back and find that man again, with his mother and Louie.

There were cars bringing home office workers who lived in the area so the streets were becoming cluttered with the rows of parked cars, sometimes two cars thick on either side of the street, but the bright headlights of the passing cars kept the atmosphere from being overwhelmingly gloomy.

Nunzio thought about Father Kelly's words. He knew his Guardian Angel was always there, but Jesus, too? That seemed a little hard to believe. For one thing, why would He spend all that time on him when there were a lot of other boys in Sacred Heart School? And girls, too. Maybe he meant that Jesus was always thinking of him. But no, the words he had used were "always at your side."

Just then, the train jolted a little and started to break as the conductor announced the next stop. "Hammonton! Next stop, Hammonton!"

Carlo woulda loved this character, Nunzio thought, smiling slightly. He'd sit there and do an imitation of him as soon as he walked by. The thought moved him back into his dark mood. When would he ever see Carlo again? When would he see *any* of his friends again? What had Pop said, "on your break." When would that be?

Nunzio closed his eyes and tried not to remember the scene that had greeted him when he had arrived with dinner from the priests. How had so much developed in such a short time? Or was he just so blind to it all that he couldn't see it happening right in front of him?

Louie opened the door before he'd even made it up the steps. "He's here," he said, looking back into the living room and rolling his eyes. "They thought you run away," he said, quietly taking a drag on his cigarette.

Nunzio looked at him with disdain and moved sideways into the house to avoid directly confronting whoever was in the living room.

"Where you been, Nunzio?" his mother demanded. "We been sittin' here waitin' for half an hour. Eddie's got more important things to do than to sit around waiting for some emotional kid."

"Where ya been?" Eddie demanded, as if he had some sort of right to know, Nunzio thought.

Nunzio looked at his mother. Had she bothered to look back, she would have seen the horror and disgust in his eyes. It wasn't lost on Eddie though, he scoffed and looked at her.

"Listen, the kid's okay. I gotta go, but have him ready tomorrow early, 'cause I don't want to go through all this waitin' around again. I get itchy feet," he said, laughing at his own joke.

"Sure Eddie," said his mother.

"Sure not, Eddie," said Nick, standing in the door with his hands on his hips. Right behind him stood Cat O'Hearn, one of the beat cops for their block.

"Who the hell is this?" Eddie demanded, turning to Nunzio's mother.

"Look," she said, ignoring Eddie's question, "I'm moving out. I can't leave the boys here—"

"You ain't leaving me in this dump!" Louie piped in. Nunzio stared at his brother. Two days ago, it was home. Now it was a dump?

"I realize that—" Nick began.

"Who *is* this character?" Eddie demanded again.

"It's my Pop!" Nunzio called out defiantly, breaking his silence.

"All right, look, I'm sorry about all this," Eddie said, "but she's got a right—"

"You ain't taking my son," Nick continued. "She don't have the right. We're married, we're not even divorced yet and you're there trying to run off with my family."

"She's got a right," Eddie repeated. "She wants out of the marriage."

"*She* may have a right," Nick said moving forward, his hands forming into tight fists. "But my son stays."

Eddie couldn't resist responding. After all, who was this little nothing? Didn't he know he was Eddie Saco? Capo of over sixteen blocks, unchallenged? "Well I'm sayin' it ain't up to you!" he yelled, moving closer to Nick.

Nick wasn't wealthy and he didn't have a team of nasty soldiers backing him up, but he did love his son, and he was not backing down. He took another step forward. "Looks like you've already corrupted Louie. He's a lost cause. Look at him over there, sucking on a cigarette, can't wait to get into your good graces. You got him doing any rough stuff for you yet? How many'd you knock off for him, Lou? Couple a dozen?" He took another step forward so that the two men were almost nose to nose. "But you *ain't* and I'm saying it just as plain as that ugly wart on your nose, *ain't* takin' Nunzio!"

Eddie started to rise to the physical challenge, but Cat unholstered his gun and stood ready.

"Aah, you ain't worth it," the fat man said, shoving Nick on the shoulder.

Nick stood his ground, one fist raised and ready and the other still on his hip.

Eddie pushed past Cat O'Hearn, who was just as tall as he but more muscular and not as fat. "Get your crap and get out here," he ordered Nunzio's mother, while Louie held the door open for him. "We leave in five minutes!"

Louie grabbed his two bags and followed his new leader. Fifteen minutes later, Mrs. DiAngelis took one last look around and left through the front door for the last time.

Cat O'Hearn shook Nick's hand and turned to go. "Sorry, Nick. I'll see ya tomar."

"Yep," said Nick.

Nunzio watched the scene unfold feeling lost in a combination of awe and declining fear mixed with confusion.

Nick shut the door as the large black car drifted away down the street. He locked it, but not before throwing the welcome mat outside to air out.

"Pop," Nunzio said.

"Yeah," said Nick, looking at his son for the first time since he'd arrived.

"Are they comin' back?"

"Nope."

Nunzio sighed. "Good."

Nick chuckled. "What have you got there?"

Nunzio suddenly realized he still had the covered dish in his hands. "The priests made us dinner," he said, putting it on the kitchen table. "Monsignor French said the angels did, but I think they did, or that lady, Mrs. Michaels."

"I had a call from Monsignor today," Nick said casually, as he looked at their supper. "Looks good! Like one of those shepherd's pies."

"Monsignor French called you?" Nunzio said. He sat down, his legs having been shaky ever since he arrived home. The house was cold from all the air coming in during the confrontation, and he started to shiver.

"Listen son," Nick said gently, turning on the oven to heat up their dinner, "you know I can't take care of you the way you need. You're still young. Not like Louie."

Nunzio shot up onto his feet. "I don't want to go there! Not to that Fat Eddie's house!" he yelled. "I want to be with you, Pop!"

Nick squatted down next to him. "I want to be with you, too," he said. "You and me are like the same, just one's big and one's little," he said smiling. "But we got a problem. I have to work all day and sometimes into the night. There wouldn't be anyone here to take care of you."

"Maybe someone could come over while you're away," Nunzio suggested.

"I thought of that, but that costs money. The way this thing turned out, I'll have to make more money just to be able to you know, hold onto the house and all."

"Maybe I could get a job," Nunzio countered.

Nick put an arm around him briefly. "Far as I know, they ain't hiring eight-year-olds in South Philly," he said sadly. He could feel his son's painful realization breaking through and it was killing him. He'd known similar pain when his own dear father had been killed in combat.

"There's a school," Nick said, "it's a little far away but Nunzio, it trains young men to be soldiers, to be generals. That's what you want to be, isn't it?"

"Yeah," Nunzio answered hesitant but interested.

"I talked to the Monsignor. He said the nuns down there in Virginia—you know where Virginia is, don't you son?"

"Yes, it's by the capital, Washington."

"Yes, it's down south a little ways. You take the train, just like when we go down the shore or over to Harrisburg. Except it takes a little longer."

"You mean I would go there every day?" Nunzio asked.

"Well, no, it's a long trip, so they set it up so that the kids have beds and a place to put their things."

"I'd stay overnight?"

"Yeah," Nick forced himself to smile. "It'd be like a big, long sleepover while you're at school."

"How long a sleep over?"

"They set it up so you get breaks now and then—we won't see each other Thanksgiving because I won't be able to afford to bring you back that soon, but maybe at Christmas."

Nunzio could see the pain in his father's eyes and hear the effort he was making with his voice to sound enthused about the notion. He knew the idea his father was telling him about was more than just a passing thought. He had already made the arrangements. After everything his mother and that man and even Louie had put his father through, he couldn't bear to hurt him.

"They teach you how to be soldiers?" he said, his voice weak with the enthusiasm he was trying to project.

"Yeah," said Nick, knowing exactly what his son was doing.

"Well, that sounds good," Nunzio said. "I guess Carlo won't be there, though."

"No, but you can show him everything you learn at the end of the year."

"Yeah."

There hadn't been much more to say, and they had sat down to have the priests' dinner. The days had followed with amazing rapidity. Nunzio had been given the next day off so that he could pack up whatever he needed to take with him. Nick had visited with Monsignor French. Nunzio suspected Monsignor had given his pop the money for the school.

In many ways, he looked forward to going to the school. It was an adventure, it was a soldier school, he loved to go places, and he loved trains. He knew he would miss Carlo and the others. But he shoved that thought to the back of his mind. He couldn't get upset about that. The plans his pop had made for him would keep him safely out of that scary man's house. Living in some rich guy's house was not an opportunity he would miss. He wondered if he would miss his mother. He knew he wouldn't miss Louie.

Carlo had given him a piece of paper with his and Frankie and Pete's addresses. He had also given him his Yankees pennant. "It's just a loan," he said. "You can give it to me when you're a soldier."

Nunzio had been surprised how hard it was to say goodbye without crying. It was as if the feeling was waiting outside and just at the precise moment, jumped through the window and choked him, putting pressure on his chest, making it hard to breathe.

The train joggled back and forth on the well-worn tracks, and Nunzio's head, so full of memories and questions, rested heavily against the window frame. In seconds, he was in a deep sleep.

Chapter Five

Nunzio woke up with a start, as the conductor gave his shoulder a jostle. He looked out the window and saw that it was nearly dark. His hands and feet were cold and his whole body felt stiff from the bumpy, joggling five-hour journey.

"Alexandria, son," the conductor called. "This is where you get off."

"Yes, Sir," said Nunzio, getting up as quickly as he could. His right foot was asleep. He pounded it against the floor of the train to try to get it to wake up while at the same time yanking at his suitcase, or his "grip" as his pop called it, which was stuck.

His movements must have looked odd, because the conductor leaned over and said in his ear, "Are you all right, son? Do you need a doctor?"

"No, Sir," said Nunzio. "I'm okay. My foot's just asleep and I can't get the grip—" he gave it one last yank, and it shot loose of what it had been caught on, sending itself and Nunzio back down onto the seat.

By then, Nunzio was fully awake and trying to figure out where to go.

"There's your exit," the conductor said, holding up a hand to stop folks behind them so he could get out. "I think that's the woman you want to see right over there."

He pointed to a woman in a sharp gray suit with blond bobbed hair who stood only about four feet tall. She looked as military as Nunzio had ever seen a woman look, especially one without a uniform. Then he wondered if maybe she *was* in uniform.

He stepped down from the train, getting help from the conductor onto the platform. The final step was a long way down, and he was grateful for the help. He turned around to see the man behind him refuse help and then go tumbling down on one knee. He sighed, relieved that he had managed to escape that pitfall.

Walking toward the woman in grey, he wondered if he was supposed to salute her. All of his problems and worries back home were quickly moved to the back of his mind as he struggled with the decision. He had heard that you could get into serious trouble for failing to salute a superior officer. He went over the form in his mind: right hand, stiff four fingers—but what do you do with the thumb? He tried to form it in his pocket where his right hand was trying to get warm. Before he knew it, though, he and the grey-suited woman had come face to face.

Quickly he withdrew his hand from his pocket, attempted to salute her, and stabbed himself in the eye. He shut his eye tightly, too embarrassed to say "ouch" but unable to avoid cringing.

"Oh!" said the woman in a surprisingly ducky voice. "Did you hurt yourself?"

"No, ma'am," he said automatically. "Well, just a little."

"Here, let me take a look," said the woman, as she peered into his eye. "What was you doin'? Reachin' for your hat?"

"Uh, no ma'am, I. . ." he felt silly saying that he was trying to salute, so he tried to change the subject. The trouble was, he couldn't think beyond his having stuck his fingers in his own eye.

"Well, I think it looks okay," the woman said, nodding. "I'm Mrs. Hardy, by the way. We're pretty informal off the field. Once you get your drill uniform, then they teach you all the soldiering."

Her accent was very comforting somehow and made Nunzio relax.

"I guess you got no idea what to expect, huh?" she said, starting to pick up his bag.

"Oh I'll carry that, ma'am," he said.

"Why thank you!" she said, which sounded more like "thank yeeou" to Nunzio. "You *are* a little gentleman!"

She drove an ancient coupe, with seats that had been covered over with a sturdy but very unseatlike fabric. Nunzio thought it might be burlap but he wasn't sure. She had a toolbox in the back seat, which Nunzio saw when he put his grip back there.

"You can set up front with me," she said. "Get a chance to see where all you are!"

They drove down the short driveway from the station, passing only a few other cars entering the station. Compared to 30th Street Station, it was a phone booth, Nunzio thought. He started thinking of Carlo and the funny things he would probably say about it, and he felt almost happy. Still he knew he must keep up his guard, this was all unknown territory. He thought of George Raft, driving in the dark, thinking the same thing.

But while it *was* getting dark, Mrs. Hardy's steady discussion of what farms they were passing and who lived there, was anything but ominous. She described what sort of businesses there were in the area and how far they were going to get to Manassas, the town closest to the school. "Some of the boys are gettin' to be right good milkers. We've got cows on campus. Did anybody tell you that?"

"Cows, ma'am? You mean the animal?"

She laughed out loud. "Yes, the animal. Do you have them up there in Philadelphia?"

"Not at the school, ma'am."

Mrs. Hardy laughed again. And Nunzio couldn't help but smile. Maybe this was going to be more of an adventure than he had thought.

When they finally reached the school, it was very dark and the lights lining the long driveway glowed gently. Mrs. Hardy put the car right up next to the big entry door and Nunzio popped out quickly to get her door. But he was startled by the appearance of a man in a coat and tie, who had been standing apparently in the shadow of the door.

"Madame," he said, as he opened her door.

"Thank you," said Mrs. Hardy. "Now honey, let's get your things and somebody will show you where you bunk."

Nunzio was again on guard. The idea of a servant at a school was even stranger than cows being there. This could still be a trap. He realized that he had failed to ask Mrs. Hardy if he could see some identification. In the dark, who knew what this place was? In fact, he just realized that she had never even called him by his name.

But before he could do any impromptu investigation, they reached a second door, which was larger when seen by the light from within, and they were welcomed by two Sisters, one tall and thin and one short and round. Both were peering at Nunzio, and neither were smiling. This is where it gets ugly, he thought.

The tall nun looked at the short one and shook her head. "That's nowhere near enough to keep him warm," she said.

The short one put both her hands to her face before reaching out for Nunzio. "Nunzio DiAngelis!" she cried as if she had known him all his life. "We are so happy to see you! Come inside where it's warm. Let's get him some cocoa, Sister Bernadette."

"Good idea," said the tall nun, smiling at Nunzio.

The two of them almost encircled him as Mrs. Hardy stood at the doorway nodding. "He has very nice manners, too," she said.

Nunzio looked from one happy face to the next, clutching onto his suitcase and hoping not to lose his balance amidst the thoroughly unfamiliar effusion over him.

"He's probably missing his mama," said Sister Bernadette. "You round up some of that cake you made today, Sister Claire, and Mrs. Hardy, would you please find him a cozy place to sit and get his bearings?"

"Yes, of course," said Mrs. Hardy, taking Nunzio by the free hand. "Here, we'll put your bag over here for now while you get warmed up. It's cold out there and Sister Bernadette and Sister Claire are two of the warmest hearted people you will ever meet!"

Oh, thought Nunzio. So that's it. They're the nice ones, and up next are the mean ones. But all he said was, "Yes, ma'am."

When the Sisters returned, they were accompanied by a priest. "So this is our star pupil! Welcome to Lexington Hall. I'm Father Boreto," said the friendly looking man in a cassock. He offered his hand to Nunzio.

But what Nunzio heard was "I'm Father *baretta*." He shot straight up, his eyes wide with fright.

"Didn't I tell you he had nice manners?" said Mrs. Hardy, misinterpreting his actions for respect.

Father Boreto reached down and shook Nunzio's hand, patted him on the back and said, "I'd like to stay and talk a little while, but the younger boys are getting ready for evening prayers. We'll get acquainted soon. Nice to meet you, young man."

"Nice to meet you," Nunzio said faintly, and sat back down.

Sister Bernadette and Sister Claire fussed over him like two mothers, while Mrs. Hardy sat back and enjoyed watching. This young fellow is not used to affection, she thought. This school will be a godsend for him.

"I think I'd best get home," she said, standing up. "I hate to leave this cheery company, but I've got chores to do, and it looks like we might have snow a little later on. I don't want to get stuck on that hill."

"Thank you so much for delivering him to us safely," said Sister Claire.

"Yes, thank you, Mrs. Hardy," said Sister Bernadette, smiling at her and then at Nunzio.

"Oh, thank you Mrs. Hardy," said Nunzio. By then, he had enjoyed a full plate of Sister Claire's cherry coconut cake and felt surprisingly revived.

"It's time Nunzio met his roommates, too," said Sister Claire, as Mrs. Hardy left. "Let's get his things and go over there."

The two nuns walked down the hall with Nunzio as he tried to catch glimpses of their feet on the sly. He knew they had to have them, but neither he nor Carlo had ever seen a Sister's feet. Sister Claire's long, wooden rosary hung very low by her side, its crucifix bouncing mercilessly as she walked. Sister Bernadette's was more humanely positioned, and swung freely with her strides, not incurring any further undeserved collisions. He wondered if Sister Claire knew. It struck him as not quite right.

At the end of the hall, they turned left and followed past one large room, and then a series of rooms with doors reaching only halfway up. Inside each were four beds arranged in bunks of two. The first two bedrooms were empty, but the following two had boys doing various things at desks or on the floor. Two boys played chess, one was reading, and another was writing something in what looked like a notebook. At the fourth door, they stopped, and as soon as Sister Claire opened the door, all of the boys immediately sprung up sharply at attention. Then, in one voice all three said, "Good evening, Sisters."

"At ease," said Sister Claire warmly. "I've brought you a new bunkmate!"

Nunzio studied the faces of the boys, looking for anything he could find to reveal something more about the school. One of the boys seemed a little lost, but the other two seemed like Frankie or Pete or anybody else he knew.

"Nunzio," said Sister Bernadette, touching one of the boys on the shoulder, "this is Carl, and over there is Donald. And you will bunk with Emil." She moved over to indicate the boy who had seemed lost. "Boys, this is Nunzio. He's joining us right in the middle of the semester, so anything you can help him with will be greatly appreciated. All right?"

"Yes, Sister," answered everyone again in unison.

Sister Claire set Nunzio's bag down and smiled as she and Sister Bernadette closed the door behind themselves. "Father Boreto will be in for prayers in a little while."

As soon as they left, Donald asked, "How old are you, Nunzio?"

"Eight and a half."

"Are you from up north?"

"I'm from Philadelphia. That's a little north."

"Yeah," Carl said nodding. "It's in Pennsylvania. This is Virginia."

"How old are you?" Nunzio asked Donald.

"I'm nine, and Carl's nine, too."

"How about him?" Nunzio asked, indicating Emil.

"Emil is eight."

Nunzio looked at Emil. The boy just sat there, working on what looked like a clay model. After a while, he asked, "Don't he talk?"

"I can talk," Emil answered sharply. "I'm just doin' something."

Nunzio brightened. Emil's was the first voice he had heard since leaving Philadelphia that sounded familiar. "Where you from?" he asked him.

"Down the market," Emil answered, clearly impatient with the questions.

"The market? You mean Philadelphia?"

"Yeah."

Nunzio felt instant and complete relief. Well, he thought, if there's another guy like me, and he ain't worried, I ain't worried. This guy can show me the ropes. He can be my eyes and ears.

"Which bunk you sleepin' in?" Nunzio asked.

"The bottom one," Emil answered.

"He has to sleep in the bottom one," Donald explained.

"He has to? How come?"

Emil turned toward him, but his eyes looked elsewhere as he answered. "Because it's safer. I can't see. I'm blind."

Chapter Six

At Lexington Hall, there were 24 students in all. Nunzio's days were spent almost exclusively with the middle grade students. But during Mass, dinners, and special events all the boys were assembled, and he got a chance to see who else was attending.

His bunkmate was rich in information, surprisingly, considering his circumstances. But, as he explained it to Nunzio, "people think if you're blind, you can't hear. I don't know why, but they do." They had both had a good laugh out of that and Nunzio told Carlo all about it in his first letter, opening with their usual sarcasm.

Hey Carlo, I hope you like the fancy writing paper. They ain't got note paper here, so you write in your notebook and tear it out. How's things at

Sacred Heart, and the church? I started classes right away, but they're easy compared to our school, and we got a bunch of different teachers instead of just one, kind of makes the day seem shorter. What I found out as soon as I got down here is that this place is on a real farm and they got real cows! We actually learn how to milk them and what to do with the milk and all that kind of stuff. I'm not serving at Mass yet. They got so many of us that my turn won't come up til after Thanksgiving. But we got a break Thanksgiving time, so I guess I'll be seeing you before you know it! It's me and three guys in my room. They call us bunkmates. They're all okay. One of them is blind, but he's okay, he's from down the Market in Philly. One thing it aint is very military. There's one guy that comes in and teaches us how to keep a clean room and making the beds and saluting and marching, but that's pretty much all. Well, my hand's cramping up. Say hi to Frankie and Pete. I'll see all you guys soon! Nunzio.

In the dining hall one night, Emil nudged Nunzio. "The guy, the one with the big mouth," he whispered, "he's got some kinda fancy father, works at the White House. At least that's what he tells everyone."

"No kiddin'!"

"No, and when he comes here, he shows up in a chauffeur-driven limousine. That's what the nuns say, and you know they don't lie. He's a pretty tough guy."

"No," said Nunzio, studying the kid with the big mouth. He was relatively short, compared to his peers, but he looked like he could hold his own. Nick had always sized up Nunzio's potential rivals in funny ways, and Nunzio could hear him in his mind "Ah, you could take 'im," or "I don't know, Nunz, look at that big thick neck."

The funny thing was, Nunzio never seemed to run into rivals of any consequence. He either didn't notice or didn't rise to the bate, but other than the occasional yelling or pushing match, he hadn't ever run into conflicts. His only troubles with people were right there in his own home. It was the same story at Lexington Hall, even though by then he had discovered that he was, as his father would say, about the hungriest duck in the pond, he got along with everyone.

"That's what I heard, and you know how good I hear," Emil said.

"Your folks got money, Emil?"

"How do you think I got here? Sure, and the settlement, you know."

"What's that?"

"After my accident, the chemical company—long story. But that's how I got here. But not like that kid. That Jimmy's family's got some bucks, let me tell ya."

Nunzio watched the rich kid for a while. He seemed like the sort that needed approval, even with all his wealth. Several of the older kids seemed that way. Maybe, Nunzio thought, that's what happens when you get older. He thought of Louie and how he always aligned himself with his mother. That's probably the same thing, he decided. She was very quick to approve of everything about her older son.

And very little, Nunzio thought painfully, of anything I've ever done.

Shortly after Emil had described Jimmy to him, Nunzio caught sight of him lending a hand to one of the younger boys. A five-year-old had fallen on his way to the dairy and cut his lip. It wasn't a bad cut, but it bled, and the boy was visibly upset.

As Nunzio watched from a distance, he gave Emil a play-by-play.

"He's pickin' 'im up. Now he's lookin' at the kid's face."

"Lookin' at 'im?"

"Yeah, I think he's trying to help the kid."

"No kiddin'!"

"Yeah, he's takin' out a hanky and wipin' the kid's mouth. Hey," Nunzio snickered. "Some tough guy, huh?"

"Yeah, a real furfante."

All of the boys had chores, ranging from sweeping and emptying trash in the dormitory to milking cows and mucking out stalls. Making sure the assigned chores were done by each set of bunks was the responsibility of one person within the 4-boy bunk. In Nunzio's bunk, that person was Donald.

Under Donald's supervision, which Nunzio suspected unveiled a burgeoning professional manager, he learned how to clean under his bed, wipe down walls, mop floors with a string mop, and get windows so clean that they required cross decals to prevent birds from flying into them. All students learned to make tightly cornered bunks, as instructed by the day instructor, Sgt. Monnahan, who was a very strict task master in the few respects actually related to military training.

Early Mass was a daily occurrence except for Sundays, when the boys slept in until 8:00. When he first arrived, Nunzio was told that the altar boys were rotated and that he shouldn't expect to be called until after Thanksgiving. But it was actually during the Thanksgiving break that he had his first opportunity—and his greatest disappointment.

The week of Thanksgiving, the classes were shortened, and the boys packed for the long weekend home with their families. The nuns helped the younger boys and some in Nunzio's section, too, but the older boys were packed and ready even before it was time to go. By Tuesday afternoon, things were clearing out quickly.

"When's your pop comin'?" Emil asked Nunzio. "They're pickin' me up tomorrow early so we can have most of the day at home."

"I don't know," Nunzio answered. While everyone was packing and getting ready, he just assumed they were all waiting to hear. But as time went on, and all of his roommates were settled in their plans, he began to wonder. "He said he'd see me when I got my break."

"You didn't get a letter or anything?" Emil asked.

"Not yet."

"You'll hear from him," Emil said, reassuringly. But he had doubts. "Maybe he's working up to the last minute."

"Yeah, that could be," Nunzio said, feeling a little better. "Everybody wants to look good for

Thanksgiving, so he's probably cutting so many heads he can't see straight."

But the next morning, just after he said goodbye to Emil as his mother led him to the car, Sister Claire came to see Nunzio, who was by then one of only four students remaining. "Nunzio," she said as nicely as she could. "We've heard from your father. I'm afraid he won't be able to come and get you this holiday. There were problems with his plans, I think. He really wanted to come, but he won't be able to make it until next time."

Nunzio was not prepared. The news hit him like a frying pan in the face. The only thing that kept him from crying while he stood there with his heart breaking was the visualization of being hit in the face with a frying pan. So his brain held an emotions tournament between laughing and crying while his body just stood there, rigid as the soldier he had intended to become.

Sister Claire had experienced the sad occasion many times before. Trying to protect his pride but still show the compassion she felt, she gave his shoulder a little pat. "We'll have a happy Thanksgiving, Nunzio. You and the other boys. You'll see."

As she gripped him warmly on both arms, the tears won the tournament, and Sister Claire held the sobbing soldier in her ample arms, patting him gently on the back.

Nunzio felt blindsided, never imagining that his pop wouldn't come for him, or at least send the train fare for him to go home. In all truth, it wasn't only his pop he wanted to see, but Carlo. And more than anything, he wanted to be back at the Sacred Heart Church.

After Sister had left, telling him that his time was his own but that she and Sister Bernadette were cooking up a surprise for the stayovers, as they were called, he stood unpacking his things. At first he was so angry he opened the bag and threw everything on the floor. But even after a few weeks of minimal military training, he couldn't bear to see the room messy and he picked them up and began to put them away.

Something must have happened, he told himself. Maybe there was an accident, or maybe they got snow up there or something. The only letter he had gotten from anyone in his family had been his father's very brief note wishing him well right after he had arrived. Nick was not one to write much, being much better with figures than with penmanship.

What Nunzio did not know was that Nick wasn't in the greatest shape, and writing a letter to his son, much less coming for him on the train, would have been a little outside the realm of possibilities.

Morris Schultz stood next to his hospital bed, shaking his head. "Well, at least you got your way. Mighta got beat up, but you got your way."

Nick smiled, nodding painfully, his left eye resembling a brown turkey fig fresh from the market, and his right arm in a cast to the elbow. "Yep," he said.

"Look, it's almost Thanksgiving, you want me ta do anything about the kid?"

Nick shook his head, wincing again. "Nah. I told the Sister, she'll take care of it. Don't let 'im know nothin', hear me?"

"Sure, sure. But you know Cat. If O'Hearn says it ain't ovah, it ain't ovah."

"Don't get in it, Mo. It ain't worth it."

"Lookin' at you I can see it ain't worth it!" Mo said, starting to laugh.

"Don't make me laugh," Nick said, trying to stop. "Dam—gotta get one of them pain shots."

"I'll get the Sister."

But the nursing Sister was already there. "I think we should let Mr. DiAngelis have a little sleep now."

Mo nodded. "See ya, Nick."

"See ya, Mo."

"I'll just give you a shot for the pain, Mr. DiAngelis," said the Sister, wincing privately as she moved his gown aside, catching sight of the mess that had been made of his ribs and chest. "And we'll keep your speedy recovery in our prayers."

"Thanks, Sistah."

Chapter Seven

That Thanksgiving, while Nick lay recovering from his reward for defiance about Nunzio, generously administered by Saco's thugs, Nunzio experienced what he would always remember as his first calling to a life devoted to God.

Carlo and he had not talked often about whether or not they might want to be priests.

"I don't think they make much," Carlo said, during one of their few discussions. "Not unless it's a big church."

"Well, I guess you don't do it for the cash anyway."

"No, it's probably a good living, but not easy street."

"Yeah. Not unless you're the boss of a place like the cathedral."

Carlo shook his head. "See, that's too much like a business. That ain't for me. Give me a small church or a medium church."

Nunzio had agreed. The way things went like clockwork at Sacred Heart, neither boy new anything different. They didn't realize that sometimes the priests fasted not only for sacrificial purposes, but also in order to make the bills. Father Kelly and Monsignor French made it their way of life to be clean, upbeat, and welcoming to the parishioners, in the spirit of St. Anthony. And that spirit is what had awakened in Carlo and Nunzio.

But on that Thanksgiving afternoon in Lexington Hall, Nunzio's first ever away from home, all four of the boys who were left at the school for the holiday were given a few moments in front of the Blessed Sacrament (which is the Consecrated host, the Body of Christ) to make their own private thanksgiving for all of the good things in their lives.

Father Boreto started them off with a prayer, a Benediction, he called it, and Nunzio and the boys were left to stay and pray as long as they wanted in the incense and candlelight. The younger boys left soon after the Benediction, cherishing visions of Sister Claire's Thanksgiving feast. But Nunzio and one of the older boys were captivated by the glory and love that touched their hearts, as the flames flickering about the sanctuary alternately grazed the faces of the Holy Family and the golden brilliance of the Tabernacle.

They continued to kneel in silence while any pain of family rejection at the holidays melted away, replaced by the warmth of what Nunzio could only express as the love sent from the Sacred Heart. After a while, the older boy stood, genuflected, and left after nodding affectionately at his fellow devotee. It was when Nunzio was totally alone in the little chapel that his heart felt suddenly filled with an urgent love and longing. It was as if he had suddenly awakened and seen and felt and heard the calling of the Holy Spirit, coming down, touching his heart. His wistfulness to serve God was complete, and took on an overwhelming and glorious resolve, where every sort of earthly thought fell temporarily outside of his senses, and he wished himself to the feet of Jesus.

Nunzio felt a kind of gentle but radiant light on his shoulders that he could neither see nor define, but he yearned with all his heart to stay there, just as he was, without end. So blissful was it that he hadn't taken a single breath since it had come upon him. While it seemed to be a much longer time, it had only been seconds. He drew in air sharply, as the spiritual intensity faded, leaving him mourning, near tears, to be losing that wealth of spiritual riches that he had only just found.

He took a deep breath and let it out again. He knew at that moment that everything was different, that a way had been lit for him; that even though the beautiful moment had lasted only for an instant, it was the start of his life's path. His old life had ended, and the new and brilliant one was unfolding.

When Nunzio finally tore himself away from the Blessed Sacrament, mostly because he heard the dinner bell tolling, it was evening and dark. As he journeyed through the halls so lovingly decorated by the nuns and Mrs. Hardy, he felt a kind of happy peace inside. He felt he was carrying it in his heart, where it sat securely perched, a warm benevolent light.

He stopped to enjoy the comical rendition of a turkey hiding behind a haystack and felt himself laughing freely. It was that merry laughter that caught Mrs. Hardy's ear.

"So there you are, Nunzio!" she said. "We're all ready for dinner, but we're missing one important person."

Nunzio smiled sheepishly. "It sure smells good."

"Oh I'm sure it will be delicious!" she answered. "I've had Sister Claire and Sister Bernadette's Thanksgiving dinners many times, and they have always been heavenly!"

Nunzio smiled at the word.

When they reached the dining room, Mrs. Hardy said, "You're over there, honey. Have a seat. We're just in time for grace."

As Nunzio went to take his place at the table, Mrs. Hardy and Father Boreto exchanged glances. Mrs. Hardy had only feigned confusion over where Nunzio had been. They both knew that of his own accord, he had been with the Blessed Sacrament for almost an hour. Father smiled at Nunzio. For Nunzio, he thought, this might be a Thanksgiving he will remember all his life.

In fact, it was a Thanksgiving Nunzio would remember all his life. That evening after dinner and the little gifts they were given, no doubt in Mrs. Hardy's way of trying to ease their loneliness for family, and evening prayers which were said in one big group, Nunzio went back to his bunk to write a letter to Carlo. By then, he was sure that Carlo knew his plans to come home had not panned out. But he had something bigger to share with him. He got out his notebook and fountain pen and sat at his desk, ready to go.

But after "Dear Carlo," he couldn't move on. How would he ever explain what had happened to him, what had begun? He realized as he sat there struggling for words, an unfamiliar plight for him, that instead of the sorrow he had felt at missing his pop, and in some ways, his mother, he now felt only a kind of thrill in his chest, dampened by his circumstances, but still very much alive. He wasn't even thinking about all of the things that had hurt him or broken his heart. He was interested only in telling Carlo about the decision, or revelation, or whatever it was.

After ten minutes of coming up with nothing, lost between remembering what had happened and beating his brain for a way to express it, he gave up and went to bed. He had the weekend to work all that out, he thought. And for the time, he just wanted to revel in his new world.

With Emil and everyone else returned by the start of Advent, time seemed to race by at Lexington Hall. By Christmas time that year, when Nunzio again learned that there was no one coming for him, he had learned to roll with the punches. He hadn't truly expected to be sent tickets for home, and he knew from his dad's letter that he was working double shifts to make up for lost time. According to

Nick, he had had to fix a lot of things in the barber shop, which cost loads of money and he had to make that up.

"You oughta tell the kid the truth," Morris said to him.

"When it's your kid, you tell the truth. When it's by kid, I'll do it by way." Nick's pronunciation of the letter "m" was disturbed by the healing of his jaw and came out sounding more like a "b". "By kid's in another state, he don't need all kinds of sad songs just now."

"Okay, have it your way."

"I will."

"When you gonna get over that cold, Nick?"

"Shut up, Bo."

But on the 27th day of December, as Nunzio shoveled the little path that led to the barn to help the Sisters and younger boys stay on their feet when traveling it, he got a very happy surprise.

"Nunzio!" called Sister Bernadette.

"Yes, Sister?" he called, setting down the shovel.

"Put away the shovel and come inside. You have a visitor."

Did she say a visitor, he wondered. He hadn't met anyone outside of the school except on the occasions when Mrs. Hardy took him and another boy with her to town to help carry groceries. Most everyone was with family that week, though, so he doubted the boy he'd befriended at the grocery store would come for a visit, even if Nunzio had invited him, which he hadn't.

He dusted the snow off the shovel, and then off the knees and cuffs of his pants and stomped on the doorstep before stepping inside. He could smell the fire burning in the dining room and hear Sister Bernadette speaking more animatedly than was her habit.

"And did you have a nice trip down?" she asked.

He couldn't hear anyone answer, but Sister Bernadette went on.

"Oh, that's nice. Were there many other people on the train?"

On the train! Whoever it was had come to see him on a train!

He rushed down the hall and turned into the large room. There to his great surprise, he found his best friend Carlo diFrancisco!

"Hey!" he called, as Carlo popped up from the chair.

"Yo Nunz!" called Carlo, grabbing his buddy for a hug. "Surprise, huh?"

"You bet it's a surprise! You came all the way down here?"

"Hey, I needed a break from the city. What can I say?"

"I bet your ma didn't like it too much, cuttin' out right after Christmas."

"No, but you know, sometimes you gotta do what you gotta do."

Sister Bernadette laughed quietly, luxuriating in the warm colloquialisms.

"Why don't you show him around, Nunzio?" she asked. "Maybe he'd like to see the barn you were clearing the path to just now?"

"Yes, Sister. Come on, Carlo. Let me show you how to milk a cow!"

The two friends spent an afternoon looking at everything new in Nunzio's life, starting with the barn and cows, viewing the classrooms and dorms, and ending with the chapel.

"Geeze, Nunz," Carlo whispered as they entered it. "Your own private chapel?"

"I wrote you about it."

"Yeah, but you didn't say. . ." his voice trailed off as he slowly explored the alcove with its statue of St. Bonaventure. He turned to Nunzio. "This a gumbah?" he whispered, smiling.

"Yeah," Nunzio whispered. "I never heard of him."

"He's in the missal," Carlo responded absently as he continued to investigate his surroundings. The Sacred Heart Church in Philadelphia had its own grandeur and beauty and had its own special devotions within, but this was something very different for Carlo. He had never been in a private chapel. It was quieter, with a great deal less floor area to carry and recarry the sound waves which create the natural and glorious depth of sound in the more spacious buildings. In the more intimate setting, he felt more personally embraced, as if huddling in some sort of holy cocoon.

He slowly moved along, studying the elaborate chair rail and woodwork framing the walls, pausing to take in every detail of the second alcove, a radiant statue of the Blessed Mother, backlit and highlighted with several small spotlights positioned varying distances from the base. The expression on her face captivated him. After a few moments, he turned to Nunzio, said nothing, but just shook his head, and continued to the altar rail.

There, Nunzio joined him as they knelt.

"You serve here?" Carlo asked.

"Yes, every couple weeks I get a turn."

"Boy," said Carlo, shaking his head again. "Boy."

Just then, the door to the outside opened, and Father Boreto entered. When he saw the two boys, he waved and smiled, but turned toward the tiny sacristy, not wanting to interrupt their prayer. He had not met Nunzio's friend, but he had heard about his arrival from the Sisters. "It must be a very good friend to come all the way from Philadelphia over Christmas!" Sister Claire had said, her eyes wide. Father enjoyed their enthusiasm, which often surpassed his own. But in this case, he, too, thought it intriguing. What he had known of Philadelphia did not include young men of this sort, ones who had interest in chapels and even prayer. Most of the boys he read about in cities seem to be more interested in movie stars, gangsters, and learning to drink.

A short while later, he heard a tap on the door and Nunzio saying, "Father Boreto?"

"Hello, Nunzio," he said opening the door. "I see you've brought a friend."

"This is Carlo diFrancisco, Father. He's come from my hometown."

"Welcome, Carlo," Father said, offering his hand.

Carlo shook it, smiling. "Nice to meet ya, Father. Love your chapel!"

Nunzio felt his buddy's enthusiasm and chuckled to himself.

"Thank you," said Father Boreto. Maybe I've misjudged today's youth, he thought. "Are you going to be with us for a while?"

"He's stayin' in Emil's bunk," Nunzio answered for him. "For at least a couple days, right Carlo?"

"Yeah, yes Father. I have a return ticket here somewhere." He looked through his pockets for it, not finding it right away.

"That's all right," Father said. "I'm glad you'll be with us awhile. I'll see you at dinner. Sister Claire is cooking up something special!"

As the two of them headed toward their room, Nunzio asked Carlo, "So what made you come down all the sudden? You never said nothin' 'bout it in your letters."

"I don't know. A change."

"A change? From your house? There ain't nothin' I'd ever wanna change comin' from your place, Carlo!"

Carlo's face distorted as he answered, trying to keep in the tears. "It's 'cause I wanted to get away from there for a while," he said, his voice tight. "Ma's got cancer."

Chapter Eight

Nunzio was incredulous. Cancer? That was what old people got, wasn't it? "No!" he responded a little louder than he expected. Then whispered. "She *can't* have cancer. Ain't that for old people?"

"I guess not 'cause she's got it. Pop told me that's why I didn't get no brothers and sisters."

"Geeze Carlo," Nunzio said. Everything he wanted to say seemed to fit into those two words. No wonder Carlo had made a sudden, unannounced visit.

"It's extra good to be here right now," Carlo said, as if reading his friend's mind. "You know, it's just every day, I gotta see her trying to act like nothin's wrong, trying to hide the pains and pretending she just ate because she's too sick to eat anything."

Nunzio tried to imagine Viviana diFrancisco, her warm smile, always welcoming arms. She was the woman he equated with being "Mom," especially in comparison to his own mother. Mrs. diFrancisco was such a bright, happy, and pretty woman. He figured her smile made her pretty. It brought out the good in her. "She don't eat?" was all he could think of to say.

"Nah, she just, you know, acts like it for my sake. I came down here to give her a break as much as me," Carlo said, flicking bits of paint from the doorframe. "Just lettin' ya know, Nunz. I don't really want to talk about it."

"Okay," said Nunzio, who also didn't really want to talk about it. "And if Sister Bernadette sees you scrapin' that paint off the door, she's gonna make you sand it down and repaint it!"

Carlo laughed. "Cripes—then get me inside and lemme hide!"

"What's goin' on in the neighborhood these days?" Nunzio asked, checking Emil's bed for sheets. "Anybody new on our corner?"

"A couple of girls were there, but I told 'em it was gangster territory and they bolted.

Nunzio laughed.

"Then pop told me that Bobby the Skunk got in an argument with Big Rio."

"Did he bump 'em?"

"No, but Bobby ratted 'em out, and Big Rio got sent down for counterfeit."

"Them guys do counterfeit?"

"Yeah, big time, like 20s and 50s."

"No kiddin'."

"Big Rio swore he was gonna get even. Nobody stood up for him!" Carlo laughed. "Some gangsters, huh?"

"How 'bout, you know, anybody takin' care of Bobby the Skunk?"

"Pop said they were all glad to be rid of Big Rio!" Carlo laughed. "Said it'll be one less greaseball!"

Nunzio laughed. "Yeah, but one less customer for Pop. I guess Pop's doin' all right."

"Oh yeah, he's good as new," Carlo said. Suddenly he drew in his breath, heartily regretting the words that he had let come out of his mouth without thinking. He hoped it had escaped Nunzio's notice, who was busily moving things around in the dorm to make room for Carlo. But Nunzio was sharp.

"Good as new? Whadya mean? When was he not good as new?"

"Just a you know, figure o' speech, Nunz," Carlo said, desperately trying to backpeddle.

"No it ain't," said Nunzio, hurt that his friend would lie to him. "What are ya talkin' 'bout? What happened to Pop?"

Carlo sighed and plopped down on Emil's bed. "This mine?" he asked, gesturing around the bed?

"Yeah. What happened?"

"Look, everything is good now, okay, first you gotta know that. You get the end of the story first," he smiled weakly.

"Okay."

"But after you left, I guess he had some trouble with a couple of Fat Eddie's goons. I heard he got in some good punches, though, knocked out a couple of teeth with that left of his. He's got one hell of left cross. You know, them left-handers always get you by surprise—"

"Carlo look, don't fool around. I'm glad he's okay now, if that's the truth, but what happened?"

"He got a few broken bones, his arm I think, and jaw."

"What was the beef?"

"Big Eddie. He didn't like not getting his way."

"His way? You mean about me?"

"I guess so."

Nunzio shook his head. "Son of a bitch."

"Yeah."

"And my mother's living at that bastard's house."

"Yeah."

"She know about it?"

"I don't know. Probably."

"And she didn't do nothin', just stayed there, livin' with that piece of trash."

"Nunzio, your Pop is amazing."

"Why do you say that?"

"His sense of humor. He told my pop he was only doin' his part to keep them guys in shape."

Nunzio smirked. "Well, from what you said, they don't look the same. Not in the mouth anyway."

"They were already ugly so what's the difference? And they got other problems."

"Yeah?"

"Big Eddie's, you know, he's only a capo. He ain't the top."

"I know."

"He's got a lotta cheech from things goin' on down the market, but there's others movin' in. And the big guys, you know, Pop says he's on his own. They don't care for him."

"No kiddin'."

"Yeah, and it's because of things he done, like your pop and other guys."

Nunzio smiled. "That's nice," he said.

Carlo smiled, too. "Yeah."

The dinner bell was ringing so they quickly washed and changed their shirts. As they rushed down the hall to the dining room, Carlo elbowed Nunzio. "Sorry I told you about all that. Now you gotta go to Confession."

"Me? What for?"

"Cursin'."

"Oh. Yeah." But he knew there was more he would have to confess. Despite his new love and devotion to God, Nunzio felt a deep disgust and loathing for the creature his mother had married. He was sure it was hate. And he knew that was wrong.

At dinner, it seemed to Nunzio that Sister Claire was trying to edge out Sister Bernadette in the unofficial dinner competition.

"Them nuns can cook," Carlo said. "I never tasted Medigán so good!"

"Yeah, I think it might be they're trying to impress you."

"Who me?" Carlo said, smiling with a mouthful of pot roast.

"They know it don't take much to make me happy."

"I always heard they fed the kids worms and old fish at schools like this," Carlo said. "You been livin' it up. How 'bout that butler that takes care of the place?"

Nunzio laughed, "Yeah." But then he lowered his voice so the boys next to them wouldn't hear. "I think the priests of Sacred Heart paid for my tuition, and you know, food and all. I heard Emil talkin' one day, and what this place costs, no way could Pop afford it."

Carlo just nodded, seemingly more interested in food than conversation.

The boys ate at several tables ordinarily, with Father, the Sisters, and sometimes Mrs. Hardy at another. But since there were so few students over the break, they had pushed two tables together for everyone.

"Are you Nunzio's brother?" one of the younger boys asked Carlo.

"No, why, do we look alike?" Carlo answered.

"No, but you sound alike."

Nunzio snickered. "He copies me," he said seriously.

"Actually, I taught him how to talk when he was real little," Carlo said. "That's why we sound alike."

"I think he sounds like Emil," said the older boy who had been left at school during Thanksgiving holiday as well. "Same accent."

"Emil from Philly?" Carlo asked, slightly surprised.

"Yeah, he's from down the market. I told ya that in my letter." Nunzio said. "He's a good guy."

"Man," said Carlo, shaking his head.

"What?"

"I told my pop maybe I wanna go here."

Nunzio was startled. "Yeah?" he said, sitting bolt upright.

"But he said I gotta wait."

"For what?"

"Well, you know…"

"Oh," Nunzio nodded. Carlo's father didn't want him to leave his mother. He wondered how sick she was and if it would be long. "I see what you mean."

Neither boy had lost anyone close to them, although plenty of older relatives had passed away. The situation weighed heavily on Nunzio and that evening at prayers, he included his buddy and his buddy's suffering mother.

Father Boreto, who seemed to always know things even though no one could remember telling him, paused during prayers to speak for a short while about working through painful things. "Sometimes," he said, "things come upon us that we don't expect. Sometimes those are things that are very hard for us to live with. We feel trapped in pain or worry, like we're in some kind of fog."

Carlo looked at Nunzio, amazed. It was as if the priest were reading his mind.

"We may not believe that it will ever get any better, but things do get better, and they do fade some in our memories—not all the way, but enough so that they're no longer making us walk in that kind of grey cloud. And the way we see our way through it is by embracing the things we've learned. We remember the Holy Spirit, who guides us, and to share our grief with the Sacred Heart, who wants nothing more than to take all of our cares from us and refresh our own hearts with His redeeming Grace. We remember the love of the Blessed Mother." He paused, looking down, thinking of how it must be breaking the young boy's heart who sat a few pews back. He looked up and gently met the eyes of the grieving soul. Carlo's eyes had clouded over, and he knew the message was directed at him. "This is the time," Father Boreto continued, "when those things lead you to God, not away from Him."

Nunzio noticed his buddy quickly flick away a few tears with his sleeve, but stayed still as a statue, pretending not to notice. The other boys truly did not notice. Father continued with the prayers for the night before saying goodnight as they all departed.

"Thank you, Father," Carlo said, shaking his hand and looking him in the eye.

Father nodded. "Call on me anytime," he said.

The last days of Carlo's visit flew by. As he smashed everything back into his suitcase on the final afternoon of their visit, Nunzio sat on it for him so he could close it.

"How's Frankie and Pete doin'?" he asked. "You haven't mentioned them."

"That's 'cause there's nothin' new. They're exactly the same. Pete still wants to be right all the time, and Frankie's got his head in the clouds."

Nunzio laughed as they headed toward the front of the school where Mrs. Hardy would pick up Carlo for the station. "How about Mr. Tucker and Mr. Finn, are they still—"

"Still workin' away on that garage! And always on different days. Pop was thinking about goin' over there and seein' if there really were two guys, or if yours and my theory is correct and there's only one."

The boys laughed. "Why didn't he go?" Nunzio asked.

"Ma said, 'Pafun, you don't do that!"

They laughed harder. "I bet it's one guy!" Nunzio said, coughing from laughing.

"I don't see how it could be. They look so different."

"They don't act so different."

As they got to the front door, Nunzio noticed that Mrs. Hardy was already in the car with the motor running. Sister Claire was on hand to wish Carlo a happy trip. He thanked her and smiled.

"Sister," he said politely, "Did you know that when you walk, your crucifix gets beat up?"

Nunzio was startled.

But Sister Claire threw back her head and laughed heartily. "No! But I'll be sure to adjust it!" she said.

Nunzio shook his head and shoved Carlo on the shoulder. "Jeeze, same old Carlo!" he said.

Carlo spread his hands. "What?"

"Say hi to your folks," Nunzio said, opening the door. "I hope, well, write when you can."

Carlo nodded and joined Mrs. Hardy. As the car disappeared, its taillights leaving thin red trails in the darkening dusk, Nunzio wondered which was worse, losing a mother you loved, or never having a mother who loved you.

Chapter Nine

When Emil returned early the following month, he brought Nunzio a giant "steak" from their favorite shop. A Philadelphia steak is different from what one usually thinks of as a steak. It's actually very thinly sliced and sits inside a long roll usually with oil, vinegar, oregano, and a lot of different kinds of cheese.

"Hey, what a buddy! How'd you manage that?" Nunzio nearly shouted, grabbing the package.

"I'm blind, not stupid," Emil said. "They sent the driver for it before I got on the train. I got one for me, too. Hey, I heard you had company."

"Yeah, it was a surprise, my buddy from Philly."

"Mrs. Hardy said he was from downtown. I wish I coulda met 'im."

"He wants to come down here, so maybe you will."

"No kiddin'. It'll be like transplant city, little Italy down here!"

Nunzio snickered. "That'd be something. So what's going on back home? Carlo told me about Big Rio and Bobby the Skunk."

Emil laughed, then stopped himself. "Yeah, it was ugly. Rio was sent up weeks ago but things are still rough. Were they part of your, well, Fat Eddie's gang?"

"I don't know. I guess they coulda been. Why do you ask?"

"Well, I heard that there's some kind of trouble for that guy."

Nunzio brightened. He knew he shouldn't be happy to hear about trouble for anybody in those circumstances, considering what the trouble could result in. But he didn't cherish the idea of having to live under his roof when his time at Lexington Hall was over. And here was the second time he was hearing the same rumor. "What did he do?"

"I don't know exactly, but I think it had to do with some cops. I was just reading my braille and there were a couple guys on the stoop next door talking about how he's upset somebody he shouldn't have."

"Do you know the cops' names?"

"No, but involving any cops is bad news as far as, you know, the bosses are concerned."

"Yeah." It was a sobering thought. Nunzio knew that even as protected as his infractions might be, a man with an ego like Fat Eddie's could step right into trouble if he fell out of favor with the bosses. And causing trouble with, as his dad used to call it, "the local constabulary," was one of the worst offenses a guy could commit in the rackets.

He wondered what would happen to his mother, or to that scoundrel Louie for that matter, if Eddie got whacked. As much as he couldn't stand the man, the idea of his dying some brutal way without warning and leaving the world in the state of Mortal Sin made him feel sick to his stomach.

I wonder if he even remembers how to pray, Nunzio thought. He's probably gotten so used to getting his way, everybody bowing down to him, that he don't even think he has to repent his sins. He's gotten accustomed to acting like he's as good as God.

Maybe Fat Eddie got wind of his brewing disrepute, because despite his ego, he did settle down, made amends such as was possible with the bosses, and kept to his own side of the street, as the saying went. For three years, he kept to the status quo.

It was Nunzio's great delight that Emil did eventually get to meet Carlo, but it wasn't until the eighth grade. Nunzio had grown several inches and his face bore the chiseled, classic Italian features that thrilled girls and made the nuns shake their heads, saying, "And he would have made such a good priest." He was naturally muscular and at age

14, his work on the farm and helping with a construction project the preceding summer at the school had helped developed him into a strong, athletic young man.

Carlo's city life hadn't allowed him to reap the same outward rewards, but his mind was sharp and through his well-focused attentions at Sacred Heart Grade School, he had developed an excellent memory and capacity to think. His mother had suffered long, and by the time she had finally gone to God, his father was worn out from the suffering along with her. Her worries about Carlo's possible loss of faith because of her early departure were needless. He had known the great support and experienced both emotional and spiritual encouragement from their two good priests throughout the ordeal. He had never wavered in his faith that God had specific plans and reasons for everything, even something as painful and sad as the loss of his mother.

It happened at the end of his seventh year at Sacred Heart, so every child in his class and their parents were present for the funeral, which was rich with beautiful music and sorrowful but heartfelt prayers. Carlo, who had borne the burden of the seemingly unending heartache, allowed himself to cry in private, feeling the relief not only from the long anticipated tragedy finally having come about, but also the pain his mother must have felt that somehow, he too, could feel but in a different way. His heart was made light by the vision of her no longer in pain and enjoying the fruits of her earthly labors, having prepared that warm home in her heart for Jesus.

He looked at his father, though, wondering how he would do without their mainstay for comfort. Never had she complained, always downplayed her pain, continuing to bring laughter and happiness into the home long after others in similar circumstances would have taken to their beds in defeat.

Pufante diFrancisco had also experienced a sense of relief when his wife died, greatly to his distress and guilt. But it was that same guilt that directed him to encourage Carlo to experience a little more childhood before he had to face the responsibilities of being a man, even though he believed his young son to already be a man inside. He immediately enrolled him in Lexington Hall.

"You gonna have a good time down there with your buddy," he said. "The two of you turn that place upside down."

The trip down to Virginia together was a happy adventure, but the ride was over before they knew it. Carlo gathered his grip, and a second bag with three giant Italian subs inside, and followed the other departing passengers toward the exit.

"I'll miss ya, Pop," he said as they reached the platform, turning his head away. He knew his father would be hurting. They had clung to each other emotionally through the last painful months, trying to keep the house nice in between visits from his aunts and neighbors. Viviana was so popular that everyone she knew was simply reluctant to let her go. But in her final weeks and days, there was little doubt about her future, and Carlo and his pop carried heartaches inside instead of the sweet rolls and meatballs they were given.

"I'll miss you, too, Son," Pufante said, his voice hoarse. "You write me, now, hear?"

"I will, Pop, right away, soon as I get my desk all set up."

"Make that a promise?"

"I promise." Carlo wanted to turn and run back to him for a hug, get one more chance to feel his Pop's strong protective arms around him and hear his laugh, but he knew it would be a mistake. Aside from the fact that there were other Lexington Hall students around, he knew that it would only prolong the inevitable.

Pufante stayed on the platform, watching his son meet up with Mrs. Hardy. His plan was to simply turn around and take the next train back home. He knew he could have gone and enjoyed seeing the school, and in fact, had been invited to enjoy a dinner and stay overnight, but like his son, he longed to get on with things. The world had come to a stop too long ago, and it was time to begin again, take on life without his wife of over 20 years.

Carlo put his things into the car and started to climb in. Unable to resist taking another look, he turned around to see his father standing and waving just outside the station. He wished with all his heart that his father had grown up the way he had, with a happy family, and a good friend, and attending such a good Catholic school where his spiritual life was fed and nurtured. He knew that his father would probably slack off as far as church was concerned.

He waved back smiling, and then turned, sat down, and closed the door.

"Ready?" asked Mrs. Hardy in her cheerful voice.

"Yes, Ma'am," said Carlo.

The old DeSoto chugged along the train station driveway and down the two-lane highway as Mrs. Hardy recited the familiar "new student" speech, which was frequently interspersed with words such as "of course, you already know this because you've been here to visit so many times."

"Yes, Ma'am," Carlo said, observing the dry, cracked earth along the way.

After a while, the conversation picked up again. "We've been in drought," Mrs. Hardy explained. "I expect at any time, the Heavens will open up and we'll be dealing with a minor flood, but for the time being, we just try not to breathe in any of that dust and go on as usual."

Drought? Flood? There wasn't anything like that back home. Carlo began to feel apprehensive. Maybe he'd gotten into something that he might want to back out of. What if the place caught fire and burned down? Or what if they ran out of water and couldn't flush the toilets? Visiting was one thing but living in a disaster prone area was something else entirely. I've just gone through one terrible ordeal in slow motion, he thought, this isn't going to be another one, is it?

Mrs. Hardy immediately regretted her words. "Oh shoot, Carlo, I just got so comfortable talking to you, I didn't stop to think you're not used to the summer weather here. It stays dry a long time, and then we have rain. But we're prepared for it. There's nothing to worry about, honey."

Carlo sighed, trying not to show his relief as he did so. "Yes, Ma'am," he said. "I understand." But it sure didn't sound like a great situation to him. He would talk it over with Nunzio when he got there and see what his buddy thought.

As soon as that thought crossed his mind, he started to feel stupid. *Stunad!* he thought. Nunzio had lived there almost nonstop for 4 years. If there were catastrophic problems, he would have told him years ago. Just then they turned into the driveway. There at the door stood his buddy, grinning brightly alongside of the smiling Father Boreto. Sister Bernadette stepped out as they pulled up and held open the door. She wore an apron that had remnants of her culinary efforts on it, and a smile on her tall, thin face.

"There he is!" she cried.

"Hey buddy! Good to see ya!" called Nunzio as Carlo opened his door.

Father shook his hand, and everyone grabbed something to carry in for him.

"You're just in time for dinner," said Sister. "Fried chicken and corn fritters."

At that moment, and for the first time in months, Carlo felt ravenous. "Sounds great, Sister," he said.

"Nunzio, get your friend settled in and we'll see you at the dinner table in half-hour," Father said. "Welcome, Carlo. It's good to have you here as a resident, finally."

"Thank you, Father," Carlo said, and grinned at Nunzio. "Let's go!"

Chapter Ten

That night after dinner, which felt like a feast to Carlo after his long abstinence, as the students prepared for the first evening prayers of the semester, Nunzio pulled Carlo aside.

"You seem okay," he said. "You know, your mom and all."

Carlo nodded. "It don't seem like it now, but that was like living in slow motion." He stood at the mirror and combed his hair. "You know, Nunz, she was in a lot of pain but she hardly ever let on. Me and Pop were sittin' with her all the time, one of us, at least. She kept sayin', go on, go eat, and motioning with her bone-thin fingers. Got the point where we'd pretend we were going to eat and then come back in a while. Pop couldn't eat except toast in the morning. After that, nothin'. I was a little better but neither of us were doin' very well."

"I wish I coulda been there, you know, done somethin'."

"I don't really wanna get into it, you know, but it was sure good knowin' I was gonna finally get to come here," Carlo said turning. "By the way, Father Kelly and Monsignor French send their regards. They're looking forward to seein' you next summer!" He started buffing his shoes so they'd be shiny like Nunzio's.

"I can't believe how long it's been. Workin' here over the summer was good though. Got the chance to put a little money together to pay them back for all the years I been here on their dime. I just wish I coulda seen more of my pop."

"He's doin' good. Misses you like crazy, but the courts tellin' him you gotta live with your mother and that didn't go down so well. Still, it won't be long before you can decide where you're gonna live for yourself." He looked up then and studied Nunzio. "You still thinking, you know, along the same lines as when we were kids?"

His question made Nunzio laugh. "Kids? What are we now, old men?"

Carlo joined in the joke but only for a minute before he became serious. "You know what I mean."

Nunzio nodded slowly, smiling happily at his friend, whose mind he could nearly always read. "There's nothing I'm more sure of in my life than the fact that I want to be a priest."

Carlo punched the air jubilantly, the buffing cloth in his fist fluttering like a flag. "Me too," he said feeling the life return to his veins. "You knew that, didn't you?"

"Yeah, pretty much," Nunzio said.

Through the years, with the overwhelming weights of Carlo's mother's illness and Nunzio's family's disintegration, they had spent little time in conversation over important matters. But in the time they did have together, Nunzio had noticed that Carlo was just as easy entering the chapel, serving Mass, and joining in prayers as the two of them had always been at Sacred Heart. He was comforted by the fact that it seemed his friend had been traveling along the same spiritual lines that he had. So he hadn't found Carlo's reaction to his response surprising at all, but there were others around them who did.

Sister Bernadette and Sister Claire were wiping down the tables in the dining room after supper and stacking up the dishes to take into the kitchen.

"It's a beautiful thing to see a young man so resolute in his faith," said Sister Bernadette.

"Oh yes, Nunzio is very devout," said Sister Claire.

"Nunzio, yes, but I was speaking of young Carlo."

"Carlo?"

"He hasn't been here as a student, yet there he was, hands folded, never a thought of sneaking bits from the fritters in front of him. I noticed several of our long-timers swiping a taste or two."

Sister Claire smirked proudly. “Yes, they can’t resist my fritters,” she said, popping a leftover from the final serving dish into her mouth.

Sister Bernadette raised her eyebrows and turned away. “Yes,” she said. “But the thought I had was that boys who have gone through the loss of a parent, and the slow loss, I might say, which is not easy to manage for such young souls, and particularly one living in the city, would generally separate themselves from things they can’t see and touch. It’s a rare child who clings to Faith for such a long and painful time, wouldn’t you say?”

“I agree,” said Sister Claire. She had not thought of the journey the boy had been forced to travel in his heart over the preceding few years. “It is rare.”

“We are fortunate,” said Sister Bernadette. “I think Carlo’s perseverance is a blessing to us all.”

“Yes.”

As the students entered the chapel that evening, there was no form to follow as there would be in the daily Mass. At Mass, they would assemble in the corridor and enter the chapel two by two, genuflecting on command as a well-formed group. But for evening prayer, they chose their own location, just as they would at their hometown parishes.

Nunzio tried to keep his mind on silent prayer, but it was hard because he was feeling such enthusiasm over Carlo’s arrival.

Carlo was straight with him, which could be tough, but it was the only way he’d know how things were going back at home. His pop wrote him letters and they were funny, and a lot of times he’d throw in a couple dollars for "extras," as he called it. But he didn't tell about what was going on there for fear of worrying him.

But Carlo elaborated about the beef that had sprung up between one of the other capos and Fat Eddie Saco. There had been trouble back when he had started at Lexington Hall, but he had not known the extent of it. Carlo explained that Fat Eddie had angered the big boss by involving a cop in a situation between himself and Nick. At first Fat Eddie was defiant, but when deals started to go awry in his business at the market, he was repentant and apologized, did some things to get back in the good graces.

Nunzio did his best not to wish bad luck on Fat Eddie, but it was a constant struggle for him. He knew the man was crooked, and he knew that that was how he made so much money. He also knew there were people getting hurt frequently because of the man's insatiable greed. He wondered how people could stand to be around someone like that. It was a different kind of world for people like that, he thought.

Years before, after hearing that Fat Eddie had assigned a pair of his stooges to visit his father, Nunzio had spent some of the hardest days of his life. The frustration over not being able to see his father and help him, as Carlo had been able to help his mother, was excruciating. He had gotten through it, though, with the help of the priest, a lot of prayer, and long hours caring for the giant bovines, whose gentle nature and unfailing gifts of milk and cream were compellingly heartwarming. In the end, it was better that he had not been there because, he realized, his anger would only have brought more strain on his father. Nick would have had the added burden of worrying about Nunzio trying to take some kind of revenge and gotten himself into trouble.

It wasn't only news on that front that Carlo brought, though. Nunzio had laughed out loud while listening to Carlo's reports of Frankie and Pete, their efforts—and failures--to con some of the younger altar boys out of their doughnuts. Pete had given up trying to be the smart one, because everybody knows that's me, Carlo had said, or, he had added generously, you, if you're there.

But now he's *here*, Nunzio thought, who's the smart one up there? It was funny to imagine Pete taking on the role. Just then he thought of the garage builders and wondered if they'd finished the project. Last he heard, at the beginning of summer, things were still temporarily on hold. He smiled at the thought of it, then remembered with a start where he was.

I sure can drift, he thought, focusing on the violet light cast through the votive candleholder.

After everyone had arrived, Father Boreto processed in song with the four boys whose turn it was to serve, one with incense, two with candles, and one leading the procession at the front of the line. Father wore his cassock, surplice, and overlay stole.

Two of the older boys were horsing around in a pew in the back. Father had only to focus his attention on them for a moment in order to restore order. They reminded Carlo of Frankie and Pete who were always cutting up in math and science classes back home. He wondered if they would graduate and go on to high school. Pete's older brother had dropped out when he'd failed 8th grade. Carlo figured that development would make it easier for Pete to do the same.

Nunzio nudged him. He had missed the cue to kneel and felt sheepish, having gotten lost in thoughts of home.

It was an embracing feeling, being there with so many other fellows his age. Even though he had been to visit Nunzio on several occasions, that first night felt very different because when Father spoke that night, he was included. He was one of the guys, and whatever opportunities or projects were offered, he could be part of it.

Just then, Father invited them to look in their missals to the prayer in preparation for Mass. "You've probably read this many, many times," he said. "We ask God to bless us and accept our offering of all of the Sacrifices of the Mass that have ever been offered. In speaking about this, we say, 'offered by the same Christ our Lord at the Last Supper, and on the *Altar of the Cross.*'"

He paused and took the time to look at each of the boys. The two in the back were quiet but he knew they were not tuned in. There were a few like that in every class, and while he longed to reach the soul of each student, he knew there would be some who would resist.

"The Altar of the Cross," he went on, "is the very life of the priest, the Holy Sacrifice of the Mass cannot take place without the priest. It is his gift of himself to God in the consecrated life that allows us all to benefit from that very altar. As a priest, you *are* the Altar of the Cross.*

"Let's try to make this year that year in which we determine if we are drawn to do God's work, if we have a calling to the sacred office of the priesthood." He paused again. "And if we hear that call, that we respond as God wills it. Now let us stand and pray."

Carlo elbowed Nunzio, who elbowed him back. Nunzio had felt ecstatic when the news came that Carlo would join him at the school. But in the moments just after Father's short talk, Nunzio realized the strength he received--that they would both receive—from their diligence as they grew in their dedication to the call to serve.

**The full prayer is below.*

Receive O Holy Trinity, One God, this Holy Sacrifice of the Body and Blood of our Lord Jesus Christ, which I, Your unworthy servant, desire now to offer to Your Divine Majesty by the hands of this Your minister, with all the Sacrifices which have ever been or will be offered to You in union with that most Holy Sacrifice offered by the same Christ our Lord at the Last Supper, and on the Altar of the Cross. I offer it to You with the utmost affection of devotion, out of pure love for Your infinite goodness, and according to the most holy intention of the same Christ our Lord, and of our Holy Mother the Church.

O God, almighty and merciful, grant us through this Holy Sacrifice, joy and peace, a holier life, time to do penance, grace and consolation of the Holy Spirit, and perseverance in good works. Amen.

Chapter Eleven

Their final year at Lexington Hall was far different than either boy expected it to be. When Nunzio had arrived, he had written Carlo about the comparative luxury of the school, its vast grounds, the huge dining room, and the many teachers that made up his days with stories, real life practice, and lessons in advanced chemistry and math that often took place not in the classroom but in special labs, one of the barns, or even in the school's vast kitchen.

But throughout the preceding years, one of the barns and the acreage that had accompanied it had been sold, and rather than extended farmland, the school had become neighbors with a real estate office and parking lot, with plans to add a small market they called a "convenience shop." The younger students knew little about how the school had changed, but the upper grades watched with a combination of fascination, disappointment, and anticipation of what would come next.

"What's a convenience shop?" Nunzio asked, as he, Carlo, and Emil sat eating.

"I don't know," said Carlo.

"I think they're like that little shop by the gas station on Passyunk," said Emil. "You know where they sell sangwiches and pop."

"How come you fellers say 'sangwiches'?" a boy from a neighboring table asked. "It's *sandwiches,* sand, with a d."

"They got sand in 'em?" Carlo asked.

"Hey, who wants to know?" Emil asked.

"Me, over here on table 3," the student answered.

"What's your name?" Emil asked.

"It's Don Higgins," Nunzio said. Then, addressing Don, he said, "Same reason you say 'fellers' but we say 'fellas.' It's regional."

"Regional? You mean ever'one up there from where y'all come says it like that?"

"Same as everybody down here talks like you do."

"Oh, I get it," said Don. He nodded to himself and finished his milk and left. "See ya, fellers."

"What's he doin'," Emil asked, "studying to be a culture professor?"

"You think they'll sell sangwiches in that convenience shop over there?" Carlo asked.

"We can't leave the property to find out if they do," Nunzio said. "School rules."

"I don't see any construction happenin'," Carlo said. "No gangsters."

Nunzio and Emil laughed.

As it turned out, nothing additional was built, and there wasn't a sangwich in sight. The purchased land remained grass and scrub with an inverted retaining fence protecting not the land, but access to the parking lot. The fence, running along the base of a modest incline, continued the full 2,000-foot property dividing line.

As autumn hurried into winter, Lexington Hall felt the chill of freezing temperatures, mixed with snow and ice. As it piled up, the seventh and eighth grade boys took turns clearing the driveway, the walkways, and the path to the barn. The work took so much time that often the boys missed several classes. That made the occasion of having snow ploughing duty very popular.

Up until just before Christmas, temperatures remained bitterly cold, with wind almost daily, building up snowdrifts along the sides of the barn and down into the valley where the milk cows would have grazed. The hills above the school caught even more of the snow as it blew across, cementing in place with the ice and freezing temperatures.

The boys were able to clear a path to the grazing fields with their shovels, and eventually clear out a circle where, once it rose above freezing, the cows could get at the grass. It was a sad day for the older boys when that job was done, as class work was once again the priority, and Sister Claire had plenty of math homework for them to catch up on.

Then, shortly before Christmas, when departures were in full swing, the weather finally took a turn. The thermometer read forty degrees at daybreak, and it was up to forty-five with the sun shining as multiple cars drove round the semi-circular drive picking up sons eager to be with family for the Christmas holidays. Emil departed happily, with the promise as usual to return with cheesesteaks for each of them. "Whole ones," he had specified.

"Does he do that every time he goes?" Carlo asked.

"Ever since the very first time," Nunzio said as they called good-bye to him. "I'm sure glad you're sticking around. This'll be my first Christmas with a buddy since I left Philly."

"I think Pop wanted me to stay put. His first Christmas without Ma, you know. It ain't gonna be a bowl a' cherries."

"Yeah," said Nunzio.

"What's it like, Christmas without family?"

"It's a bowl a' cherries!" Nunzio said, laughing awkwardly.

Before Carlo could respond, Mrs. Hardy called out to them on her way to her car. "Boys, Sister wants you to lead the cows out to the pasture. With this warm weather they'll be able to get at the grass. It's fifty-two degrees!"

"Yes, Ma'am," said Nunzio.

"You take Gracie and Clover, I'll take Bessie, Bella, and Clara," said Carlo.

"I don't think we'll even need to lead them," Nunzio said. "As soon as we open that barn door, they'll go crazy to get out there. Gracie might even skip her way out."

"Oh, after all that time cooped up in there. I get it. Do we need to use the rope leads?"

Nunzio thought about it. They really didn't. These old cows could show Carlo and him the way out there. But something urged him to take the added precaution. "Yeah, let's do that, just in case." Just in case what, he didn't know. But he was developing a sense of instinct. It couldn't hurt, it wouldn't take much time, and his instinct suggested he do it.

Most of the local farms had only a few cows for dairy, as Lexington Hall did, but being private homes rather than a school like Lexington Hall, where the personnel in the field were constantly changing, they didn't have any need for keeping anything to lead the cows, although a couple of them had tied bells around their necks.

As Nunzio suspected, as soon as the boys had readied the cows, all five cows knew what was up and headed straight for the barn door. Carlo and Nunzio positioned themselves flat against the open door and laughed as the aging, bony-hipped animals strolled as fast as their stick-like legs could carry them through the narrow passage. As the miniature herd sachéd down the path, Gracie giving an extra sort of kick after every four steps, the boys shut the door as best they could against the moving drifts of snow, which were quickly sliding down the sides of the barn. The late afternoon sun was bright as they took their time following the cows out to the field.

More area was available for grazing than they had thought.

"Did you clear another section?" Carlo asked.

"No," said Nunzio. "The other guys must have been out here yesterday before they packed up."

They watched the cows tearing into the grass and listened to them chewing, which never failed to make Carlo laugh. "Sounds like they got motors in there!" he said.

It was getting to be time for dinner, and with most of the students gone, Nunzio looked forward to what they would find in the dining room. One year, they had actually enjoyed steaks. They were small, but they were definitely steaks, and the taste of that rare luxury had gone a long way toward cheering up two of the middle grade fellows whose parents had been unable to come for them.

"Was Father Kelly still giving up his doughnuts to the altar boys when you left?" Nunzio asked as they walked back up the path.

"Yeah, believe it or not. And staying thin and trim. He plays basketball with some of the guys now. What made you ask?"

"I don't know. I just thought about him and Monsignor French. They're both doing okay?"

"Last I knew. Monsignor has been extra nice to us long-termers." Carlo paused. "But he still hasn't given up them doughnuts!"

They laughed. The fifty-some degree weather with the warm sunshine made the cruel winter seem almost unreal, as if it had never happened. A breeze had kicked up but it was still a pleasure to stroll back to the school. They changed out of their wet clothes and found their places in the dining hall. Three small tables had been repositioned to accommodate the much more intimate group in a very cozy arrangement with Father Boreto and the two Sisters each at a table. Only Carlo and Nunzio of the older group had remained at school. Two of the middle group were there as well, and three of the younger ones, who were receiving special care from Sister Bernadette who treated their homesickness as if they were her own children.

"We might not be home," Nunzio said, trying to cheer them, "but we're sort of a family here anyway."

"Yeah," Carlo added, smiling at them, "I don't have any little brothers. It's nice to be with you guys."

Sister Bernadette smiled as one of them wiped their eyes. "I wasn't crying," he said to Carlo.

"Oh I know," said Carlo. "You've probably got a cold or somethin'."

"Wait 'til you see what's for dessert!" Sister Claire said.

"Sister, please," said Father, making a fearful face for the younger boys to see. "Don't tell me we're skipping dinner! I want to taste that pot roast dinner I heard you talking about!"

The boys giggled, as Sister Claire rose, exaggerating hurried movements to get to the kitchen.

"Oh yes, Father!" she said. "I'm on my way."

But the kitchen helper was already rolling things in, and she stood and began the customary placement of things on the table. Once everything was in place, heightening not only Father Boreto's, but everyone else's eagerness to get started, Father said grace. Then they passed the food from Father, to Sisters, then from oldest to youngest, a traditional method that dated back to the beginning of Lexington Hall in the early 1800s.

After dinner, Carlo and Nunzio hurried to put on their snow boots and overcoats to bring the cows in because it was getting dark quickly.

"You weren't kidding about the food," Carlo said. "It ain't ravioli, but it sure is good."

"Yeah," Nunzio agreed. "For Medigán, they do all right. How 'bout that ice cream dessert?"

"That was—hey!" Carlo suddenly shouted. "What's that!"

As they approached the door to the outside, they spotted a stream of water coming into the building and down the hallway.

Nunzio was puzzled, but he knew it couldn't be good. "Let's get out there!"

But when they opened the door, they had to stop sharply. Water was everywhere! The path to the barn was a stream, and seemed to be growing deeper.

"What's goin' on!" yelled Carlo.

"I don't know!" Nunzio said.

"Boys," they heard Mrs. Hardy call out as she moved carefully from the other end of the building. "Are the cows in yet?"

"No!" Nunzio yelled.

"We have to go and get them," she said. "The snow is melting so fast it's flooding. They could be lost!"

"We're on our way," Carlo yelled.

"I'll follow you," Mrs. Hardy said.

"No, stay here," Nunzio said, "Ma'am." He could feel rain drops and as he looked up into the darkening sky, he saw no stars at all. "Carlo, let's go. There's rain coming on top of all this!"

They stepped into the growing stream, carefully at first to get a feel for the current. Then Nunzio grabbed a couple of shovels left behind from the day before and handed one to Carlo. "Use that to stay up," he said. "This is gonna be tough."

"No kiddin'!"

They headed down the path in the flow of the stream which had reached halfway up their calves just as the rain began to fall for real. They were familiar enough with the way to know not to step too far to the right, which would lead to the gulley that was rapidly filling with water. But the path was obscured by the growing darkness and the flowing water, so they used their shovels to make sure they weren't stepping off of it. It was a frightening business as the wind and rain picked up urging them forward, but nothing could have prepared them for what they saw when they rounded the corner to the pasture.

Where they expected to see cows in a pasture covered with water, what they saw was a raging river. The pasture itself sloped slightly, and the further into it, the greater the slope. The cows must have been grazing at the far side of it when the flooding began, because there was not a single cow in the pasture.

Through the driving rain, Nunzio yelled to Carlo, "I think I see something down the hill there. That could be them!"

Carlo nodded vigorously as they tried to hurry without giving way to the current that was growing ever stronger at the backs of their knees and splashing into their faces with not only dirty water, but small rocks and bits of dead grass. Just then, it seemed like a wave snuck up fiercely from behind, taking Carlo completely by surprise and lifting him then dropping him. He went underwater for a moment, but held onto his shovel, and quickly recovered.

"What was that!" Nunzio cried. He turned to look toward the hills and finally got an understanding of what they were up against.

The hills were no longer snow-packed and icy. Everything was grey or the green brown mixture of evergreens. The warm weather must have melted so much of the snow all at once that it had formed a kind of water avalanche. It was coming in waves behind them. "Look out!" he screamed as another one rose behind them.

They stayed up for it but knowing that their time to save the cows was extremely short, they returned to their struggle to go downhill to them. After what seemed way too long, they spotted the retention fence and possibly their animals.

The waves had diminished behind them somewhat because the land rose slightly in one spot, but the rain continued to pour down hard, obscuring their view. Making it closer to the edge of the property, Nunzio could see what looked like the shape of a cow, or maybe two. “Come on!” he yelled. “I think I see Bella!”

Carlo caught up to him and yelled, “There’s two of ‘em, Bessie, maybe.”

“Yeah, that’s Bessie. She’s scared to death, Carlo. We’re gonna have to drag ‘em by their ropes.” Just then he felt a chill reach down through his shoulders and into his shins. The ropes. He was instantly aware that his instinct had been directed by God, probably via his angel. Even as he struggled to stay on his feet pulling the animals away from the retention fence, he vowed to always listen, always hear that instinct from that point forward. Without those ropes, the animals would have eventually drown, floating into the torrent below them, unable to save themselves.

“We should go up that ridge,” Carlo said, pointing to a higher area. “It’s gonna take all we got, but otherwise, there’s just too much water, and where there ain’t water, there’s mud.”

“Good,” said Nunzio.

They each pulled hard on the ropes, pulling the frightened animals toward safety. But as they did so, they found that Clara and Clover were also there, obscured by their barn mates’ struggling bodies. Too tired to laugh the joy he felt at seeing two more of them alive, Nunzio retrieved Clara’s rope and passed it through the wind to Carlo, who just shook his head and grabbed it, and turned to move toward the higher, rockier area, leading his two charges.

Nunzio’s heart was filled with hope as he searched desperately for the one remaining cow, the entertaining Gracie. He felt around with his shovel, thinking maybe she had been plastered against the fence in the deeper water, where the ground was rapidly eroding away downstream. He knew if he didn't get Bella and Clover back to the barn soon, they would get sick and die. Sadly he gazed for a moment in the direction of rushing water, whispering a mournful goodbye to Gracie, and followed behind Carlo with his own two animals in tow.

Chapter Twelve

Later, inside the barn, Father and their ranch hand rubbed down the four remaining cows and urged them to restore their strength with corn and a mix of soybeans and hay. The cows seemed to sense something was different and were reluctant to eat. The rain had returned, and the wind was making wild sounding noises outside the barn, but it seemed to Father that it was their missing companion, Gracie, that was responsible for the cows' true hesitation.

Gently, he stroked Bella's ears and head. He knew that she was more or less the leader. If he could get her to dig in, he suspected that the others would follow. His attentions brought him a gentle nuzzling after a while, and then the familiar nodding of the head, as Bella seemed to be mulling over the idea of a late dinner. He chuckled and nodded back at her. The ranch hand laughed.

"Do you know a special cow language or something, Father?" he asked as Bella stuck her head into the feed bucket.

"I didn't think so," Father answered, smiling at Bella. Then quietly into her ear, "St. Francis told you to eat, didn't he?"

As if in response, Bella pulled her head out of the bucket and nodded again as she chewed.

Father burst out laughing. Soon after, the other three cows joined in as the men had hoped, and the crisis was fading for the four survivors.

Inside, Mrs. Hardy enthusiastically related the heroism of the two boys as Sister Claire bustled around, taking their wet clothing to the laundry while Sister Bernadette stacked fresh towels and socks outside their door. "Once you've had a good hot shower," she called from the hall, "use these clean towels out here and dress warmly. We'll have something hot waiting for you."

Carlo grabbed his heavy robe, opened the door, and grabbed the towels. "If only we coulda found Gracie," he said. "I feel sick about leaving her out there."

Nunzio nodded slowly, taking one of the towels and drying his hair. "I tried the best I could, but I don't think we had any more time. We woulda lost all the others to cold and maybe just death from fear. Did you see them? They were terrified!"

"I know it. We did everything we could. It's just, you know."

"Yeah."

Carlo smirked. "If you'd 'a told me six months ago I'd feel like cryin' over a lost cow, I'd 'a socked ya."

Nunzio laughed in spite of how he felt. "Yeah!" he said. "Me, too!"

As they headed back to the dining room, they heard someone sniffling inside the young boys' dorm.

"Hey, what's the problem, little guy?" Carlo asked, squatting beside the boy. Carlo's muscular physique dwarfed the appearance of the seven-year-old. From a distance, it might have looked like a father speaking to his son.

Nunzio tried to imagine Pete comforting the child. More likely, he'd stand in the doorway and tease him, he thought. And Frankie, forget about it. He'd be hiding under the bed and jumping out. "It's Christmas time," he said to Carlo when the child didn't answer. "He's got a right to be upset. His folks couldn't come for him."

"They miss you as much as you miss them," Carlo said. "I can promise you that."

"It's not that," the little boy managed to get out.

"What is it then?" Carlo said. "Me and Nunzio gotta get back to the dining room. They're making us something hot to drink after being out on our adventure with the cow rescue."

At that, the little boy began to cry again.

"Hey, Carlo, maybe he's scared," Nunzio said. "Come on little fellow, we'll share with ya."

"It's Gracie," he said. "Poor Gracie the cow!"

Nunzio and Carlo looked at each other.

Carlo took the boy's hand and they walked together toward the dining room. Nunzio explained the situation to Mrs. Hardy who had decided to stay the night.

"Oh, well, we'll just have to avoid that subject!" she said, straightening out the collar on his robe.

Carlo and the boy, who had cheered up by then, were seated and in animated conversation.

"Well!" called Sister Claire in a cheerful voice, entering the room with a tray full of hot cocoa and sugar cookies. "Here's a nice reward for the cow saviors!"

"Oh!" whined the boy and the tears began again.

Carlo leaned over toward Nunzio and said in a low voice, "You wanna take a turn now?"

Nunzio raised his hands and laughed. "You're doing great!" he said.

After the younger boys were asleep and the halls were quiet, Carlo stole across the way to the chapel. Even though he had been at Lexington for several months by then, he had not gotten used to the beautiful Presence so close to them all day long. He stood at the back of the chapel for a few moments, just looking around at the statues and inhaling the lingering incense. Then, unable to resist the beauty of the statue of Our Lady, he approached and knelt directly in front of her, and looked up into her eyes. "Ma," he said softly," I can't imagine you're anywhere but up there with the beautiful Mother of God. I'm glad you're finally home, but I sure do miss you."

He stared into the eyes of the Madonna, who seemed to be filled with understanding and light. He knew of many apparitions of the beautiful Lady, and he hoped to study them in depth in his lifetime, but for that night, just her calming gaze was enough. It had been a wild day, and while he mourned the loss of the one funny cow, he felt peace kneeling there in the candlelight. After a few minutes, he heard the outside door open.

"We done our best," Nunzio said, just loud enough for him to hear.

"I know it," said Carlo.

Nunzio joined him on the kneeler. "I knew I'd find you here," he said.

"I still can't believe how great to have all this," he raised his hand in a circle. "You had all this all them years."

"We both do now," Nunzio said. "We gotta make the best of it, Carlo. I don't know what it's gonna be like in high school back in Philly."

The two boys, unlike so many they knew, stayed a few more minutes, feeling the presence of God both in their hearts and right there in front of them. Then fatigue set in as the cost of their long adventure in the water took its toll.

As the chapel door closed behind them, Carlo asked, "You think there's a cow heaven?"

By breakfast time, the clouds were long gone, and the sky had turned a crystal clear blue, but the temperature had fallen back into the thirties and was predicted to land in the twenties again by nightfall.

The young boy who had been so inconsolable the night before seemed to have forgotten completely about the cow reduction and loudly expressed his approval of the pancakes and hot syrup being offered with sausage patties.

"It's a miracle!" whispered Nunzio to Carlo.

"What can I say?" he whispered back. "I got the gift."

Sister Bernadette heard the conversation and snickered. She wondered if it was vanity to think that she had really been the one with the gift, as the one who stayed with the child for an hour after his bedtime to get him to forget all about the storm snatching their Gracie away.

"Fresh milk!" called Sister Claire, setting glasses in front of them. "Boys, you did an outstanding job. Everyone out there in the barn, I won't mention any names so as not to upset certain younger folks, was up and ready for milking today. So you two boys get the milk with a little cream still in the mix."

That was indeed a reward. The chapel is the best thing about Lexington Hall, Nunzio thought, but this fresh milk with cream still in it has to be the second best.

"We'll be popping up some corn later," Sister Claire announced. "So we hope you will all join us back here to string it as well as the cranberries. We want our Christmas tree to look nice! There isn't much time!" She hurried back into the kitchen.

The telephone rang and Mrs. Hardy ran down the hall to catch it.

"And after we finish putting up our popcorn and cranberry garland," Sister Bernadette added, "we have candy canes for the tree!"

"Candy canes?" cried one of the little boys. "I love candy canes!"

Just as they began an excited discussion about what St. Nicholas might put in their stockings, Mrs. Hardy came down the hall and into the dining room almost as rapidly as she had gone. She was out of breath and her expression said something was up.

She stood puffing for a moment, and then said, "That was the real estate office."

"Yes?" said Sister Bernadette.

"Said they'd like us to come claim our property."

"Our property?"

Mrs. Hardy had started to giggle under her words. "The secretary said that we were actually trespassing."

"Now what is this all about?" Sister Bernadette said a bit starchly. "We haven't even been off the property this morning!"

"I'm just having a little fun," Mrs. Hardy said. "It seems someone we know has been eating their grass."

"No!" said Sister Bernadette, her eyes bright.

"Yes!" said Mrs. Hardy.

"How *ever* did she survive?"

Mrs. Hardy shrugged.

"You mean—" Nunzio began, unable to voice his hope.

Carlo looked at him. "That ain't possible."

"Well it must be," said Mrs. Hardy, looking at the little boy who had become interested at the mention of something eating grass, "because Gracie is standing there beside their parking lot, having her very own fresh grass breakfast!"

The seeming miracle of the Christmas cow would become legendary as the years passed, and Carlo would remember it in sharp detail for the rest of his life as the first time he recognized a prayer happily answered. For him, it was easy to understand; his prayer for Gracie's survival had not been for himself, but for the little boy whose heart seemed to break at her loss.

Nunzio would remember it as the Christmas that he first experienced having a real family to celebrate it. The boyhood friendship had matured, and as young men, both intent on giving their lives to God in His service, the friendship had become more of a brotherly bond.

Chapter Thirteen

Following the solemn procession of Corpus Christi, and the emotion-packed graduation from Lexington Hall, Carlo and Nunzio had packed up and gotten on the train to Philadelphia for the last time. Strengthened in their faith, as well as in practical and even some military skills, they were more like men than fourteen-year-old boys.

The journey home had been a kind of unpacking of energy and excitement about what would come next. High school.

"I feel like a Roman already," Carlo said jokingly.

"I'm takin' Latin," Nunzio said, "and some other languages. They say you got a better chance at gettin' into the seminary if you are good at languages."

"Oh yeah? Well don't worry, I'm gettin' in!" Carlo answered.

"You doin' ROTC?"

"Oh yeah. I kind of liked that military stuff, after I got used to it."

"Yeah," Nunzio said. "I left here thinking I was going to become a general. I think the closest I got to a general was that retired Sergeant Monnahan and his dog."

Carlo laughed. "Yeah, but he knew his stuff."

"Sure he did. He was a Drill Sergeant. But I'm sure Sister Bernadette told him to go easy on us."

"Up at dawn before Mass to do PT? That's *easy*?"

"Compared to what he probably would have preferred, like marching us around the entire campus ten times!" Nunzio answered.

As the train pulled into 30th Street Station, they looked for their fathers on the platform. Carlo immediately spotted Paffuto, leaning toward the cars looking in each window for his son. But it was clear from the relatively low volume that time of day that Nick was not there.

"I wonder what happened to Pop," Nunzio said. "I told him we'd be in today."

"He mighta had to work," Carlo said. "Him and Mr. Schultz are probably real busy."

Nunzio continued to scan the area, holding out hope that his father had come to welcome him home. He craned his neck to see along the distant platform but without success. As they stepped out of the train, bumping their luggage awkwardly and finally setting it on the ground to get reorganized,

Carlo's father caught sight of them and hobbled over joyfully as quickly as his old legs would let him. He grabbed ahold of Carlo and hugged him tight, kissing him on the cheek and hugging him some more.

Nunzio observed the pure joy in the old man's eyes. He wondered what it would be like to receive that kind of love from someone. It wasn't an envious thought, just a genuine curiosity.

"Hey, come 'ere, you too!" he called to Nunzio and gave him similar treatment. "Sorry your pop couldn't make it—they're packed at the barber shop. He might even have to open another shop!"

"No foolin'?" Nunzio said. "That's great!"

"Yeah, him and Mo can do it right. Let's get going. I didn't drive, I got a cab waitin'."

"All this time?" Carlo said. "What happened Pop, did your horse come in?"

The cab went first to Nick's barber shop, passing through the neighborhood and by Nunzio's former home. He was struck with a surprise wave of painful nostalgia being back there, and knowing he would never live in that house again. When they got to the barber shop, he braced himself for the crowd of customers he'd have to get through to get to his dad.

"Tell him hello from me," Paffuto said as Nunzio got out.

"Me, too," said Carlo. "I'll see you tomorrow, okay?"

"Yeah, sounds good," said Nunzio.

He grabbed his two heavy cases, filled with so many things he had worked on over the years that carried memories he would never forget. It was a struggle getting through the shop door, but when he got inside, he was shocked. Instead of a throng of customers, there was one old fellow sitting in Mr. Schultz's chair, and his pop was doing something at the counter with his back to the door.

Nunzio stood there for a moment until Mo called out without bothering to look over, "Have a seat Mack, Nick'll be with ya in a minute."

The same radio that had been there before played music through the dominant static, and the air was heavy with the smell of burning cigarettes, and old cigarette ashes. The floor was so dirty that Nunzio was sure it hadn't been swept since he left, and the trashcan was overflowing and surrounded by wads of newspaper or racing forms, paper cups, and what looked like an old dishrag.

When the song on the radio ended, Nunzio decided to compete with the static, and called, "Pop?"

Nick turned around with a start. His face showed a combination of surprise, annoyance, and embarrassment, and Nunzio could not help comparing it with Paffuto's reaction to seeing Carlo. In fact, Paffuto's welcome to Nunzio was world's beyond what Nunzio came upon that day from his own father.

"I thought you were goin' to your mother's," Nick said.

"I told you," Nunzio said. "I didn't tell her."

"Oh. Well." There was a moment of silence, and then Nick shook his head as if trying to get rid of a headache. "I'm sorry, Nunz. I guess I got mixed up. Where's, is Carlo gone already?"

"Yeah, he's gone. They took a cab."

Nunzio was still standing there, holding both suitcases and wondering if maybe it would be better if he turned around and got a cab himself.

"I guess you'll have to get a cab," Nick said. "Mo, we got any cash?"

"No," said Mo. "Hiya kid."

"Hello, Mr. Schultz," Nunzio said, his chest heavy. "It's okay, Pop. I saved some from my summer jobs. I'll get a cab."

"Look, we can go around the corner for a soda or something, after I get, well, don't we have anybody coming today?" Nick finished, directing his question to Mo.

"I don't know," said Mo.

Nunzio suddenly remembered the church. He had missed the two priests there as much as he had missed his father. He knew something was wrong with his father, and he had come to know it a little bit at a time since he'd left for Lexington Hall. But he didn't know what it was. Still, he had never seen the barber shop look so bad. It looked as if it was on its deathbed and only days to its final rest. And both the men looked whipped.

I wonder if he'll give me a hug before I go, Nunzio couldn't help thinking. Maybe shake my hand, congratulate me on graduating? His thoughts ran to the presents his classmates had received on graduation. He knew Carlo was to receive something, but he wouldn't see it until he and his pop got home. Looking around him there at what used to be a thriving business, Nunzio knew there would be no graduation gift. But he longed for at least a smile or just, something.

Finally, Nunzio let out the breath he didn't realize he was holding and said, "Well, I guess I'll do what you say. Good to, you know, see you and all."

"Oh yeah, Nunzio. Good to see you!" said Nick, wiping his hands on his pants as he came forward to offer a half-hearted handshake.

The feebleness of the gesture almost made Nunzio cry. He turned and quickly left the shop, rushing down the walk with his suitcases, grateful for the strength he had built up in school, and even more grateful that he had somewhere to go where he would be wanted.

The church was quiet at that hour of the day. Nunzio stood in the vestibule almost hearing the voices of Carlo, Pete, and Frankie as they got dressed on cold mornings years before. Despite the ugly shock he had just experienced, the memory of those days gone by with old friends made him smile. Pete and Frankie, he thought. I should find out where they're going to high school, get together maybe with them and Carlo.

As he breathed in the lingering incense, it brought back the days of being the chosen altar boy to carry the incense burner for Father Kelly or Monsignor French. He cherished the simple memory of watching one of them add the incense over the charcoal. That was his favorite service. And in the grand Sacred Heart Church, with its beautiful stained glass windows and ceilings so classic and rich in history, it was like a sacred privilege to swing the incense and fill the area with the lush translucent blanket of holiness.

He passed through the vestibule and set his suitcases down just under the holy water font, made the sign of the cross and practically fell to his knees in the very last pew. Sometimes when a person doesn't let himself think of something he loves or wants, they can forget how precious it really is to him, so that when they have it again, the love of it overwhelms them. That is what happened to Nunzio.

He felt as if he were grieving for lost time, lost opportunities, lost friends, even lost family. So much had happened during those four years away from Philadelphia. If he had felt grown up leaving Lexington Hall that day, by this evening, he felt twice as grown up. After a while, he took a deep breath and let it out, filling his lungs with the beloved incense. He stood up and walked more easily to the edge of the sanctuary and knelt down at the Communion rail.

"Father," he prayed silently, "I don't know what's happened, but I know I don't like it. I don't know what to do to make things better. I almost wish I could go back in time and have another year at Lexington Hall not knowing how bad things would be here."

Again, as so many times had happened in his life, he felt the symbolic hand on his shoulder, urging him to go on, to stay strong through the pain. It was at that moment that the door to the Sacristy opened and out stepped a happily surprised Father Kelly.

"Nunzio!" he half-whispered, half-cried out. "Welcome home!"

Nunzio got up and greeted the priest who had not put on one pound since he'd last seen him, although his hair did look a little thinner. "Hello Father Kelly!" he whispered.

"Come on back! We're getting ready for vespers, but let's talk a bit. Then can you stay?"

"Sure," said Nunzio, energy returning.

Father moved a pile of laundered surplices to a side table and pulled a chair over for Nunzio. "I was going to hang these up so that they're not so much trouble for Mrs. Michaels in the morning," he said, "but that can wait. So you've graduated! Congratulations!"

"Thank you, Father!" said Nunzio.

"How long have you been back?"

"I just got in."

"When, yesterday?"

"No, I mean just about maybe half-hour ago."

"And you came here right away? Better let your folks—your father, that is--know that you're home," Father said, wondering what was going on.

"I seen Pop," Nunzio said, indicating his suitcases at the back of the church. "He told me to go to Mom's. I don't even know where it is. But I think I got the address somewhere."

Father Kelly's face fell. "I'm so sorry, Nunzio."

They sat there in amicable silence for a few moments. Then Father sprung into life. "Well, come on, we've got something back here that'll fit you. You can serve for vespers, and then I'll drive you home. All right?"

"Well..."

"What, don't you serve at Mass anymore?"

"Oh, yes, I do, but when I'm here..."

"When you're here?"

"Wasn't there a certain part of that deal, you know—" he began, cocking his head as if trying to remember something.

"Oh!" Father Kelly laughed merrily, and Nunzio, finally feeling the loftiness of being home, joined in. "The doughnuts! I'll be back in five minutes. Bring your suitcases up here in the meantime."

The service was such a salve to Nunzio's broken heart that he didn't want to leave the church. Still, it might be good to see his mother after all this time. Maybe she would have softened now that she's got the things she wanted so much.

As Father drove, Nunzio told him about the school in Virginia and how it had taught him some of the most peculiar but helpful skills, such as how to milk a cow, or how to tie special knots with only a little rope.

"It must have been a great experience," Father said, smiling. "I know your father really wanted you to be able to go there."

"He did," said Nunzio as they arrived at the address his letter specified. "But I know the money probably came from you and Monsignor, and I earned a little over the summers there. I want it to go back to you and Monsignor." He took out an envelope from his pocket and handed it to Father Kelly. "And don't worry, I saved a little out for me," he said with a grin.

"Nunzio," Father began, putting up a hand of refusal.

But Nunzio insisted. "For the next kid like me," he said, his smile breaking momentarily.

Father nodded and accepted the heartfelt gift.

Then as Nunzio started to say good-bye, he turned and caught sight of the house he was to live in. It was startlingly large and surrounded by a wrought iron fence. He looked back at Father and shook his head. "I'll figure out how to get the bus to Mass," he said. "I'm going to the Catholic High School in the fall."

"Looking forward to seeing you soon! Let us know your phone number as soon as you can."

Father waited for him to get inside the big house before driving sadly away. Nunzio had heart, he thought, but he still had high hopes for him. He knew the reputation of his stepfather, and he knew his road was not going to be easy.

Chapter Fourteen

The next morning, Nunzio awoke and silently got dressed, put his money in his pocket and headed out to the street to find the bus heading downtown to Sacred Heart. He made it out of the house without encountering anyone, for which he was grateful.

As he exited through the gate, feeling the discomfort of being surrounded by something so imposing that seemed to indicate he had something to hide, he avoided looking back at the mansion that was to be his home. It was very heavily furnished and the rugs inside were thicker than any he had ever walked on. Each room looked like a commercial for new linens, with wallpaper and décor that seemed so overdone it almost made him dizzy. He had become accustomed to simple accommodations and religious art, and he liked to hear his own footsteps when he walked. The new environment was foreign to him in every way imaginable.

Still, he would not have minded if there had been a feeling of welcome about it. It had been nearly four years since he had seen his mother or his brother, or Fat Eddie for that matter. He had not expected a big welcome, but the reception that he did get was even colder than what he had encountered at Nick's barber shop.

He could still remember the expression on his mother's overly made-up face when he joined her in what he assumed was the living room. Her hair had become very blond, and instead of one of the housecoats he had always remembered her in, she wore a very suave looking evening outfit, very like Susan Hayward or Dorothy Dandridge in the movies. But it was the expression on her face that he didn't think he'd ever forget. She looked downright disgusted.

"Well, weren't you supposed to be here earlier?" she demanded. "I assumed if you didn't show up that meant you were staying with your father."

"Yeah Nunz," Louie had chimed in, having slunk in from the shadows. "Give us a break!"

Even with his earlier disappointment, Nunzio had not been prepared for their reaction. He had wanted nothing more than to turn and go back to the church. Thoughts of trying to manage that were going through his head even then. But instead, he held his ground, showing twice the strength of character of those two put together, and politely asked how they were.

"Well, tired, if you have to know," said his mother. "Della," she called to the maid bringing in a tray of iced tea. "Don't worry about that now. Show Nunzio where his room his." She shook her head and standing up lazily announced. "I'm going to bed."

Louie just sat in his dark corner, drinking and looking at what Nunzio assumed was a television set. If Louie supposed Nunzio would be fascinated by the magnificent technology, he was in for a surprise.

"All right. Good night," he said, and followed Della up a set of stairs that were narrow and seemed to lead to a higher level than the wide staircase his mother used.

"You in the attic level, Mr. Nunzio," she said, forming her words very carefully. "They set you up in one of the upper rooms since you the youngest."

"Okay, thank you, Miss Della."

Della snickered, but not meanly. "Oh honey, you don't have to call me *Miss* Della. Della's just fine.

"And Nunzio's just fine with me," he said smiling at her.

She opened the door to his bedroom, motioned him in, and waddled down the hall mumbling, "Two peas in a pod they *aint!"*

From that point forward, Nunzio worked out how often he would be able to be out of the house, including school time in the fall, and altar serving in the meantime, visiting Carlo, and finding a job to work for the money he would need at the seminary. He didn't know how much it would cost, but he and Carlo had decided back at school that they should start saving right away. He didn't know how soon he could work, but at fourteen, soon to be fifteen, he already had good skills and discipline and he planned to put them to work.

But his primary goal was to get out of the house. He had never expected to be embraced, but he had expected things to be different after all their years apart. That hope had quickly vanished. As he walked along the sidewalk, he wondered how it was possible that two people could go four years without having changed at all.

Just then he caught sight of the downtown bus and ran to catch up to it. He paid the fare, bought some extra tokens and sat down near a window, watching to see what things had changed and what places were still there. As they got near his old neighborhood, the bus stopped and Nunzio smiled to see a familiar person step up to pay his fare.

"Pete Costello!" he called out gaily to his old friend.

"Hey! Nunz!" Pete called back. "What are you doing back in town?"

"I'm back home," Nunzio said. "I graduated. Starting high school in the fall. Where are you and Frankie going?"

"I ain't goin' nowhere!" Pete announced triumphantly. "I'm done with school!"

"You're kiddin'! How come?"

"Pop says I don't have to go. My brother dropped out. So I'm dropping out. He's working down the docks, and I'm seein' about a job at the drug store at 5th and something."

"No kiddin'! Well, that's great. How's your family and all?"

"Everybody's good. Frankie's trying to talk his pop into lettin' him quit but so far, he's going to you know, the Catholic High School."

"Yeah, me and Carlo are goin' there, too. You sure you don't wanna?"

"No! Not me, boy. I've had it with school. Workin's gonna be great!"

"I gotta get a job, too."

"Now's the time. You get somethin' soon, you beat out all the other guys lookin'."

"Yeah I'll be out there!"

"Okay, just don't come by the 5th Street Drug Store, least not 'til I got the job!" Pete laughed.

His stop came up soon after, and then Nunzio's.

Seeing the Sacred Heart Church during the day brought a lump to his throat completely unexpectedly. He could see himself and his buddies running in, shivering from the cold, back when he still had a home in the neighborhood and his family still lived in one house, together. But even through those memories, he could see the cracks in the picture. When had his mother ever joined him at Mass? How many times had his brother given his father the song and dance about having a cough and not wanting to disrupt the Mass? How many times had pop simply not shown up?

Inside the heavy wood door, he took his time, looking at the statues in the vestibule, knowing he had arrived far earlier than necessary. He thought again of what it would be like to live in a church. I wonder if it feels like they live *in* the church, he thought of Father Kelly and Monsignor French. They can come over any time they want, and they must know the place inside and out. Then he laughed lightly remembering how many times he'd seen Monsignor shifting through drawers and closets trying to find things he was sure he had left right there. Maybe, he thought, they didn't quite know it that well.

He had nursed the hope of being able to see Father Kelly, try to make sense of his new situation because he felt that he knew more than he had said the night before, but that he wanted Nunzio to try to settle in. As it turned out, it was Monsignor's Mass that day.

"Well!" cried Monsignor French. "I heard our star altar boy had returned from distant shores!"

Nunzio grinned. "Yes, Monsignor, I'm back from distant shores."

"And a good lad," Monsignor said, lowering his voice. "You are a credit to Sacred Heart. So, are you here to help me out this morning?"

"Yes, if you have room for me."

"We will *always* have room for you, Nunzio," Monsignor said with a smile.

Just then, things began to brighten for young Nunzio. He thought of his years at Lexington Hall and how maybe he had been protected there, not only from the rough times with little to eat and loud arguments, but also receiving the daily reinforcement from his teachers, the house mothers, and the priest in his Roman Catholic faith. The city had felt cold in such stark contrast, but that morning, after being heartily welcomed by his old buddy Pete, and then his very first words with Monsignor, Nunzio believed he could see his future laying out before him.

Father Kelly had already arranged a spot in the cloak room for him, so he was falling right back into place. The other fellows were new to him as altar boys, but he remembered them from lower grades at school. The church seemed empty compared to what he was used to seeing in the chapel at Lexington Hall. He tried to remember what size congregation they had usually seen for daily Mass at Sacred Heart before he had suddenly left. Maybe it was the same, he thought. That part was hard to remember.

At the Consecration, as he touched his forehead to the marble sanctuary floor, he felt filled with the Holy Spirit and new hope, as Jesus' promise quoted by the Apostle Matthew seemed to sprint across his mind. *I am with you always, even unto the ends of the earth.* The high school days would be just as good as the earlier days, he resolved. One way or another, he would follow his path, his calling. His fellow altar server rang the bells again, as Monsignor genuflected before the Blessed Sacrament. Nunzio took a deep breath and let it out. Everything would be all right. He was sure of it.

Chapter Fifteen

"What will you do on your first day home?" Father Kelly asked as Nunzio hung up the surplice he had been assigned.

"I'll talk to Carlo, I hope," he said, "and maybe get a job for the summer."

"That sounds like a very good idea," Father said. "Not too early in the morning, though, I hope."

"Oh no, I want to be here in the mornings," Nunzio said. "That's for sure. Most of the jobs are in stores and things. I saw Pete today. He's trying to get something at the drug store at 5th."

"Pete Costello?"

"Yes."

"I was hoping to see more of him, but he hasn't served since, I guess it's been a couple of years now."

"He hasn't?" Nunzio was startled. "Why not?"

Father Kelly smiled. "I guess we're not all called to the same duty," he said. "And sometimes family duty forces changes."

Nunzio felt sheepish. "Yeah." After all, he'd been forced to leave himself. But he had the feeling Father Kelly was hinting at something. "You mean maybe their family was struggling, too?"

"I don't really know. All of my families are in my prayers, though. Did you have a nice visit with your mother last night?"

Nunzio was ashamed to tell the truth, embarrassed that his family had so little regard for him. But he didn't want to lie, and certainly not to a priest. "It was pretty short," he finally said.

Father Kelly nodded. "Nunzio, I know you were struggling with your father's reaction yesterday."

"Yes."

"You might have felt that he had let you down."

"I, well, it was so, I don't know the right word. It really, it made me feel bad…" his voice trailed off as he tried to keep control over his emotions.

"Sit down for a minute," Father Kelly said. "Here, have another doughnut."

Nunzio laughed in spite of himself. "No, Father, that's yours."

"Oh I don't need it," he said, pushing it back toward Nunzio. After Nunzio gave in and started into the prize with vigor, Father took the opportunity to plead with him. "Try to be compassionate toward your father. He needs your understanding. The breakup of his family, which he loved, hit him so hard, and the things that happened along with that—"

"I heard about the beating he took," Nunzio said, his head down and voice hushed.

"Yes, those things," Father said gently. "Sometimes a man chooses to go away from God at hard times, the worst time to make that choice."

"Why do they do that?" Nunzio asked, almost whining. "Don't they know God could help?"

"Some do, others don't. But a helplessness sometimes turns to anger, and outside of all reason they listen to temptation. Some men drink too much, others get lazy and don't work, and others," he paused, "turn to gambling."

Nunzio expected him to continue, but when he stopped, the reality of it started to dawn on him; the empty look in his father's eyes, his physical weakness, and his seeming disorientation. He'd seen it somewhere, in a movie maybe. The man was so obsessed with gambling that it tore up his life. The nightmare Pop went through, Nunzio thought, our family breaking up, and me going away. That's what caused him to start gambling.

His expression gave him away.

"Nunzio, it has nothing to do with you," Father said.

"I shoulda been here when all this was going on," Nunzio said.

"Number one, you could not have. It was not up to you," Father said sternly. "And number two," he continued more gently, "it was your father that came to Monsignor and me. He wanted help. He wanted to get you out of the grip of the man your mother married, at least until you were a little older. And that's why you went." He paused. "From the looks of you by the way, I'd say it did you a lot of good!"

"Yeah, it was a great school, and really nice people," Nunzio said, calmly, thinking through what he'd been told. "He loved me that much, huh?"

"Yes."

As the conversation continued, Nunzio found a kind of rocky peace in knowing that while his father was struggling with the urge to gamble, he wasn't a bad guy, and he did still love his son. It wasn't the comfort Nunzio had anticipated or desired, but he knew it was the best he could expect.

Father became serious again just before he had to hurry away on his errands. "A man can lose his soul just as easily by gambling as he can with drink or loose women," he said. "Pray for him, Nunzio."

"I will, Father."

Carlo showed up just then, and Father welcomed him warmly as well. "Nice to see another one of our boys!" he said, shaking his hand. "I am sorry to say I can't stay and talk, but maybe we'll meet *before* Mass tomorrow."

Carlo laughed. "I'm sorry, Father. I planned to serve this morning, too, but I didn't wake up on my own and Pop was cooking breakfast. Tomorrow for sure!"

"All right, that sounds fine, Carlo. Good to have you both back home." Father Kelly hurried off across the walk and through the rectory door.

"I never figured they had other things to do when I was younger," Carlo said watching the door close behind him. "I thought all they ever did was say Mass and visit the sick."

"Me, too!" Nunzio laughed. "I still don't know what else they do, but it must be a lot."

"Hey, what are you doing today?"

"I think I'm gonna try to find a job for the summer. What about you?"

"Me, too," said Carlo. "Pop wants me to work close by so I don't have to take the bus. He says it's a waste of money."

Nunzio laughed. "Yeah," he said. "That sounds like your pop."

"I hope I don't turn out that way," Carlo said as they began to walk along the main street.

"Well, it's kind of up to you, isn't it?"

"Yeah, but sometimes stuff just happens to you."

Nunzio gave him a sidelong glance. "Yeah. Stuff."

Carlo knew that Nunzio knew what he was hinting at. He wasn't sure if he should say anything more or just keep quiet about it.

After a few minutes, Nunzio said, "I didn't stay with Pop."

"Huh? Where'd you go?"

"I had to go to the other place, where my mother lives."

"No kiddin'! What was it like?"

"Big, I guess. It wasn't a whole lot of fun. A lady named Della brought me a burger and some chips in my room because everybody had eaten by the time I got there."

"How far away is it?"

"It just off Broadway, but I didn't go directly. After Pop basically told me to get lost, I went to the church."

Carlo shook his head. "Jeeze, Nunz."

"Yeah. It was good to be there, though. You shoulda come for Mass."

"I was kickin' myself that I didn't wake up. But I felt like after he made breakfast and all, even though I coulda made it, it wouldn't be very nice to leave him and say see ya!"

Nunzio chuckled. "I guess not."

They had arrived at one of the busier sections. "I'll take this side, you take that side, and we'll meet on the corner after we apply everywhere, all right?"

"Sure Nunzio. You're such an operator."

It took no time at all for Nunzio to find a job delivering groceries, and as he waited for Carlo, he spotted one of the girls Louie used to spend time with when he was in fourth grade. Before he could step behind the post, she spotted him and came marching over.

"Where is that boy, your brother?" she demanded, acting as if she had just seen him maybe the day before.

"Huh?"

"You heard me! He calls and tells me get ready, I'm coming over and we're going out, and I got all ready and sat there, and sat some more. Do you know how long I waited? Hours!" she shouted, in a voice that sounded more like "ou-ahs!" She pointed her very red nailpolished finger at Nunzio. "You just tell that [boy] that if he ever calls me again, my big brother's gonna come aftah him!"

"Well, he don't live here no more," Nunzio said, amused but trying not to show it.

"I know that!" she continued in an excited state. After a few moments, with her standing there looking very ignorant of her surroundings while Nunzio watched the cars going by to see if he could spot anyone he knew, she said, "Well, where *does* he live?"

Nunzio chuckled again.

"What's so damn funny!" she demanded.

"I was just wonderin' how your brother was gonna come after him if he don't know where he lives."

Her face got red and she pursed her lips and shook her head in frustration. "You're just as bad as he is!"

Nunzio took exception to that, praying that he would never be like Louie. "Oh don't say that," he said.

"You give him my message," she said, ignoring his remark, and turned to march off.

"Wait," said Nunzio.

"What!" she said.

"What's your message?"

"Tell him," she puffed and turned to the side, then "Just tell him to drop dead!"

Nunzio nodded as she stomped off, thinking he wouldn't mind giving Louie that message. He had grown to at least his height, might even be taller, and he had no doubt that he was in far greater condition than his lazy brother.

Carlo popped out of a drug store on the other side and crossed the street. “You’re looking at the next stock boy and floor sweeper for Becker’s Drug Store,” he said proudly.

“That’s great! I’m a grocery delivery guy.”

“For Joe’s over there?”

“Yep.”

“Hey, we did all right,” Carlo said happily. “Not bad for 15 minutes!”

“When do you start? I’m supposed to go there tomorrow morning,” Nunzio said. “And guess what? They give me a sangwich at lunch.”

“Ah you lucky stiff,” Carlo said. “I start tomorrow too, but he didn’t say nothin’ ‘bout no lunch.”

“I’ll share it if we get the same lunch time.”

“What a guy. You seen Fat Eddie yet?”

“No, let’s go by my old house as we walk.”

“All right. The reason I ask is, if your Pop musta told you…”

“He didn’t tell me nothin’ but I heard that he’s gambling. He didn’t look too good, Carlo. I wonder if we could work it out that I live with him.”

“I meant he musta told you what Fat Eddie did.”

“The beatin’, oh yeah.”

“Well that and then telling all the guys, their guys, don’t be going to that barber, there’ll be consequences.”

Nunzio was startled. “No! I didn’t hear that. He blackballed my dad’s shop?”

“Yep.”

“What the hell is his problem!” Nunzio yelled.

Two passing ladies stopped in their tracks to stare him down for using that language.

"Oh, sorry," he mumbled.

"That's what made him get so tangled up in the horses," Carlo continued, lowering his voice as well. "They can't get past just the bare essentials to keep the place going. And whenever he gets a few bucks, he goes off hoping to make a big win."

"Somebody ought to do something about that creep." Nunzio paused. "And I gotta live with 'im!"

Carlo shook his head. "At least you'll be at the job, serving Mass, you might hardly ever see 'im."

But when Nunzio got home that afternoon, he did see him, bright as day and larger than ever, sitting at the dining room table ordering his mother around as if she were a servant. "I don't like that much garlic. I like garlic, but you go overboard. Try to get that right, wouldja and also don't cut the bread so thin."

"You said you like it thin—" his mother began to object.

"If I said it's too thin, it's too thin!" Fat Eddie roared. "I'm the one eatin' it!"

Nunzio stood in the dining room doorway, surveying the ugly scene, but feeling a certain dark satisfaction at hearing his mother take the abuse for a change.

"What are you waitin' for, some kind of invitation?" Eddie said to him. "Come in, your mother'll make you a sandwich."

"You ain't from here, are you?" was the first thing Nunzio said. He didn't pronounce the word "sangwich" correctly.

"Huh?"

"You got a different accent."

"Oh, yeah, well, I'm from Cherry Hill," the giant said. "Make him a sandwich, wouldja?"

His mother gave him a dirty look and said, "Sit down. I'll get to you."

"You don't get to him, I wanna talk to him," Eddie said with the edge in his voice returning. "Sit down, kid."

Nunzio sat down two seats away from the man, as there were 12 chairs around the large table in the dining room that should have held one with six.

Fat Eddie observed his individualistic behavior and made a note of it.

Nunzio's sandwich also had too much garlic, but he was hungry, so he ate it.

"I got work for you," Fat Eddie announced, "down the docks."

"I just got a job," Nunzio said.

"When? Today?"

"Yeah," Nunzio responded, fully aware of his lack of respect toward the man.

Fat Eddie stared hard at him. Who was this kid? Did both boys have the same father? "Where'd you get a job so quick?"

"Downtown, the grocery store."

"Your brother says he's been looking for a month and he can't find a thing. I'm having him work down the docks."

"Well, I found one. Maybe it was just a good day for it," Nunzio said.

"Yeah, don't get too sure of yourself, kid."

Nunzio wasn't sure what to make of that response, so he just continued to eat his sandwich, regretting that for the first time in four years he had forgotten to say grace before it. As he did, he wondered what grace was ever uttered in that house and by whom. The only crucifix in the whole house was huge and plastered right at the entryway so that anyone entering would be sure not to miss it. Other than that, he had not spotted a single indication that it was even a Christian home.

His stepfather's attention returned to a short stack of documents he had in front of him. Nunzio could tell from a distance that they were some sort of invoices, like the ones he'd learned about at Lexington Hall. He figured his stepfather was sending out bills. But he seemed to be struggling with it. Good, he thought darkly. He could see the man's hefty gold gunagila hanging around his neck, looking like a carrot that Jack and the Beanstalk might have found in the giant's garden. While most people would have felt instant envy, Nunzio was repulsed by it. He didn't know the concept of vulgar, but if he had, that's what he would have assigned to it.

As he started to get up, Fat Eddie addressed him again. "I think you oughta work down the docks with me," he said. "It ain't up to you where you work, it's really my call."

Louie had come then. "Oh don't bring him into the business," he whined.

Nunzio hid his resentment toward Fat Eddie, and to wind up Louie, he said, "You want me to work with my brother Louie?"

"No!" Louie shot out emphatically. "You said I'd have that office to myself, like a professional," he said addressing Fat Eddie. "We don't want some kid still in high school coming in there, messing everything up, saying the wrong things."

Fat Eddie thought it over. The kid seemed pretty smart, but someone that young might be just ignorant enough to say things he shouldn't about things that nobody should know.

"Yeah, you go to your little job for now," he said to Nunzio, as if he were in charge of the world. "We'll see how it all works out." He looked back at his frustrating stack of papers and yelled, "Damn, where is that woman? I need something to drink to wash down this dry sandwich!"

Louie gave Nunzio a dirty look. Nunzio smiled sweetly at him as he left. So far, so good, he thought.

Chapter Sixteen

Within a couple of months before Nunzio realized that at his new home, family meals were never to be as they had always been at his previous home. They were not even as they had been at Lexington Hall. In fact, there would only be family present when guests were due to arrive, and the semblance of a happy family was necessary. Otherwise, which was most of the time, Della or one of the other ladies who worked on her day off, would create a kind of cafeteria array of food, ranging from hearty meal selections to sandwich and salads. Often a soup tureen would appear as well, holding one of Fat Eddie's favorite soups.

Residents of the house would wander in at will and eat what they wanted and then wander back out. Occasionally, two people came in at a time, such as Nunzio's mother and stepfather. It was during the presentation of one of these food conglomerates that Nunzio witnessed his first fight between his mother and stepfather.

Della had set out a tray of sliced meat, another of mashed potatoes, and was struggling to carry in the large soup tureen. Nunzio saw her trying to push open the door from the kitchen passageway and jumped in to help. His mother, seeing the chivalrous move by her son, was reminded of the fact that her husband no longer showed her that kind of consideration.

"What kind of soup, Della?" she asked.

"Minestrone, Mrs. Saco," Della said as she put the ladle onto a plate beside it.

"Minestrone again?" Mrs. Saco whined. "Why is it always *your* favorite? You know I can't stand that," she said, addressing her husband.

He said nothing but waited for Della to bring him a bowl of soup. Unlike the others, which he regarded as his underlings, including his wife, he sat like an overgrown mushroom in his chair, waiting to be served.

"Why don't you ask for gnocchi or even the chicken pastina," his wife persisted. "Why is it always something *you* want?"

"I like minestrone," Fat Eddie said, shrugging, seemingly indifferent to her, as Della set a bowl down before him, and returned with two large rolls on a plate. He began to eat, producing the loud slurping sound of a man thoroughly indifferent to those around him. Tearing chunks off of the bread with his pudgy fingers, he slopped them into the soup and back up to his mouth recklessly, dripping soup from the table to his chin and everywhere in between.

It was a very slight sound, almost imperceptible. From where Nunzio stood, because he had not yet decided whether or not he wanted to eat in that company, he could better see his mother's face than hear the disgust in her snort. It was a sample of the disdain he had grown up with. It had accompanied most every effort his father had ever made to please her. He cringed, sensing that the man to whom her disgust was now directed would not respond in the same manner his father had always done.

Nunzio's reckoning was on the mark.

The first thing he heard was the slamming of a fist so hard on the table that it jarred everything from plates to glasses and even utensils, all of which seemed to do a short dance and land back down on the table, and not all in the upright position.

"Do you have something you wanna say?" Fat Eddie roared at her with the energy of an industrial meat grinder. "'Cause I can hear ya, and I'm listenin'!" His eyes looked wild to Nunzio, as if he had lost part of his eyelids, and his mouth had become empty, leaving traces of what he had intended to chew and swallow across the table with the fallen glasses. He sat there, as forward in his chair as his girth allowed, fist in the air, waiting for her response.

As Nunzio watched transfixed in the doorway, the mother who had always had a mouth full of abusive comebacks, complaints, and healthy insults said nothing, but shrank back in her chair until the monster at the other end of the table leaned back in his chair and resumed his soup shoveling exercise. At that point, she got up, pushed past him and ran down the hall like a frightened squirrel.

Thoroughly unrepentant, Fat Eddie continued with his feeding and threw out the remark, "That's how you gotta treat'em. Otherwise they gonna walk all ovah ya."

Nunzio quietly left. It wasn't a good time for a meal, he decided. And the emotions the scene created were puzzling. As he left the house, unsure of where he was going, he wondered with a degree of guilt, if maybe Fat Eddie had a point. As disgusting as he was, Nunzio's mother didn't walk all over him. She certainly had done that to Nick, on a regular basis, leaving the man so broken that he'd lost himself in gambling.

Equally confusing was the fact that he could not muster up any sympathy for his mother. A man should never yell at a woman that way, he knew. That was one thing his pop had taught him. It was just wrong in all kinds of ways. So why wasn't he more upset over that?

The more he wandered, the more he recognized that the happiness his mother had complained for years about not having was still evading her. Nunzio's earlier years had been spent trying to please her with his drawings, his superlative classwork, his excellent behavior. But walking the sidewalks that afternoon, he wondered if he would ever be able to please her. If Fat Eddie, with all his money, minions and other worldly goods kept her the same old sourpuss, anything he could offer her would certainly not bring her happiness. As long as she only wanted those types of things. That was the key, wasn't it? He pondered the idea, wondering how a son could affect the values of a mother, and should he even attempt it? Wasn't part of the Fourth Commandment to respect the wishes of the parents?

After a while, Nunzio realized he had nowhere to go. He missed walking down to the barn to spend time with the giant, gentle creatures that had provided such glorious milk and cream those four years. By that time, he figured, they'd be slowly making their way back up to the upper pasture, stopping to nibble a little more and "think about things" as Mrs. Hardy had described it. He couldn't count the times he had sat and thought about things with those cows. They had welcomed his presence from the start. It wasn't the first time he found himself wishing he were back at Lexington Hall.

When I was there, I wanted to be here. Now I'm here, I want to be there. There's no pleasing me, he thought with a start. I'm like ma! A kind of shadowy guilt seemed to hover over him then; guilt over the feeling of wanting to be nothing like her, and guilt over his immediate reaction to want to denounce that part of himself that bore any resemblance to her.

He sat on the newspaper dispenser next to the payphone at the bus stop and stared at nothing as the traffic passed by. "Great," he said.

At home that afternoon, with Fat Eddie out at one of the mysterious meetings Nunzio had come to accept as his job, Louie and their mother sat lounging in the sunroom that sat overlooking the pool. Louie was drinking, and his mother was working on her fingernails.

"What are you doing home?" she demanded when she saw Nunzio. "I thought you had a job?"

"I'm off today," Nunzio said, unperturbed.

"Well, listen," she went on. "We're having a party this evening. A last-minute thing."

"Last minute because the oaf is out of town," Louie said, sitting up dreamily then lying back down.

"Louie's invited a few of his friends," said his mother, "and I know it's late but—"

"Oh that would be nice," Nunzio interrupted, surprised and pleased to finally be included as a member of the same family. Since he had arrived, he had felt very isolated, living on a different floor from them and having no meals as a family. At last, a little warmth had arrived. He smiled, all thoughts of his disdain for his potential similarity to his mother quickly dissolving.

His mother scowled at him for a moment, and then returned to the important work in front of her. "It's late in the day, but I think you could still do it," she said. "The pool man is gone for the day and there's an awful lot of scum on the shady side. Go out there and clean it so that Louie's not embarrassed in front of his friends. I think you can get it done by the time people start coming." She paused. "This is a party for *adults*."

Before he could respond, his mother turned to Louie. "And you'd better sober up and get in the shower. Tell Della to put on a fresh pot of coffee. Oh go on, I will then." Then she noticed Nunzio still standing there, trying to take in the situation. "Well what are you waiting for? Hurry and get busy. You can get the cleaning things out of the shed out there. And don't track in any dirt when you finish. Use the back door."

Nunzio was numb. Vulnerable to the core, it couldn't have hurt more if someone had punched him in the face. "You want me—"

"Yes, yes, now go!"

Louie waddled over, very inebriated, and leaned in close to him, "You ain't in fairyland no more," he said gleefully, and continued on his way to the main staircase.

But still he stood there. Why should he do that? With all their money, there must be someone who was paid to do that sort of thing. Why didn't she just call the pool man back? No, he wasn't going to do it. They could clean their own pool. He turned around, unsure of what he would do.

"And try to be out of there by the time our guests arrive," his mother added. "It looks awful when people are arriving, and workers are still hanging around."

That was it. He would go, maybe catch a bus somewhere. He went to his room and gathered his earnings from the previous two months' work and left the house by the back way. At the bus stop it occurred to him that he should go and see Father Kelly.

He said if I needed anything, he would do all he could, Nunzio remembered. His heart began to fill with hope as he worked on a strategy. As soon as the downtown bus arrived, he popped on, feeling giddy with new freedom.

Chapter Seventeen

It wasn't a long ride to Sacred Heart, but it was hot. Several windows were open, which brought the welcome breeze when the bus moved, which did less than Nunzio hoped. The passengers on the bus were different from those who rode during the week. On a Monday morning, for instance, they would clomp up the steps, drop their fare into the slot, and clomp down the rubberized carpet to find a seat as the coins jingled down the fare tube. If anyone made eye contact at all, it was only the person whom the new arrival chose to sit beside. It was a quiet, somber ride. But on that afternoon, the mix of passengers was surprisingly loud, multi-aged, and multi-lingual.

"You gotta get a haircut, Georgio. You look like a bum."

"*Non ti preoccupare, Maria. So come prendermi cura di me stesso!*"

"Yeah, you can take care a' yourself! What's that you got all over your shirt?"

On any other day, Nunzio would have enjoyed the exchange. He loved the sound of spirited conversations between loved ones. But he was urgent to get to the church that day. Despite his bold move, he was afraid. He knew he had no right to disappear from his home and there would be trouble if his plan went awry. But that wouldn't happen, he reassured himself. After all, Father Kelly had as much as offered to help him.

A little voice in his head tried to get his attention with the message that this might be one of those times when acting impulsively would give him trouble. He sensed it, but he side-stepped it. The pain in his heart and the anger in his head at being so deeply insulted, especially when he had mistaken his mother's first remarks to have been welcoming, were simply too much to bear.

He hadn't lived with them for such a long time, and by contrast, *had* lived with such supportive and nurturing people, that he had been thoroughly unprepared for the cruelty. But as he rode along, his heartbeat began to slow, and return to normal. He would keep working, he decided, even when school started, to make sure he had money to give the priests for staying there. He could serve every morning, just have the doughnut that Father brought, have cafeteria lunches, and he'd only have to provide for dinners. Maybe cereal, that would be cheap.

The bus stopped at Sacred Heart Church and Nunzio hurried out and down the sidewalk to the church. It was empty. Unlike during his last visit, he did not stop to pray, and was so intent on setting his plan into action that he even forgot the Holy Water and hurried down the side aisle to the Sacristy.

He pushed open the door, expecting to see his fellow servers or one of the priests at least, but that room, too, was empty. The table was bare and the lights turned off. He stood in the doorway for a moment, coming down a little from his adrenaline and passion heights. Who would he talk to about his plan? Should he go over to the Rectory?

With no one immediately there, he had time to think about what he would say. But formulating the words that went with his rebellious thoughts was not easy. In fact, he began to feel a little foolish. Yet, he knew, or at least he thought he knew, that he had to take action. He couldn't live in that awful situation, being made to feel like the servant under the stairs. The one consolation at having to live away from his father was that there would be a certain degree of comfort. Taking away that consolation, what was the point in staying there?

Just then he heard the door to the outside open, and he turned to see a very surprised looking Father Kelly appear.

"Well, hello Nunzio! It's nice to see you in the middle of the day. No work this afternoon?"

"No, Father. I have the day off," Nunzio began.

But then Monsignor pushed through the back door and Nunzio suddenly felt uncomfortable. He hadn't counted on speaking to both priests, even though he was fond of both. All of his imaginings of the situation involved Father Kelly alone. Telling them both about his troubles felt sort of like standing up and reading his composition in class.

"Well, what a surprise!" called Monsignor. "Father Kelly and I were just heading over to make some plans for September's special Masses. I hope you'll still be able to join us, even when you're in high school. The Exaltation of the Holy Cross is always one of my favorite holy days."

Father nodded. "Maybe you will be able to serve that morning, at least."

"I hope so," said Nunzio, feeling very awkward.

"Yes, well," said Monsignor, continuing toward the Sacristy. "Excuse the interruption, Nunzio.

Father moved to join Monsignor, but hesitated. "Was there something else? Did you want to talk about something?" He sensed that the boy was struggling with something but wasn't sure if it was a matter for discussion or if Nunzio preferred to spend some time in prayer.

"Uh, yeah, Father," Nunzio began. "I've just come from uh, the bus."

He stopped, focusing instead of on his thoughts, on an imperfection in the pew beside him that caught his eye. He ran his finger over it, as Father waited patiently for him to continue.

"I imagine it was hot inside the bus this time of day," Father said.

"Yeah, it was hot, and there were a lot of people."

"Mmhmm."

"Father…"

"Nunzio, what's on your mind?" Father asked gently.

"I just came from home. And it was such a, it was so bad. I can't express how awful it feels to be there now," Nunzio went on, the words pouring out freely then as if a bottle had been uncorked. "The people, my family, Father, they're rude and ugly, they treat me as if I'm beneath them. They never come to church, they don't even think about church or God or anything anymore."

"I'm sorry you're having such a hard time," Father said.

"Today, when I came in, I found out that they, my mother and my brother, are having a party. I guess it's because my stepfather is out of town, and—"

"They are having a party because he's out of town?" Father asked, not understanding. It would seem more likely that they would have a party to welcome him home.

"I guess so. And I'm not involved, as far as my mother is concerned. I don't have guests to invite, I'm separate from her and my brother. I wasn't so surprised by that, but Father, then she told me I had to clean the pool. Get in there and scrub out the pool so that my brother won't be embarrassed when his guests see a little bit of algae on the sides of the pool. I'm not invited to a party being held in my own house, but instead, made to clean the grungy scum off the pool! I can't live there anymore. It's just not possible."

Father listened, and motioned Nunzio to join him in a pew in the rear of the church where it was cooler and further from the Blessed Sacrament. "Let's sit down," he said.

When Nunzio sat, he began to feel uneasy again. Father Kelly seemed to be reserved, different from the indignant supporter that Nunzio had imagined.

"Nunzio," Father Kelly said, "I can see there's a problem with your family. I guess there are lots of problems. Monsignor and I both anticipated that you would have a rough adjustment because of the differences that have grown between you and the other two members of your family."

"There's three of 'em," Nunzio said.

"In the eyes of the Church, only two are actually members of your family," Father reminded him. "Even so, your stepfather is part of the picture. As such, regardless of his behavior, and I suspect that there is much that is objectionable, you have to show him some degree of respect. In this case, it seems as though he is also being left out. In any case, the situation you describe, as unpleasant as it is, is actually an opportunity."

"An opportunity?" Nunzio asked blankly.

"Do you know what Our Lord's favorite quality is?"

Nunzio stared at the floor. One of the tiles was just slightly out of alignment, and a tiny bit of dirt had gathered in that space. His wanting to flick it out of there drew his attention slightly away from the conversation that was not yet going in the right direction. "No," he said.

"Humility," Father said gently. "Being able to accept being put into situations such as this and acting with individual dignity, honoring Our Lord and offering up the external indignity. This is an excellent chance for you to make an important choice. Do you understand what I'm saying?" As he continued, reminding him of Jesus' many indignities even before the Cross, he couldn't help noticing that Nunzio seemed to be turning off, no longer listening.

"I can't live there, Father," Nunzio said, looking at him suddenly. "I can't stay in that house."

There were tears in his eyes and Father's heart was breaking for the boy. His own parents had been quite different, so he never knew the kind of pain this devout young man was suffering. Without fully grasping Nunzio's plans, and with an eye toward pointing out the futility of his intent to live elsewhere, Father asked, "But where would you live? Your father's already indicated he can't afford to have you there, not yet at least."

"I could live here," Nunzio shot back, almost pleading. "I could pay, I'll keep working. I'll go to school, then to work at the store, and pay my way."

Finally getting the picture, Father felt overwhelmed with sorrow and sympathy for the young man. The law would never permit someone his age to leave his family home, and they would never be able to house him even if it were legal. Nunzio was in a crisis, and he had gone as far as working out the practical details in his head, which told Father that he had created a picture in his mind of how to solve his problem. And now it had come to him to destroy Nunzio's rescue.

He closed his eyes, asking for help from God. The task was one he had not tackled before, and he knew the stakes were high. If he missed a step, like a man on a high wire, he could ruin the whole direction of this young man's journey through life.

But Nunzio sensed he was about to be rejected. He had sensed it earlier, and he had even somehow realized it before he had said a word. But it was still making him angry. The humiliation and rejection of his mother seemed to come roaring back, laughing cruelly as Father spoke.

"You're such a responsible young man," he began. "I don't doubt for a second that you would keep your promise and pay your way, as you say. You'd probably be very neat and not a problem in the least." He paused. "But not only would it be illegal for you to move away from your home, it wouldn't be all right with the Church either for you to live with us. There are rules about these things that we all have to follow."

"But can't you find out? Can't you ask Monsignor?" Nunzio persisted, even though he knew the answer.

"I already know the law. I know what his answer would be, Nunzio. Of course, the way things are," he added, "you're here with us mornings to serve Mass, then you'll be going to school, and if you continue working, the amount of time you would be spending at home—"

"So the answer's no, then," Nunzio interrupted sullenly.

Father nodded sadly.

Nunzio angrily wiped away tears of frustration.

"But I want you to feel that you can come to either of us, especially now with the situation being as it is, and feel free to talk things over—"

"Talk, yeah," Nunzio said in an ugly tone he'd heard his mother use more frequently than not.

Father sighed. He had failed. "Talk can be very, very good for you—"

"I got friends for that. Thanks anyway," Nunzio said, getting up to leave.

Father watched him walk rapidly toward the door. "I'll see you tomorrow morning then," he said hopefully.

But Nunzio was already gone.

Chapter Eighteen

Be humble, sure, that's easy for a guy like him. He don't have to live with it every day. Bitterly Nunzio reviewed Father's words of consolation as if they were heartless and unfeeling arrows aimed at his execution. *Yeah Jesus was betrayed, that don't mean I have to be. He was doing something important, and he knew how it was all gonna turn out. I'm a nothing, doing nothing, with no idea what's gonna happen, living in a house full of heathens. What's the point of it all? I thought Christians were supposed to stick together, help each other out. Even the mafia stands up for their guys. What have I been doin' all my life? Top of my class so I can clean the scum for my no-good brother!*

The bus bumped through the city to the stop near Nunzio's house. He got off, carrying an attitude and a cross at the same time, sneering the best he could at a woman on the corner collecting for St. Christopher's. But after he passed her, his breath caught in his throat and he felt sick. He breathed deep to try to regain his equilibrium, and then walked more slowly. Still angry and disgusted, but less sure of his own reasons. One of Father Kelly's promises nagged at him, *"after you've finished the job, if you have taken the proper attitude while doing it, your soul will be multitudes richer for it."*

Nunzio hated that the words rang true. He hated that to gain grace he had to subjugate himself to the fools that he was living with. And they were fools. His mother had longed for riches all her marriage to his father, and there in her new marriage of sorts, she had them, but only complained that they were not exactly to her liking. And his brother. Nunzio shook his head. How long was he going to hang around his mother like a little puppy, waiting for pats on the head?

"What important choice am I supposed to make?" he said, walking up the long driveway to his house. He shook his head, trying to ward off the continuing nausea he felt.

When he stepped inside, there stood his mother. "The guests will be here any minute!" she commanded. "Go out there and do that job. You have nothing to do all day long, and now when you could show a little appreciation, you disappear. Get out there now and take care of it before anybody sees you." She clapped her hands for emphasis. "Now! Get going!"

Nunzio walked by her without a word, heading for the back of the house to the pool. It was a large pool considering the size of the house. Despite his mother's urgency, he felt very little need to rush. As he stood outside next to the clear water, he felt refreshed. He found a scrubbing brush with a long handle and set to work, the nausea gradually drifting away as he worked.

About halfway through the job, he heard a commotion inside, and stopped to listen. He couldn't make out the words, but it was definitely the voice of his stepfather, and he was not happy. Leaning closer, he almost smiled, feeling like an old gossip, but he felt a kind of sinister glee at the idea of his stepfather catching his mother and brother having their secret party while they thought he was out of town.

"You thought what? That I wouldn't find out? What kind of a chump do you think I am? I know everybody in this town!" the man roared. *"EVERYBODY!"*

Nunzio heard a smack, followed by a mild bump. "You don't arrange things to happen behind my back, because that is one thing that will get you in trouble. You hear me? Every time. Every time. I'm surprised you didn't learn from the time I caught you out at the bar that night."

"That was innocent," he heard his mother saying, her voice riddled with emotion. "It was totally innocent, Ed, I'm telling the truth!"

"Yeah. Well, how do I know?"

"She wasn't meetin' nobody," Nunzio heard Louie say in a small voice.

"How would you know?" Fat Eddie responded disdainfully. "Go pick up that mess your mother knocked on the floor. I gotta get dressed. I guess we're having a party!" he finished, his voice falsely elevated.

Nunzio wondered what the mess was. Whatever it was, he decided, the storm seemed to be over. The conspirators were caught and were going to have to pay the price, meaning acting like they were having a good time at their ill-fated party. Good, he thought. Serves them right. He went back to the scrubbing project; his farm-developed arm muscles no match for the algae hoping to take up residence on the swimming pool wall.

All of the sudden he felt a hand on his shoulder. He jerked with a start and looking up he saw the face of Fat Eddie looking down at him. "What are you doin'?" he asked, genuinely curious.

"Scrubbin'," said Nunzio, and went back to it. What does it look like, he thought.

"You part of this party thing? You don't look like you're dressed for it."

"No." He wanted to say I'm doing this for the ingrates inside, but he left it at "no."

"Hey," Fat Eddie said without hostility, "don't waste your time cleaning up for that sissy brother of yours. Come on, forget about this. Go and do whatever you want. I got a charge account at the drugstore there on the corner. Take your buddy out. Go on, get out of here."

Nunzio was shocked. Was that a side of Fat Eddie he hadn't known? Was he actually a nice man under it all? But then he remembered the report of his father in the hospital, and his subsequent descent into complete degenerate gambling, and the fact that he was about to lose his business despite his popularity as one of the city's best barbers.

"Okay," he said, standing up but showing no emotion. He put away the brush, closed the shed, and left the pool with Fat Eddie standing there nodding in admiration. Nunzio was glad for the reprieve and satisfied that his brother's pool would not be 100% spotless. He even considered giving Carlo a call and arranging to meet him at the drug store counter for a hamburger. But the mist of confusion had descended on him, and the nausea was back.

That night, after everyone had left the house, and the maids had finished vacuuming and stacking the chairs to be returned the following day, Nunzio finally fell asleep. He had decided against going for a hamburger, and instead visited the kitchen and had a peanut butter sandwich. The act of making it reminded him of how his life had been four years before. He wanted to lament the changes, feeling them tug on his heart, but he also wanted to be tough, tell himself it didn't matter what hit him now. He could handle anything. Maybe his whole life had been a series of mistakes. His dreams were like leaves of multiple colors, untrue to nature, blasting red and purple, navy blue, and black. After a time, they grew faces that he recognized. He found himself in the church again, sitting and unable to leave. Someone was talking, “Even Jesus was betrayed by his own people. Remember Judas?” the voice said. “But He was humble, He stayed strong and carried out God’s plan.”

Nunzio tried to talk but he wasn’t able. He could see the face of Father Kelly then, who was still talking but his voice was growing dim, “We have talked about your future, of your choosing Holy Orders. Nunzio, this is an excellent chance for you to make an important choice.” His voice was almost inaudible, and Nunzio wanted to hear what he was going to say next, so he leaned in. As he leaned in, he could hear better, but his face felt hot. “Be humble, and stay strong. Cleaning the pool itself is respectable work. Set aside the fact that you aren’t invited to the party. Enjoy an evening doing some reading or make plans for tomorrow, and feel the love of Christ grow with …” and his face had changed, darkened, and faded. Grow with what? Nunzio wondered. What was he going to say?

It grew hotter and hotter, and in his agitated sleep, Nunzio kicked off his covers. The outside temperature had risen, and although his window was open, the air in his room was still and heavy. The other portion of the house, the section where the others lived, was cooled by a continuous fan system, a fact that added to Nunzio’s continuous internal turmoil. As he lay in sleep, the heat began to subside, but the leaves returned, their harsh colors mixed together then, making an ugly wet mess, plastering itself on his head.

He awoke, feeling hot and dizzy, the sounds through his open window unfamiliar; a hound baying continuously and someone way down the street frantically yelling, "Shut up!" He got up and walked around his small attic room. He went to the bathroom and wiped the sweat from his face and neck, and splashed cool water on himself. He felt hot and wondered if he had gotten a fever. But after enough cool water, he decided he was well, just overheated.

The images of the dream were fading, and he was left remembering the gentle words of Father Kelly. He knew that his urgings were correct, and that he should try with all his might to stay strong and grow with, what was it he had said? Grow with what? Had he finished that thought? How am I supposed to listen to him if he doesn't even finish his sentence, Nunzio thought angrily. Then he realized it was a dream, not the real Father Kelly, so why should he listen anyway?

I've become angry, and bitter, and I have not served the Lord in humility as I should. I have not forgiven those who have hurt me as I expect to be forgiven. Was it his angel? Nunzio didn't know, but he just couldn't listen, there was too much inside his head. As he got back into his bed, leaving off the covers, he tried to concentrate on the following day's work at the store and push everything else out of his mind.

Chapter Nineteen

The next day after work, most thoughts of the preceding nightmare gone from his mind, Nunzio met Carlo and walked through the old neighborhood. Nunzio had wanted to see his father, not to talk, just to see him literally, through the window at his shop.

"I guess I just wanna make sure he's still there," he said sheepishly to Carlo. "You never know."

"You never do," Carlo agreed, nodding.

Before long, they reached the shop. Mo Schwartz's old car still sat out front, and they could still see the men inside, but there were no men waiting as in the early years. Only a few youngsters and a woman waiting to have her boys fixed up for school.

Nunzio studied Nick, his posture, his profile. He couldn't make out his expression, but he didn't feel that he needed to. His father was a vision of despair, his own hair too long and his shoulder sagging. The profile suggested the defeated appearance of one whose hopes had been raised and then dashed too many times. Nunzio stared, thinking about his pop as Carlo stood nearby, kicking at a loose screw at the base of the railing post.

This is what happens, Nunzio thought. That's what you get from holding onto hope too long. In his heart, he knew that it was not genuine hope that had eluded Nick, but the hope of winning at the racetrack. It was the man's only vice, yet from the looks of him, Nunzio thought, that was all it had taken to eat him up from the inside out.

He shook off as if just climbing out of a pool, and said, "Well, I guess he's still there."

Carlo slapped him on the back but said nothing.

Continuing on, they came to the perpetually rendering garage of Mr. Finn and Mr. Tucker. It was Mr. Finn's turn to sit outside that day. He was trimmed down, wearing a pair of dark work pants, a long-sleeved shirt, and a baseball cap, but no jacket. Even earlier in the summer, they had sometimes seen the men wear coats or jackets.

"I guess it's too hot to disguise himself in a coat," Carlo said, his voice low.

Nunzio grinned, eager for the distraction from his thoughts about Nick. "Yeah, but can you see his face, I mean really, with that cap down over it?"

"Nope," Carlo answered. "But he's drinking Mr. Finn's summer drink, the lemon on the ice tea."

Nunzio nodded. "Hey, did your pop ever go over and ask them if they were two different people, or just the one, changing clothes? Wasn't he gonna do that?"

Carlo chuckled.

After they passed by, he turned to Nunzio. "No, he chickened out!" he answered, laughing out loud.

Nunzio joined in.

"Hey, how come you weren't at Sacred Heart this morning?" Carlo asked abruptly. "I thought you were servin' today?"

"Well, you know, they had this party at my house last night. It went so late. I couldn't sleep, and it was so hot!"

"Yeah! It was roastin'!"

They walked for a while in silence as they passed by Nunzio's old house. Someone had moved in and changed the color of the shutters. There were a child's toys lying on the front lawn.

"So you'll be there tomorrow?" Carlo asked.

"Oh yeah, I'm sure I'll be there, you know."

But that night, there was another argument at the big house. Nunzio's mother was pouting about something when Nunzio arrived. What now, he wondered. Somehow, the terror of the evil stepfather, as he had thought of him, was fading. He didn't bear him any goodwill, but his fear of the man's dark and unknown character had greatly diminished following the previous afternoon.

"So what's he supposed to wear?" his mother was demanding.

"What he always wears. There ain't no reason for him to change," came his stepfather's response.

"Listen, honey," his mother said, trying to soften her tone, "You can't get one kid something and not the other."

He could hear Fat Eddie laugh meanly after that. After a long time of snorts and coughs, he came back with, "So you figured that out, huh?"

Nunzio didn't want to find it funny, but it was hard not to. It sure had taken her a long time to realize that.

His mother was quiet. Nunzio wasn't in the room, so he couldn't see, but he imagined that she had assumed her pouting position. Trying to gain sympathy for her desire.

"Get me a sandwich, would you?" Eddie said. "When does the kid get home?"

"I don't know."

"You don't know when he gets in? He's not an adult yet, you know. You should keep better track of 'im."

"Around 5:30 I guess," she said.

Nunzio heard the cabinet open and he could just picture her sullenly handing him the plate with the sandwich. The argument was low level, but he was feeling sweat forming at his temples. He knew it was about him, and nasty or not, he didn't want a thing from that man.

Just then Fat Eddie came around the corner chewing his sandwich, half in his hand and the plate nowhere in sight. "There you are. Come on, get in the car. I'm gonna get you some clothes for school."

So that was what it was. What a relief. He couldn't get him any clothes for school. "They don't let you wear street clothes," he said. "We wear a uniform, it's a pair of pants, white shirt, a tie, and a blazer."

"Oh! Uniforms, huh." He turned his head, his mouth still full and called out to Nunzio's mother. "They got uniforms! You got your wish!" He studied Nunzio. This was one hard-to-figure kid, he thought. Thread bare, works like a man, and don't seem to want nothin'. How can them two kids be brothers? How can they even be related?

"Thanks anyway," Nunzio said. And he went upstairs.

"Okay," Eddie called after him. "I'll contact the school and let 'em know you get whatever you want, hear?"

"Okay," said Nunzio. What I want, he thought. I wonder what that feels like. He was intrigued by the idea of feeling like a rich kid for a short time, but it also made him uncomfortable, and at first, he couldn't understand why. I'm not stealin' nothin', he thought. He's offerin'. It would be nice to go to school in a shirt that wasn't the exact same one he had worn the day before. And the idea of getting the blazer was just a dream. But he'd get that too, a change of shirt, the blazer, maybe even an extra tie.

Somewhere nearby was his angel saying, remember, the devil takes on pleasing appearances. This may make you happy for a short while, but remember what kind of man this is, and be on your guard. He may come to think he can tell you what to do once you've accepted enough gifts from him.

You can listen to your angel, or you can ignore him. Nunzio was in an ignoring frame of mind and concentrated instead on how he was going to look in his sharp new uniform. He'd get the cufflinks, too, if they had 'em, the tie with the school emblem and even socks. Louie never wore the blazer with the emblem. And he had sure wanted it! The thought brought an unfamiliar but darkly appealing feeling. Louie would be envious. And he, Nunzio, would be the one lookin' sharp and keepin' pace with the affluent kids. He smirked, realizing that Louie probably wouldn't even know what the word 'affluent' meant. But there his thoughts stalled for a moment. What about the rest of the ensemble? Socks would be good, and he'd order a few pairs, maybe even six, but shoes. He only had his old, scuffed shoes, and they were actually getting to be too small. They weren't likely to sell shoes at the school. If it was like Lexington Hall, you brought your own shoes. Black ones, polished and clean.

He hunted them out of the closet where he'd simply thrown everything when he'd arrived earlier. The summer was coming to a close and he'd have to get organized anyway. He found them in the back of the closet. The heals were good but the rest of them was in serious need of polish. He'd find some shoe polish somewhere and they'd be good as new. They were old, and some parts wouldn't look that great even after polishing them, but he felt intensely repulsed by the idea of replacing them. They were his, he'd had them for years, and he intended to keep them. No matter what.

His angel, exhausted by the tiny victory, sighed in relief. Little victories were better than a dead loss.

Just then the thought of what it would be like to live in the rectory guest room came to Nunzio's mind. It took his breath away, which angered him. He hated the fact that he had wanted to do that, that he had revealed that part of himself to Father Kelly, it was embarrassing. And most of all, he hated that he had been rejected. But the way it all came together, he just plain hated Father Kelly. He knew it was a sin to hate, so he modified the thought to dislike. You could dislike someone, just not hate them. And why shouldn't he dislike him? He had acted like a friend, but then when Nunzio had needed him, he'd let him down. What kind of friend was that? They still want me to serve? He shook his head. In that moment, his pride began to separate him from all of the things he truly loved. He wanted to stop all the things he was doing wrong, but yet, it felt good to be treated like someone who mattered. Did Father Kelly treat him that way? Well, he didn't know, but he knew Fat Eddie did.

Again he felt a nudge in his brain. Why is Fat Eddie doing it? Because he cares about you? But he turned off the voice and went downstairs to the dining room for a quick, cafeteria-style dinner. There was only a short time before school started. At last he had something to look forward to.

The next day, when he saw his buddy on his way to work, Carlo was a little cranky.

"I thought you were comin' to church today," he said. "You said you'd be there."

Nunzio had thought about what to say in response because he had felt a kind of guilt that morning, having bacon and toast while he knew that Carlo and the others were at Sacred Heart, getting dressed to serve Mass.

"I was gonna, but I had to get everything ready for school."

"It ain't 'til next week," Carlo said, narrowing his eyes. "What's the matter with you?"

"What do you mean?" Nunzio felt cornered. He hadn't contemplated more questions from Carlo. He figured if he didn't go to church, the priests wouldn't ask him anything because he wouldn't see them. But Carlo was a different story.

"You know what I mean. Every day as long as I can remember, we serve Mass in the mornings. You and me. All the sudden, two days in a row, you ain't there."

"Well, I'll probably start doin' it again," Nunzio said. "I guess I'm just takin' a break."

Carlo continued to look at him suspiciously. "What's goin' on? Did something happen? Is Fat Eddie pressuring you to stop going to church?"

Nunzio scoffed. "Fat Eddie! What's he got to do with it?"

Carlo didn't respond. The day before, he had had a feeling about Nunzio. They were pretty close, and he could tell when something was brewing in his brain. Usually it was some worry about getting something done on time or something about his dad. But this is different, he thought. And I don't like it. "That's what I'd like to know," he said after a time. "Are you gonna tell me or not?"

Nunzio glanced at Mr. Tucker sitting there smoking as they passed by. For once, he did not feel like chuckling. Carlo was his best buddy. What was he doing, shutting him out? But what could he say? "Carlo, it's just something, I figure I have to work out for myself."

"Okay, work it out yourself, but what is it? Maybe I got some ideas or somethin'."

"Yeah," Nunzio said.

"So. What could cause a guy who's gonna be a priest to suddenly stop going to Mass? If it *is* that Fat Eddie, you don't have to listen to him. You know that, right?"

"Oh yeah, I know. He's just. . ."

"Is he tellin' you not to go? Not to serve Mass?" Carlo persisted.

That might be a good way to slide out of this without revealing his embarrassing experience with Father Kelly, Nunzio thought. Carlo didn't have to know the whole story. As long as he understood that Nunzio wouldn't be serving Mass just then. "Well, you don't *have* to go except on Sundays, right? Isn't that right?" he asked, glancing at Carlo briefly without meeting his eyes.

"Yeah," said Carlo, as they reached the shop where he worked. "That's right." And he stepped inside, shut the door behind himself, and did not look back.

The orientation to Catholic High School was much the same as his orientation to Sacred Heart Grade School, except with bigger students and more of them. But there was one very specific difference.

This time, Nunzio was not the poor kid wearing a threadbare, hand-me-down uniform. The fact that he ever had been such a student had never occurred to him before he was no longer such a student. His glorious wardrobe had included not only everything he had imagined, but a second blazer, with personalized stitching of his name inside, having been insisted on by Fat Eddie, and not two shirts, but six, as well as six pairs of pants, and several ties that were hung on hangers with the other things by Della, who explained it was Fat Eddie's orders. Nunzio had resisted the urgings to get new shoes, explaining that he wanted to make the most of what he already had and not go overboard.

Fat Eddie had argued that with a new set of clothing, it was only appropriate to have shiny new shoes. "They'll set things off," he claimed with the urgings of a Fifth Avenue salesman.

But Nunzio refused to go to a shoe store, always seeming to be gone or otherwise engaged when his stepfather was available. Eventually, Fat Eddie lost interest and let things rest. Nunzio told himself there was no need to get new shoes and that he hated shoe stores, which was true enough. The funny contraptions the salesmen made him stand on always tickled and despite his struggles not to laugh when he was younger, he had never been able to hold it back. Likewise, his mother had never failed to slap him in response, which turned the memory of the experience to the typical grey haze that most of his memories with his mother seemed to generate, perilously dangling, like sopping wet men's room hand towels stuck to the lavatory wall.

In the back of his mind though, he knew he kept those shoes because they represented a piece of the past, of the longing for something he had convinced himself that he had given up. They had been purchased with money sent from the priests at Sacred Heart right before he started his last year at Lexington Hall. He had needed new shoes for a while and had not used his earnings because it had been so securely set aside to pay back Father Kelly and Monsignor French. And then in a surprising twist, Sister Bernadette had tapped on the dormitory door one night and explained that he would be going shoe shopping with Mrs. Hardy the next day; that they had received a letter and funds with instructions. He had never loved a pair of shoes with such fervor. And even with things having gone so differently, he wasn't about to give them up.

Nunzio managed to stay in the top twenty percent of his class, remaining strong in even Latin and Spiritual Studies, much to his own surprise. When he saw Carlo, it was most often in class rather than outside of school. Those few times they did cross paths outside of school, Carlo managed to make the encounters brief, although always cordial.

After one such brief conversation one afternoon, Nunzio walked down the block to his house thinking about it. It wasn't as if Carlo was rude. He just didn't want to spend time with him. He probably don't wanna catch anything from me, he thought. He's worried he might stop servin' Mass himself.

Nunzio had continued to attend Mass on Sunday as required, but often times he would spend time wondering what the altar boys were talking about, what Carlo and his pop were going to be doing that day and if there was anyone else in the congregation he knew. Despite his intentional aloofness, Nunzio's heart remained heavy when he saw the others attending Father Kelly and Monsignor French. While he knew that he could also be doing the same thing, he denied himself, telling himself that he had done his share, and that while they were all very nice people, he had decided to move on.

Carlo was doing very well in school as well, and while he did not have a second blazer, with or without his name stitched inside, he presented an attractive picture to those in the girls' side of the school. He was never without female accompaniment, although he never sought it, and was very polite to everyone. And Nunzio hated it.

The girls were just as interested in him, especially since he had stepped up in the material world, so that was not the problem. Nunzio hated the idea that Carlo treated him with the same polite and kindly, but removed interaction that he treated the new, unfamiliar people of Catholic High School. He felt a bar had been placed between them, separating their easy honest friendship that had once been so natural and reassuring. It frustrated him.

You put it there, a voice insisted. *It's up to you to take it down.* But in Nunzio's self-pity and self-isolation, he simply could not hear it.

Chapter Twenty

A few years later, Fat Eddie stood watching the graduation at Catholic High, basking in the admiration he observed on the faces of the young girls. Their admiration wasn't for him, though, it was for his handsome stepson who didn't seem to be capable of doing anything wrong. The kid looked good, he thought, got good grades, didn't hang on the corners with the rough kids, even had a couple of offers from colleges. And he seemed to have given up the foolhardy idea that he'd carried around for a while of joining up with the priests.

He turned to one of his cronies, a narrow-faced individual who hung around Fat Eddie, making himself available for whatever tasks needed doing. "He's a good lookin' kid. We could use a guy like that around the docks. What do they call it? A girl magnet?"

His crony laughed. "Well, yeah, but he ain't likely to, you know, bring girls around."

"What do you mean?" Fat Eddie countered with enthusiasm. "Look at 'em! Them broads is all over him!"

"I can see that," the man responded. "But ain't he looking for a, what do you call, vocation?"

"Oh, no, I think he gave all that up. Thought better of it when he saw what money could buy. Huh?" Fat Eddie shoved the guy on the shoulder. "Huh?"

"Yeah," the man said. "I guess so!"

"He ain't no dummy," Fat Eddie said, nodding. "We could use a guy like that down the docks," he repeated. He studied the scene for a while, keeping his eye on one particular blonde. His wife had long since been nothing more than a boring nag, and rather than divorce her, he'd simply decided to play the field. Who was gonna stop him? Her older son Louie couldn't care less, and even Nunzio acted as if he expected the situation. Yes, having him around might just turn out to be a good luck charm. Pay back for all the money he'd shelled out over the years for the Catholic school uniforms.

As Fat Eddie leered at the blond, imagining improvements he'd make to his office, Nunzio looked down at the diploma he held in his hands. It was nice to be graduated high school, and he was glad to be free to take the next steps in his life. But he felt as if he were at loose ends—unsure of what to do next. His high school years had consisted simply of lots of homework, working at the store, and attending classes during the day. The fancy dances, those that he did attend, were more like something he observed than something he took part in.

Living in the big house, where his uniforms were always perfectly clean and pressed and always the right size, and where if he closed his door, he could have all of the time in study that he needed, he wanted for nothing. But he was deathly lonely. When high school began, he had told himself that he'd make new friends. Yet, something kept him from moving forward, and he found that he really didn't care whether he hung around with people or not. It seemed so involved to work out new friendships. And he was slow to admit to himself that he missed Carlo. The other two altar boys were not around either. Frankie had gone to Southern, another high school, and Pete had taken a job like his brother, so he rarely saw them. When he walked the neighborhood, he didn't even look at the Finn and Tucker house anymore. It only made him lonely for a past that he had shut away.

He was a thousand miles away when Fat Eddie and his mother stopped to congratulate him. "You did a great job, kid," Fat Eddie said. "Now you can join the real world."

Nunzio was used to the man's insensitivity. He simply nodded. "Thanks."

"Yeah, congratulations," said his mother. And then to Fat Eddie, "Are we gonna eat or what?"

"Yeah, yeah, hold your horses," he said. "Hey kid, how about you come and work down the docks for me? Good pay, easy commute."

"The docks?" Nunzio said, his distaste not well disguised. "Oh, I don't think so, Eddie."

Fat Eddie was startled. "Huh?"

"I don't know about starting in somewhere new. I gotta decide on school and I already got a job, you know, with the store."

Fat Eddie snorted roughly. "That's kid stuff!" he said. "They ain't payin' $125 a week are they?"

"No."

"Well, that's what you'd get with me. More if you do a good job." What's wrong with this kid, he wondered. Getting offered a job right out of high school that'll make him independent if he wants, and he stands there and tells me no. What am I doin' beggin' him to take this gift?

"Thanks, Eddie. I'll think about it. I don't really know what I want to do yet."

"Come on, let's eat," his mother said. "This graduation thing took forever. I'm starving."

Fat Eddie was not pleased. The ever-present cronies beside him moved to try to calm the situation.

"He's offering you a good deal," one of them said to Nunzio. "Don't think about it too long, 'cause it might not be there forever." He gave Nunzio a little shove on the shoulder meant to look congenial, but was actually delivered aggressively.

Nunzio tightened up and stared the crony down. He'd lived in the big house long enough to know how things worked. What Fat Eddie wanted, he intended to get. But Nunzio had determined that he would take no aggression from one of Eddie's minions, as he thought of them. How would it feel, he wondered at times, to be nothing in yourself, and only a reflection of some dark spirited honcho?

The crony withdrew, nodding as if he'd made some sort of point, but actually concerned that he might be knocked out cold by an eighteen-year-old kid.

The whole situation brought out the vile temper in Fat Eddie who yanked his wife's arm stomping away saying, "Come on, you wanna eat, don't you?" and completely disregarding his stepson, but nodding to crony on his right.

Nunzio was already exiting the hall. That's graduation, thought Nunzio. As he slipped his diploma into his jacket, he thought he felt the eyes of one of Fat Eddie's minions observing his actions, but he didn't see the man when he turned to look.

The local clubs never bothered about age limits on alcohol, and for once, Nunzio felt he would take advantage of the situation. He walked casually down the sidewalk, enjoying the thought of being a newly graduated young man even if he didn't have any idea what should come next. One thing he knew for a fact: He would never work for Fat Eddie. That was one racket he intended to avoid entirely.

Suddenly, he thought of Lexington Hall, remembering the endless fields of pasture, the soft, silky-eared cows, and the scent of clover in summer. Maybe if he were to become a teacher, he could return and work there. He decided to take a seat on the city bench outside the little bar. There was no rush. The sun stayed up for hours in June.

The buses and cars hobbled by, frequently stalled in traffic and pedestrian crossings, and he remembered his early morning experiences on his way to Mass as a younger boy. He and Carlo had triumphed in the fact that when traffic was really stopped up, the two of them were able to travel the distance from Nunzio's house to the church faster than the cars could. He smiled thinking of it. Of course, the fact that it was so often ice cold from October to March kept them moving at a pretty rapid pace, anyway.

Eventually, Nunzio decided to go into the bar and find a place to sit and eat for a while, think things over. As he stood at the bar, motioning the bartender that he was about to take a table, he was startled to see Carlo sitting there. Carlo spotted him at the same time.

"Nunz," he said in his old familiar tone that Nunzio hadn't heard in years. "Have a seat. I'll buy ya'a beer."

Nunzio sat down. "How ya doin' Carlo? How 'bout it? All graduated."

"Yeah, completely gradiated," Carlo said, revealing the slightest slur in his pronunciation.

He's snookered, thought Nunzio. "I don't think I've ever seen you here before," he said.

"Nope. Thought I'd celebrate."

Nunzio studied his old friend. As happy as he was to see him, and to hear him talk so amiably, he sensed there was trouble. Carlo wasn't any more interested in alcohol than he was himself. But he knew it would take some finessing to find out what was going on, so he simply sat down and ordered a beer. "On him," he said smiling, pointing to Carlo.

"You got that right," Carlo said. "I'm the big sender today, spender."

"So," Nunzio began, sipping from the heavy glass mug. "Congratulations."

"I thank you. And to you as well. I notice your pop was there."

"He was? Did you see him?" Nunzio had not spotted Nick, although he knew that had he been there, he would not stick around afterwards.

"Oh yes, but he left. He probably had to go to work."

"Yeah, probably," said Nunzio, thinking probably he had to go to work and then to watch the horses race.

"He's a good guy your pop," Carlo said, staring at the bottles on the wall. Then suddenly he turned to Nunzio. "I'm sorry I wasn't your friend."

Nunzio coughed, startled by the stark candor of the admission. Secretly he felt grateful to alcohol, if only this once. He smiled, nodding. "Yeah, buddy, I'm the one who's sorry. Stupid. Just because we go, you know, different directions…"

"I don't care about that stuff right now. I just wanna have my friend."

Nunzio was torn between taking Carlo from the bar to a restaurant to eat and listening to whatever he had to say about what it was that was bothering him. "You seem a little, well, annoyed about something," he said finally, deciding on trying to help Carlo. "Anything on your mind?"

"You mean besides my best friend falling away from the Church?" Carlo asked and then laughed out loud.

"I didn't fall away," Nunzio said patiently. "I still go to Mass."

"Oh yeah, and all that." Carlo took a deep breath and leaned on the bar. "You see my pop anywhere?"

It was the first time that that fact had occurred to Nunzio. "Gosh, your pop. No. Where is he?"

"Where he is, I don't know," said Carlo, almost singing it, "but he's out, he's on a date." He finished the sentence with particularly sharp pronunciation, expressing the final "t" as if a student in elocution class.

So that's it, Nunzio nodded. Puffate has decided to start seeing someone. He cringed. There had been no one between Puffate and his son ever since Carlo's mother had died, going on eight years. The sudden introduction of a new woman, and painfully on the very night of his son's graduation, would certainly pack a wallop, as Mrs. Hardy would say. "Geeze, Carlo," he said shaking his head.

"Yep, he's got a date. Probably an evil painted lady." Then he chuckled at the thought.

Nunzio did, too. "With bright red lipstick and spike high heels!" he added.

They laughed, Carlo finally releasing some of his anxiety over the situation.

"You wanna go to a restaurant or something, get some dinner?" Nunzio urged as Carlo started to settle down.

"Okay, soon as I finish this one," Carlo said.

The bar had become crowded, and there were several fellows sitting at tables waiting to be served. Nunzio noticed a man sitting placidly observant, the outline of his thirty-eight pistol perfectly visible through his sport jacket. Two other fellows sat at the table, both drinking beer.

Just then, a heavyset fellow stumbled against Carlo, knocking his beer forward and over onto the bar. Startled, Carlo peered at the beer still flowing from the mug, which lay on its side at his fingertips. Realizing the guy had lost him his drink, he spouted out, "What'd you do that for?"

"It were a accident," the man said, sounding fully inebriated.

His friend leaned in and said, "Yeah, it was an accident. He didn't mean nothin'."

Carlo, still taking stock of what was left in his mug, tried to stand and stumbled, his mug landing square in the face of the same fellow who had knocked into him, catching him on the nose with the heavy glass.

"Yo, ya mutha!" yelled the man in pain, clutching his nose.

"What'd ya do that for?" his friend demanded, approaching him.

Nunzio tried to intervene. "Hey fellas, it was an accident, he's had a little and he just lost his balance."

"Yeah, accident all right!" yelled the heavyset friend.

Carlo licked his lips and squinted, still processing the response he had received from the man with the injured nose. "Would you like me to procure your mother?" he asked, exaggerating his pronunciation as he had earlier.

That was it. The friend knocked him off his feet as the heavyset fellow joined in, while Nunzio did his best to equalize a very bad situation. Carlo was a good athlete, but fighting had never been one of his fortes, and he was losing rather unpleasantly. After Nunzio got in the middle of it and leveled the friend onto his back, he got caught square in the jaw by the first guy, who took advantage of Nunzio's disorientation to continue to pummel Carlo.

Just as Nunzio started to panic, two new individuals entered the ring and quickly neutralized both of the offending men, holding them in abeyance as Nunzio struggled to get Carlo up off the floor. The heavyset man tried to break away, taking a swipe at Carlo but missing.

"That's enough boys," said the calm man sitting at the table. He stood up and simply removed his pistol from his coat and held it in his hand as if he were showing them a shell he had just discovered on the beach. The bartender, seeing the man's display, turned discreetly away. He knew both the action and the actor, and neither were meant to be visible to anyone but the fighting gentlemen.

The heavyset man recognized the man at the table and began to shake. "Let's get outta here," he said quietly to his buddy.

As they left, Nunzio was heartened to see that his efforts had at least yielded a deeply blackened eye on one ruffian and a bloody lip that could only be described as hamburger-like on the other. But his satisfaction was short-lived.

The two interveners waited by the door for the man with the gun.

"Thanks," Carlo managed through his own bruised mouth.

"Nothin' to it," he said as he approached Nunzio, nodding. He paused, smiled and straightened Carlo's collar. As he sauntered out toward his associates, he looked over his shoulder at Nunzio. "Compliments of Fat Eddie."

As Nunzio recovered from the unpleasant revelation, recognizing the ominous dictum of *a favor for a favor*, he slung Carlo's arm over his shoulder, dropped cash on the bar, and supported his buddy toward the exit.

"Let's go somewhere for a nice dinner," he said.

"You know," said Carlo as he stumbled along, amazingly untouched by the incident, "I don't usually fight much."

"No kiddin'."

Chapter Twenty-One

At the restaurant, Carlo began to feel the pain that came along with his bruises and Nunzio suggested he splash a little cold water on his face in the men's room. Nunzio didn't hang on corners as a rule, but through the high school years, he'd had his share of confrontations, and had partaken of that particular remedy himself, especially if the altercation had occurred on his way to class.

When Carlo returned to the table, he was closer to his old self, but with a slightly redesigned mouth. "This hurts," he said pointing to his lip as he sat down. "That guy musta really hit me."

"He hit you a bunch of times," Nunzio said, chuckling. "But I don't think he got any satisfaction 'cause you didn't feel it at all!"

Carlo chuckled, despite the pain. "Good," he said.

Nunzio shook his head. "I thought I'd lose it when you offered to call the guy's mother."

"I did what?"

"You don't remember? You asked the fellow if he'd like you to *procure* his mother!" Nunzio managed to say through his laughter.

Carlo looked at the ceiling. "Ah—no wonder the guy clobbered me!"

As the waitress took their order, Nunzio couldn't help remembering the grim message he had received from their portentous intervener. Now he owed Big Eddie. If he hadn't seen the two ruffians run from the scene, he would have suspected that his stepfather had set the whole thing up from the start. It was bad enough though, sending those others. If there hadn't been a fight, they probably would have arranged one. As it was, he would have to be very stealthy indeed, intellectually speaking, in order to wriggle out of this one. Otherwise, he'd find himself at the docks, getting in deeper and deeper, now that he owed Fat Eddie.

"Good thing that guy showed up," Carlo said as the waitress disappeared into the kitchen. "We'd a both been on the floor!"

"Yeah," Nunzio said weakly. But the feeling of unease didn't last long. "Hey, this is great, Carlo. I don't see you for four years, and then we have beer, a fight, and dinner all on the same night!"

Carlo laughed. "Yeah." Then as his alcohol haze continued to ease, his face was more serious. "I'm sorry I kinda, you know, moved away like."

"Yeah, it's okay.

"Everybody's different. You gotta do what you gotta do. You weren't givin' me a hard time about what I wanted to do."

"Listen, it's in the past."

"It's just, I honestly didn't understand how a person could change so fast. One day we're servin' together, next day you're out. But maybe that's how it happens for some people."

"I guess."

"You can have a change a heart, you know. Being a priest, it ain't for everybody. I can see how you woulda changed your mind there."

Nunzio looked up at Carlo. "Yeah, well, I'm not 100%, you know. I haven't, I mean I haven't decided on something else yet."

"Well, deciding is one thing, but if you don't have the calling, that's another." Carlo smirked inside. He knew what he was doing and he was enjoying the responses he was getting.

"A calling can you know, come and go, kind of hang there in the air for a while, and—" Nunzio began.

"No, no, I think if you got it, you know it. And like I said, it ain't for everybody."

"No, it ain't, but who are you to say who's got it?" Nunzio shot back, surprising himself.

Carlo palmed his hands up. "Hey, I'm not trying to say who's who—"

"No, no, I know, I'm sorry, Carlo." Nunzio shook his head. "I don't want to start a fight over who's called to the priesthood!" he started to chuckle then stopped. "I don't know."

Carlo smiled inside as he took a sip of water and thought, I knew it!

Fat Eddie wasn't a patient man. When Nunzio arrived home later that night, Fat Eddie met him at the door.

"Been out carousing?" he asked in an offensive tone.

"Just dinner with a buddy," Nunzio said, knowing that his stepfather knew full well every detail of his evening.

"Oh yeah, how's he doin'?"

"Doin' all right."

"I hear he has a fat lip."

"Yeah."

"You look okay. Get in a few good punches?"

"A few."

Fat Eddie had to admire the kid's cool. He don't ever get roused up, he thought. If it was Louie, he'd be shakin' in his shoes. "I hope you 'preciate my help."

"Oh yes, absolutely," said Nunzio, heading for the stairs.

"We'll talk in the morning," said Fat Eddie, feeling satisfied with himself.

That's what *you* think, thought Nunzio.

The next morning, Nunzio was at Mass when Fat Eddie lumbered expectantly into the dining room. "Where's the kid?" he demanded, as Della filled the chafing dish with crisp bacon.

"He's gone to church," she said, raising her eyebrows.

She's enjoying this, thought Fat Eddie, angrily. "Well is he coming back here before his penny anty job?"

"I don't expect so," said Della as she returned to the kitchen, smiling out of his view.

Nunzio met Carlo after Mass in the changing room.

"Hey, I was surprised to see you out there!" Carlo said.

"You shouldn't a been lookin'," said Nunzio. "Oh hello, Father."

Father Kelly stopped at the entrance to the room, his eyes wide. "There's a sight for sore eyes—Nunzio DiAngelis in the altar boy changing room! How long has it been?"

"Four years!" shot Carlo, looking away to hide his smile of joy.

Nunzio gave him a look. "It's been a while, Father, but I been to Mass."

"Oh I know, I've seen you." He set a bakery box onto the table. "I hope you remember what's in here."

Nunzio smiled and nodded. "But I don't wanna take yours," he said. "I don't deserve it," he added.

"I insist," said Father.

Nunzio was famished. He'd eaten light the night before, and knowing that he was headed to Mass and Communion, he'd refrained from having anything at the big house.

"Go on," said Carlo. "I'll share mine with Father."

"No, you boys go ahead," said Father Kelly. "What are your plans now, Nunzio?"

"Well, I'm still thinking things over," Nunzio said. "Gettin' a little pressure to work at my stepfather's business, but I think I should go to college, maybe here in the city."

"College is a good choice for a lot of young men," Father said. "It gives you the background for a whole lot of careers."

As they continued to talk, while Nunzio enjoyed a rich cherry Danish pastry, he was surprised at how easily the conversation came with Father Kelly. It was as if he had never left. And no mention was made of the whole ugly disagreement they'd had years before. The comfort went deeper though, as if he had returned to a place where his life had had more kindness. He suspected that that was how people with normal families felt when they were at home. With a jolt of irony, he realized that he was addressing the man he spoke with as *father*. Maybe this is a kind of home. I certainly feel more welcome here than at the big house, he thought.

But that brought back the whole debacle four years earlier and his longing to live there. He shoved it from his mind. The atmosphere was too warm and welcoming to allow any unfurled pains of the past to be rolled out and untangled just then.

Before they knew it, it was time to head off to work, and Nunzio departed, feeling happier than he had in years.

Carlo waited for Nunzio to clear the door by about twenty feet, and gave Father a look that seemed to say *Didn't I tell you?*

Father Kelly smiled and nodded. "Go on, you'll be late for work, Smarty."

After work, Fat Eddie met him at the door.

"Kinda late for the mornin'" he said flatly.

Don't he ever go to work, Nunzio wondered. But from the smoke he imagined coming out of Fat Eddie's ears, he decided to refrain from expressing that thought. "I had to go to work," he said, crossing the entry hall and heading for the back stairway to his room.

"Hey!" yelled Fat Eddie. "I'm talkin' to ya!"

Nunzio stopped. He turned around and faced the large man who stood smoking hot tempered the full distance of the hall away. He was just Fat Eddie, Nunzio decided then. He was also Ugly Eddie. His eyes were ever so slightly crossed, which, when fired up the way he was just then, looked as if they might pop out of his head. His little bit of hair was like a corkscrew pigtail on the top of his head, and grey buzz cut on the sides. When he was angry, his complexion that was ordinarily somewhat ruddy came close to a full blossom of crimson.

If he weren't so large, Nunzio thought, I could knock him on his can and just exit. But that left all the little devils who worked for him on the streets, dealing out retribution at will. And I probably couldn't knock him down anyway.

"Yes?" he said, as innocently as he could.

"Why weren't you here when I told you to be?"

"I don't remember you telling me to. But I just come from work."

"I said to you last night, 'we'll talk in the morning.'"

And I said "that's what *you* think," Nunzio thought, but instead of saying it, he said, "I didn't know you meant actual morning, Eddie. I thought you knew I had a job."

"I know you have a job!" Fat Eddie yelled. And then more calmly. "I expected you to quit. That's all."

"We never discussed that," Nunzio said, "so I really didn't know."

Fat Eddie studied him. The kid was giving him the business, he knew that. But he was so darn convincing. He had a face that could calm all your worries while he robbed you blind. I could really use a kid like that, he thought. Tough, girls love 'em, and a perfect liar.

But he was still angry. "Well, we discuss it *now!"* he demanded, pointing to the dining room. "I want somethin' t'eat and we're gonna talk about it."

"Whatever you say," Nunzio said. He was hungry and the food was usually pretty good. He turned and followed behind his stepfather who jaunted awkwardly toward the dining room. His anger assuaged moderately by his anticipation of a feeding experience, he grabbed a plate from the stack that was always kept available, just as the food was.

Just as Eddie began piling barbecued ribs onto his plate, Nunzio was startled by the loud voice of his mother coming from the opposite side of the room.

"I thought you were gonna wait for *me*," she said, strutting toward them. She had put on quite a bit of weight, so her strut was about as awkward as Fat Eddie's, and to Nunzio, a little bit pathetic. "What are you doing here?" she asked Nunzio.

"We're eatin'," said Fat Eddie. "I don't need any permissions to eat."

"It might be nice if you spent a little time with your wife," she responded.

"Yeah, and then again, it might not." Fat Eddie laughed.

Nunzio's mother sneered at her son. "I suppose now that he's graduated, he's going to be your next project. You know he doesn't like you." As Nunzio looked up at her, she said to him, "You should be grateful instead of running off all the time. You know he paid for all your school crap. Louie never needed all that stuff."

Nunzio wanted to say, oh yeah? What did he do, go to school naked? But he knew it was useless. He didn't understand her antagonism, but he had long since come to accept it. That didn't mean that it didn't hurt. But on that day, he decided to ignore it. He had bigger problems.

"Go on, get what you're havin' and get outta here, wouldja?" Fat Eddie said to his wife. "We got stuff to discuss."

After she filled her plate, his wife scowled at him and left the room, turning to issue one last comment. "You wouldn't a' told *her* to leave!"

Fat Eddie didn't tolerate jealousy, no matter how justified it was. "Get outta here!" he roared.

Nunzio heard the clitter clatter of her heels as she scampered down the hall. She sure was a slow learner, he thought.

The discussion that Eddie was so eager to have, began with seven words.

He shoved a chunk of pork into his mouth, and before even chewing it, he said, "So when ya gonna come to work?"

Nunzio looked at his plate, wishing he had taken more time to prepare for this onslaught. He knew that in gangsters terms, he owed Fat Eddie. But if there was a way he could make a different deal, or even put it off, he would go in that direction.

Eddie mistook his silence for opposition.

"You know you owe me. Your buddy, he's not so tough."

The implication was menacing enough to see.

"A guy like that, don't seem like he could even defend himself with one guy. I wonder what kinda harm a couple a guys would do," he went on.

"Eddie, I ain't saying I won't work for you," Nunzio lied. "I'm just lookin' for a little time. I just graduated. Even the poor kids get a few weeks off after they graduate."

Eddie leaned back, still chewing but ceasing the shoveling temporarily as he thought. "I see, so you thought why not take a little vacation or something."

"Yeah."

"I never thought of that. Yeah, okay. I see what you mean."

Nunzio could tell that his stepfather knew it was half a lie, but he could also tell that the man sought to dig him in deeper and could see opportunities to do that.

"How 'bout I pay for a nice vacation, somewhere foreign, like Miami or somethin'?" he said slyly.

Nunzio wanted to laugh but didn't. Yes, the foreign shores of Miami, Florida, he thought.

"That's okay, Eddie. I just want time off. I don't need to go nowhere."

The kid's onto me. He knows how to work it, don't he, Eddie thought, frustrated.

"All right," he said out loud, but his tone was sharp. "Just remember, it's not what I did for you, it's more like if you don't return the favor, what we *could* do for you."

Nunzio pretended he'd missed the threat. "Yeah, okay," he said. "These are good ribs, huh?"

Chapter Twenty-Two

Lucky for Nunzio, Fat Eddie had other problems. The slothy bodyguard who accompanied him everywhere, had reported that one of his so-called enforcers, named Stevie Bingo, had started sharing information with outsiders. Big Rio mentioned it one time first, which annoyed Fat Eddie, who thought Rio was an idiot who was just spreading gossip, trying to get even with everybody for getting sent away for six months.

But it started to get to him when he heard it from Bobby Skunk, too. He had his bodyguard check it out. The man was well-built and loyal, with a typically stupid expression on his face, reminiscent of the 1940s-style gangster. *Lumps* is what everyone called him and Fat Eddie neither knew nor cared what his given Christian name actually was.

After some awkward investigation, Lumps reported that in fact, Stevie was sharing with a doll whom he reckoned to be close with another family, not necessarily a rival, but not an insider.

The situation wasn't anything new. And it wasn't anything Eddie couldn't handle. Sometimes, he thought, you gotta be tough on these guys. Somebody might have to get hurt, or yeah, dead, but that's how you gotta run things. You can't go soft.

As he mulled the situation over, it got to him that an eighteen-year-old kid could effectively talk circles around him. It was annoying, and in any other situation, he would have just had the kid taken care of, or at least knocked down a peg. But he saw the value that Nunzio represented, what he could do for his business, and the kind of help he could be to him personally. And of course there was the contributing irritation that he was his wife's kid. The fact that Nunzio couldn't stand him and had turned down the offer to work for him didn't seem to influence Fat Eddie's thought process at all. In fact, it never entered his mind. He hadn't fought and murdered his way to the top to be concerned about what other people wanted. The kid would be his inside enforcer, kind of a secret weapon, put the pressure on those louses down the shore who were slow payin', and maybe see about the Stevie Bingo situation. The kid owed him and he'd do it.

Fat Eddie discussed the situation with Lumps the next day while sitting at an outdoor café.

"You wouldn't be in any way affected," he assured his long-timer, "I just feel like I gotta get something back after all the investment I made in the kid."

"Sounds fair," said Lumps, nodding continuously.

"He'll do a good job. He'll support us, take care of things we don't have time for."

Lumps smiled. "Yeah." He stopped nodding in order to think. He'd have someone to shove around, he thought. Briefly.

"But you won't give orders. Only me. I'm the only one givin' orders. Understand."

"Yeah, yeah," Lumps answered, his nodding picking up again. Maybe next time, he thought.

"Now pay the check, let's get outta here," Fat Eddie said, getting up to go.

Lumps paid the check. It never occurred to him that his boss's millions should have paid. He was only grateful to be the one that sat next to him and even was allowed in the house.

As the oaf and the stooge, headed off toward Fat Eddie's next destination, a copy of the day's *Inquirer* was slowly lowered at a table next to theirs, over which Mo Schultz studied the pair, shaking his head. He made a point of running into Nunzio on the street that evening after work.

"Hey how ya doin'?" he said out loud for the benefit of any observers Fat Eddie might have assigned to follow Nunzio. "I haven't seen you in ages!"

"Hey Mr. Schultz," Nunzio said. Boy he looks haggard, he thought. I wonder if he's started gambling, too. "How are you?"

Mo lowered his voice. "Listen, kid," he said smiling as if talking about something casual, "I heard your stepfather makin' plans to rope you into his business. He was talking to that stupid muscle of his."

Nunzio followed suit, smiling and nodding. "Thanks, Mo. I had a feeling he was gunning for me. I'm trying to find a way out of it. They've put Carlo on the bargaining block."

"Oh geeze!" Mo said, forgetting to smile. Then remembering, and smiling absurdly.

Nunzio really did laugh at the sight, but continuing to smile, he shook Mo's hand. "Thanks so much," he said. "Say hi to Pop for me."

"You go and talk to him," Mo said. "He seen ya graduate. Proud of you."

"I heard he was there, but he didn't stick around."

"I guess he's not too fond of guys beatin' 'im up, putting him the hospital."

Nunzio found new strength in his anger toward Fat Eddie. "I'd kill 'em," he said, his eyes even. "They'd kill me, but if he touched my pop now, Mo, I'd kill 'im."

"Nah, you won't do nothing, and he ain't gonna do nothing. But go and talk to your pop. He's not such a bad guy."

"I know it," said Nunzio. But the anger he felt at the thought of anyone messing with such a vulnerable man as his father scared him. That's hate, he told himself. And I'm not supposed to hate. He struggled to get the feeling under control and said a short prayer to St. Joseph. In a flash, he realized that feeling like killing was one thing, but actually doing it was very different. A chill ran through him as he realized that his prayer had been answered almost before he had said it, a fact which at once thrilled and frightened him.

"You okay, Nunzio?" Mo said. "Maybe I shouldn't a' said nothin'."

"No, no, I'm fine," Nunzio said, coming back to the present. "I was just thinking. I appreciate it. Don't worry, you did the right thing, Mr. Schultz." He shook his hand again. "I really appreciate it."

Fat Eddie's cronies were busy with other housekeeping issues, but if they had been watching, they probably would have reported that his stepson wasn't feeling well. He'd lost color for a moment or two, and before assuring Mo that all was well, he'd stared off into space as if he were about to faint.

The incident had caught him entirely off-guard. His mind had been so far from anything related to prayer or God, or certainly St. Joseph, that the occasion to pray was astonishing. He felt sick, realizing how his life had taken such a wide turn away from prayer. But at the same time, he was enlivened by the fact that it was still in him; the prayer had simply jumped to the foreground of his mind as it would have done back at Lexington Hall.

Walking toward the bus stop, he paused and changed course, and walked straight toward Sacred Heart. He didn't care what time it was, if there were vespers or a funeral or whatever was going on, he wanted in. Even if he could only stay a short while, he was suddenly and heartily desperate to be in God's House.

Only one block away, who should catch sight of him but his brother Louie. He called out in his unmistakable nasal voice, “Nunzio, come over here!” He held out an envelope.

“What?” Nunzio called.

“Come ‘ere!” repeated Louie, stopping at the edge of a department store. “I’m sposed ta give ya this.”

When Nunzio took it from him, he could see that the envelope was from the draft board. He looked at Louie.

“Yeah,” Louie grinned. “We gotta go. And we gotta pick a place first or they’ll put us in the Army with the grunts.”

Nunzio’s heart sank. He’d been thinking of other things, brighter horizons, and only just felt the return of life to his worn out, battered brain. And now this! I asked for a way out of Fat Eddie’s clutches, he thought. I guess this is one way.

He abandoned his notion of visiting the church and headed home, where he gave Carlo a call to see if he had received the same notice.

“Yep,” said Carlo. “We were supposed to get a chance to sign up for college so we could delay it, but they caught us on a technicality. Apparently we had to be signed up for higher education by the time we graduated high school.”

“Oh,” said Nunzio. “I never knew that. Drafted.”

“Well, not yet. If you go to like the Air Force or the Navy, you can jump the gun,” Carlo said, “it don’t have to be the Army.”

“Yeah,” said Nunzio. “I’m thinking Air Force.”

“I would, but Pop wants me to be Navy like he was,” Carlo said.

"Louie's going Army, but they got some kinda connection, sending him over to Europe."

"Why not the both of you?"

"It's ma's doing," said Nunzio. "She had one choice."

Carlo started to chuckle.

"What's so funny?"

"I'm trying to imagine how long it'd take you to recover if she'd picked you!" Carlo laughed.

"Yeah, that'd be a real twistoflex."

"Where's this War?" Carlo asked. "It's not in Germany again, is it?"

"No, it's called Vietnam. Hey, at least we've had a little training, huh?" Nunzio said, remembering his earlier yearning to be a General. "You think I'll make General?"

Carlo laughed again. "Yeah and I'm gonna be an Admiral!"

"That'd be some military with you and me in charge!" Nunzio laughed.

"Yeah, hey I heard from Frankie and Pete. They're goin' too. How 'bout we all meet down at Pat's Steaks?"

"Yeah, good," Nunzio said. But the idea of the four of them meeting before going into the service gave him a heavy heart. He had read a little about the War they were entering. There were loads of casualties, and it was in a place where the people didn't speak English. Or even Italian. The thought came to him that it might be the last time they all saw each other. "See ya 'round twelve okay?" he said, wanting to get off the phone.

"Okay, see ya then, buddy."

Next day, as the summer breeze shifted the paper on their sandwiches as they stood in the shade of Pat's Steaks, eating their subs with one hand, and holding their drinks with the other, Carlo raised his paper cup.

"Here's to the Altar Boys Four!" he said in false solemnity. "May we all return to serve again!" Everybody laughed.

"Yeah," said Frankie. "If we remember *how*."

"If we remember the way there!" Nunzio laughed.

"If we even *get* back," said Pete, making everyone's smile drop.

After a few minutes, Frankie, oblivious to the change in dynamic, paused in his chewing to call attention to a very attractive woman in summer clothing, pushing a baby carriage. "Look at that!" he said.

Carlo laughed. "That's a sight for sore eyes!"

"Built!" was all Pete said. But then he repeated it, nodding, "Built."

Nunzio looked, and nodded. "Oh, yeah, that is a good one. Most of them carriages are real rickety these days." And he went on eating his sub as the woman smiled at them and walked by.

"Is he for real?" Frankie asked Carlo.

"Yep, that's Nunzio, he don't miss nothin'," Carlo answered, chuckling.

Pete shook his head back and forth. "A broad like that with a figure that won't quit. And he won awards at school for being bright?"

"What?" said Nunzio.

The following week Nunzio received instructions on where he was to report, and before he knew it, he had said good-bye to Carlo and the others, and was on a bus to Ft. Dix for basic training. Two weeks later, Carlo would depart for Texas, followed by Frankie and Pete on their way to Louisiana. Keeping in touch would be difficult, but Nunzio promised to write to Carlo as soon as he arrived at Ft. Dix, and Carlo would then share the information with Frankie and Pete.

They had no idea.

Chapter Twenty-Three

The bus rattled and jolted as its ancient tires collided with clods of dirt along the dusty road that led out from the training grounds toward the airport. Nunzio leaned his head against the side wall, grateful that he wasn't one of those sitting on the bus floor. He cast his eyes down to the stripes on his arm, still wondering how he had been given Sergeant. Was there that much weight in attending a private military school?

"It's a matter of confidence," his CO had told him when Nunzio had shown his confusion. "The others in your squad look like scared rabbits. I don't see an ounce of fear in you. You can march, you know the drills, you've got stamina, and I've seen a good propensity for leadership. That's why. Now take it and return to your hut."

Nunzio had taken it. After all, it meant more pay and better quarters. Anybody would have taken it. He wondered why it meant so little to him. The guys were all punching him on the arm, joking how they were glad they'd been nice to him. But when it was time to ship out, he saw what the major had described earlier; fear, almost panic the night before. And that morning, he was the only one of his squadron in the Mess Hall. He'd been glad for the coffee and a bacon sandwich.

I know where we're headed, he thought. I know about our chances. We're really up against it. I don't know why I'm not jittery like these guys. I should be. I know I'm not Superman. I don't have any special powers.

Special powers. For the first time in years, he remembered the special power he had wanted as a priest. The tenth promise of the Sacred Heart. *The priest has the ability to touch even the hardest heart.* He thought of his mother. She had not seen him off to Basic in Ft. Dix, and he had not seen her at Ft. Dix. He had had no visitors at all, in fact. And that had not bothered him either. With a sudden shock he wondered if *he* had become exactly that—a hardened heart!

No, that's not the case, he thought. I still feel stuff, I still care about Carlo, and Frankie and Pete. Monsignor French, Father Kelly. At the thought of Father Kelly, he remembered an important conversation they had had on his final visit before leaving town. Ironically, it had brought him a good amount of peace, even under the circumstances.

It had begun with a short reminiscence of their earlier years together. Even though Nunzio remembered those times with fondness, talking about them was painful. He didn't know why, but he accepted it and tried always to avoid those conversations. Father had sensed it and gone on to another time, which for Nunzio, was even more difficult.

"I will always remember with sadness when you came to me with your plea for help," Father said.

"Oh, yeah, but we don't have to talk about that—" Nunzio had begun.

"Yes, it took me a while to come to the realization that you wanted to be here not only to be away from your family, but because you felt your calling so acutely. This *was* your family. I should have seen that."

Nunzio's eyes filled with tears of sorrow and shame at the memory. In fact, he had wanted only to escape his stepfather. Yes, he would have been happier at the rectory with the priests, but he had not even considered it being connected with his calling. He just wanted to be there.

He regretted that he had not confessed that to Father Kelly. He should have said, "No, Father, you were right. I was only trying to escape a bad situation." But he had kept mum, just happy to know that Father Kelly had given the whole conversation so much thought.

And here I am, going off to some foreign place and I may not get another chance to level with him, he thought, disgusted with himself. At least I know I don't have a hardened heart.

It seemed too soon, but suddenly they were on the tarmac, loading up the planes heading for the West Coast and then on to their missions in the strange and unknown land of Vietnam.

The flights were long and uncomfortable, which worked to their advantage because no matter how uneasy they were about landing in enemy territory, it was a relief to be able to stand up and walk around. However, despite the turn of season, it was still smolderingly hot in Da Nang, the city where they were stationed, and the jungle terrain kept even the clearings humid and uncomfortable.

Compared to Fort Dix, the base was tiny, with a perimeter that needed nonstop patrolling even though it was located in friendly territory. Nunzio was immediately on alert. He knew from the wisdom of Lieutenant Monnahan, back at Lexington Hall, that patrol missions were performed to secure the area, and beyond the actual patrol line, there was no security. The word on the base was that it wasn't a "hot" zone, and that the only reason the French soldiers who had established the post had moved on was because they were tired of the climate. Monnahan had also warned the boys several times to beware of "easy answers." *Be on your guard and sharp enough to spot when you're being lulled into taking a mission on false pretenses.*

Nunzio's squadron was only newly under his command, and his new CO was more involved in the nightly poker games than in running his outfit. When Nunzio reported, any delusions he had maintained about the integrity of the assignment were quickly washed away.

"Sergeant Nunzio DiAngelis reporting, Sir!" he shot out when announced by the new Major's sergeant.

"Hello DiAngelis," said the major, as he continued to sift through things on his desk. "How was your flight?"

Nunzio maintained attention, answering, "Fine, Sir!"

"Yeah, how do you like the weather here?"

"Fine, Sir!"

The major looked up at Nunzio whose eyes were straight ahead. He looked beyond him then, and casually asked the sergeant. "Did they send me a Marine? He's got Air Force insignia."

The sergeant laughed and closed the door.

"At ease, Soldier," said the major. "We're a lot more casual out here in the woods. It's smelly, hot, and every kind of uncomfortable. If you stay that stiff all day you'll be dead in a week."

Nunzio stood at ease, but his immediate reaction to the command was resentment. How could the man be so casual about something so serious? "Yes, Sir," he said.

The major explained the tentative objectives to Nunzio, apprised him of the current status of the camp, how many prisoners they were holding, and what the facilities capacities were, including the hospital facilities.

"You just take care of your men. You're going to find a lot of nervous nellies, which is only natural. Your men never even heard of this place before they enlisted. I can guarantee you that."

"No, Sir."

"But there will be missions to the jungle, and experienced soldiers will accompany groups of yours. Same goes for walking the perimeter. Those missions are essential for this camp to achieve its objectives. Understand?"

"Yes, Sir."

"All right, soldier, go unpack, get your guys acclimated and there will be a few soldiers sent over to show you around.

As Nunzio returned to the hut they'd been assigned, he drew the damp air into his lungs. It was just what the major had said, and worse. It smelled like oil and sulfur most of all, but also the scent of burning cabbage or some kind of herb seemed to fill the air. It wasn't long before he learned that the unfamiliar herbal scent was the very plentiful recreational drug that regulars referred to as *hash*. The users got a kind of high from it that kept them lucid but not so serious. He knew it was an illegal substance, but he gathered from having caught the scent of it in his commander's office, that there was no actual enforcing of the regulation against it.

"Hey Sarge," his corporal called one afternoon. "Special orders. Who gets to go first?"

Corporal Mifsud was a city kid, like himself, but he had had a much more rough and tumble early life. Nunzio admired his guts and had high hopes for him in the squad, especially with regard to keeping the other soldiers in a good way. After only a few weeks on the base, he had heard about desertions, in-fighting, and guys so frazzled by the environment that they had to be treated for shell shock before they ever saw any action.

Nunzio took a look at the orders Mifsud handed him. They'd be going on a mission that evening. "Who *wants* to go first?" he asked Mifsud with a smile, knowing what he would say.

"You know it's gotta be me," he said.

"Who would you take with you?"

"Well, you Sarge, naturally," Mifsud answered immediately.

Nunzio chuckled. "Appreciate that. But I gotta go no matter what. Which soldier would you choose? You know, from the squadron? Or should I pick?"

"Probly Citta," he said. "He's got guts."

Nunzio shook his head. "You Italians aways stick together," he said.

"Oh yeah, us Italians!" Mifsud laughed. "Who gets to give Citta the good news?"

"Relax, Corporal. I'll take care of it."

That night the three of them headed out with blackened face behind their American and South Vietnamese guides. "Remember," said the Vietnamese guide they all called King Kong, "he like to sneak up on you, like dat," he said, shoving Citta on the shoulder. "He there before you know it! So keep sharp. You see something, you hear something, stop! Go down!"

"That's about the size of it," said the American lead. "Tonight, we're just hunting for the area. Tomorrow, we come back and get our man."

Nunzio immediately objected to the plan. How idiotic, he thought. If the enemy was smart, they'd simply watch what they did, where they went, and shanghai them the next night. But the American guide was a superior and an experienced one. So he kept quiet, expecting to learn something he didn't know about.

After a rocky beginning during which Corporal Mifsud managed too somehow snap a piece of brittle branch, the five soldiers stealthily entered the woods just beyond perimeter. Unknown to them, they passed by four American and two Australians disguised within the perimeter there to support the patrol units making the rounds.

One of the Americans watched in disgust, having developed the same opinion as Nunzio, that the method was stupid. His opinion, however, was based on having observed casualties that he believed no doubt would have been avoided if they'd simply gone in, done the job, and gone out.

The mission followed a line they had marked out during daylight hours in order to check a suspected area. King Kong had spotted sections of the ground that he had felt were suspicious. Some of the soldiers who had preceded these fellows knew nothing of the jungle, or *guerrilla* fighter, expecting them to be hiding out in clumps of trees, caves, or hastily built huts. But Kong knew to look down. "Find the enemy in the ground," he whispered to Nunzio. "Looking down."

At first Nunzio suspected a language problem, but as he observed Kong skulking along with his head low and his feet smoothly testing every area of ground, he realized that the man must have meant the enemy was underground. He followed suit.

Then suddenly the American stopped and gave the signal to go down flat. The five of them were silent as ice and then slowly becoming audible was a soft scratching sound. It had to be the American prisoner, signaling them. Nunzio looked at Kong. Kong nodded, pointing right below where Nunzio lay. He felt a chill run through his body from his feet to the top of his head. He turned to Mifsud who grinned at him.

They lay inert for ten minutes, their bodies feeling fully charged with a kind of energy only a soldier experiences. Then slowly they inched backward without a sound until the American lead felt it was safe for them to withdraw on foot. They returned to camp, hearts still beating like drums gone wild, and washed off the black paint.

Afterward, as Nunzio lay in bed, fully awake, still wearing off the adrenaline, he couldn't shake the feeling that going back to the same exact spot was madness. Still, he thought, Kong seemed to know the enemy, and so did the GI for that matter. He struggled against the urge to correct a situation he didn't know enough about to have an opinion on. Eventually he drifted off into a light sleep.

The next night, the group reassembled, taking extra care to be fully camouflaged, mentally prepared, and weapons ready.

"Whose got the lead?" Nunzio asked before they set out.

"I'll do the same, with Kong," the American instructed, "then maybe you stay in between your two men. When we get in, you grab the kid. He's a red head, Irish kid, so he should be easy to spot in that kinda light."

"Right," said Nunzio, nodding, not remembering much light at all. And then to Mifsud, "Your eyes on the lead. Watch everything around them, anything that moves I want you to alert, got it? Citta, you watch the woods beyond them, and eyes and ears sharp. Keep in mind, we may have been spotted last night, so be ready for anything."

Kong jerked his head around at that statement, looking fierce for only a split second before he shot Nunzio a smile. "Good idea," he said.

Nunzio smiled back. But he did not smile inside. After passing through the security perimeter, as the company inched forward to the spot that they had confirmed the night before, he kept his eyes not only on the dark jungle, but also on Kong.

The air was less humid for a change, providing a freedom from the usual mist that tended to overtake Nunzio's vision, requiring him to clear it by blinking. Later, he would be grateful for that very singular factor. Had he struggled with the fogginess, he would most certainly have missed the suspicious motion Kong made.

As in the previous evening, Kong and the American gently sifted the ground, but just as they reached the mark and the leader was signaling them all to silence, Nunzio caught Kong's left hand shove something through what had to have been a thin hole in the ground covering. It made the slightest of noises, but a noise completely foreign to the jungle they trekked. As soon as he did so, there was a burst of sound, and Nunzio knew they were in terrible trouble.

Chapter Twenty-Four

Immediately the jungle burst with the sound of blood-curdling yells coming from three different directions. There was no time to regroup, and the men were forced to fight straight from the ground where, had they not had their weapons ready, they would all have perished. Nunzio, never having shot a man in his life, fired at the trees. He wasn't sure if he had hit his target, but it was clear from the decrease in screams that their visitors were being less vocal as a group. As Mifsud and Citta shot just as wildly, the Aussie sentries who had been given orders to follow, appeared behind them, and quickly took out the offending element. One fell from where he had hidden his small body in a tree and landed right at Nunzio's feet.

It was then that Nunzio realized their American lead was dead. He signaled Mifsud to collect the man's body, and then he turned to check on Kong. But Kong was nowhere in sight. The man had betrayed them, led them right into a trap. And then, like the rat he was, he had scuttled off into the jungle to join his vile guerilla mates. Realizing what had happened, Nunzio was instantly inflamed with a wild, angry passion, the power of which he had never felt before. Pounding the ground hard with his boots and rifle in his anger, he immediately discovered the hole that had been dug to hold a bamboo cage. Inside lay the soldier they sought, buried alive without food or water, there only for the pleasure of the Vietnamese torture crew. He was still breathing.

He didn't need to signal the Australians who were already extracting the soldier and rolling him onto a kind of sheet with handles. And in seconds they were off, rapidly withdrawing through the dark under the careful watch of the five American guards still fully camouflaged and completely unknown to all but their fellow sentries.

At his debriefing, Sgt. DiAngelis reported exactly as everything had happened. The major was angry at having lost his forward lead, on whom he depended for training and tracking. And he was angrier still at having been fooled by the Vietcong by a person who brazenly called himself Kong. They're probably having a good laugh about it in their filthy shack somewhere in the jungle, he thought. If we run into that slime again, we'll be sure to show our appreciation. Out loud he said, "All right, Sergeant, good work in retrieving Conway. You couldn't have known about the traitor."

"No, Sir."

"All right, that's all."

"Sir?"

"Yes, Sergeant?"

"Regarding the method, in which we return to the exact same place via the exact same path the second night."

"Yes? That ensures that the soldiers know where they're going and where to stage the attack or make the rescue, or whatever the mission is.

"Yes, Sir. But it also alerts the enemy to our tactic. Wouldn't it be better if we studied the situation from a distance and made the first mission and rescue all in the same night?"

"Sgt. DiAngelis, you've only been here a short while. Let's let the experienced fellows make those kinds of decisions. Once you've had a little more experience, I'll hear your thoughts."

"Yes, Sir. Thank you, Sir."

"Okay, DiAngelis, that's all."

As Nunzio returned to the hut, he went over the whole debacle in his mind. That lead guy never had to die, he thought. He shook his head. Maybe they'd all have been hit if they'd done it his way, though. He really didn't have any experience, just an opinion, and a rage growing inside against an enemy that was apparently too chicken to come out and fight. A soldier didn't have to respect his enemy, they taught at basic, which was a good thing because he sure didn't.

One man he did respect was that spunky Irish guy, Milt Conway. The capture record showed he'd been held in that box for almost a week, immobile in the heat with the jungle rats and biting pests the size of which Nunzio had never seen before. He'd been punched and kicked, and had internal bruising and a broken wrist. And he also needed to have his shoulder reset surgically. But when the major interviewed him, Nunzio heard him say, "Yes, Sir, I was injured, but they didn't get me eyes—that's what they like most, but they was saving that for last, and we got 'em, Sir, before they got to mine!"

The major, who had requested the Purple Heart for Corporal Conway, simply said, "We're proud of you, Conway. You do your country proud."

Afterwards, Nunzio visited the patient who was worse off than he admitted. The internal bruising was causing other problems, and it looked like he was going to be sent home. He needed more advanced care than could be offered in a jungle hospital or even the facilities in Honolulu.

"Sergeant," said Conway, as Nunzio approached.

"I never seen a guy as tough as you," Nunzio said, not sure how to show his admiration. "I seen some characters, wild, hot-blooded Italians where I come from, but they'd be weeping in a puddle on the floor after what you been through. Where's it all comin' from?"

Conway chuckled. "You're puttin' me on, Sergeant," he said. "Trying to bolster me feelings."

Nunzio smiled. He shook his head. "If my time comes, hope to be the man you are," was all he said.

That night, Nunzio tried to write a short letter to Carlo. He heard that Carlo was aboard the *Ranger*, a supercarrier awaiting action in Subic Bay, the Philippines. Carlo had not gone to flight school, but he wanted to be on the carriers to learn about radar. It fascinated him.

There's LSTs and those speedy numbers in and out of here all day long, Nunzio wrote. *They're all Navy guys. Too bad you didn't pick that as your specialty! Anyway, so far I'm okay, but the guys are still nervous after that mission. You oughta see this character Conway, the guy we rescued. He's got more guts than all the guys at Fat Eddie's workshop and the rest of Philadelphia combined!*

Nunzio stopped to think about that. He figured it was true. The gangsters had money, but it seemed like they always worked in pairs, and with weapons, sneaking around in the dark. Like the rats in the jungle, he thought. Never face to face like the soldier combat he'd read about during the World Wars. It seemed that the US was fighting with honor against an enemy that didn't really value honor. They didn't seem to value anything other than finding soldiers and either killing or taking them off to torture them.

The thoughts of the victorious general, with his bravery and strength, protecting America from its enemies was fading. The dream was the same, but the enemy had changed, metamorphosized into a kind of snake that traveled underground, behind bushes, and hanging from trees.

He put down his writing and glanced through the open door. About 20 guys were hanging around outside, including Citta and Mifsud. He joined them, enjoying the unusual breeze and cooler air.

Some of the men were sitting on their hooch rooftops smoking hash, while radios played softly. Danang was primarily a supply post, and had frequent interaction with Navy personnel and Navy vessels. It was not considered a target area, so the men were free to relax outside provided all stayed well within the secure perimeter.

"Why don't we go up top the hooch?" Citta said. "Get a chance to see what's around us."

"You're not thinking a smokin' any of that funny stuff, are ya?" Nunzio answered.

"Me? Hell no, I'm funny enough as it is."

Mifsud laughed. "Come on Sarg."

"I'm comin'," said Nunzio as the three of them climbed from the tops of waste cans, and using the gaps in the walls for footholds, sprang to the top, careful to avoid the thin sections of thatch at the top. "You're right, this is nice," Nunzio agreed.

"How's old Conway doin' today?" Mifsud asked as he lit a cigarette. "I bet he's rarin' the go!"

"He's somethin' else," Nunzio said.

"They say he's gonna have to go, though," Citta said. "Shame. He ain't afraid a' nothin'."

"He said he's got God on his side, so he's gonna win either way it goes," Mifsud said, taking a drag and staring up at the sky.

Nunzio was startled. Conway hadn't said anything like that when they had spoken. "He said that?"

"Yep. Makes you wonder, huh?"

"Yeah."

"He's right though," said Citta. "Stuff's gonna happen to us, but—"

But Citta's sentence was lost in a sudden blast of firepower. Seemingly out of nowhere, shells were falling, and explosions were blasting structures apart all over the camp.

"Get off the roof! Get off the roof!" Nunzio yelled. But it was too late. A mortar hit so close that the little hut rose and fell, puffing out its temporary passengers into the dark sky, where they were lost from each other as they landed. Another mortar exploded painfully close to where Nunzio had come down, and he instinctively rolled over to shield his ears. But doing so created a violent shock of pain in his left shoulder so intense that he lost consciousness.

"Get him inside!" screamed the major to several men. Blood was heavily racing across Nunzio's face clogging his mouth from a head wound, and unconscious as he was, he was unable to clear it. "Turn him over, get him inside!" the major repeated. "And come back out and get Citta. He's hanging from that damn clothesline. Move!"

The surprise attack overhead lasted only ten minutes, but the damage was sizable. After everyone was inside the central Quonset hut, the major laid down the law. There would be no further recreation outside at night. Those outside at night would be only those on maneuvers or security.

The medical staff tried to assess the most seriously wounded before moving ahead. They had lost one guard who had been hit running across the field to try to set off the alarm. That was the first round fired. Citta was laid up with broken ribs, and several others had injuries, but Nunzio's was the most severe. His open head wound needed rapid bandaging and x-ray, but he had also severely broken his collar bone.

The temporary setting of his collar bone had only been begun when the guards sounded the alarm warning; the Vietcong was approaching the base.

"They're in formation, Major," reported the guard breathlessly. "They got us partly surrounded and are trying to block off the last escape to port."

"Thank you, Sergeant," said the Major. He radioed for assistance immediately, and then told all those who were mobile to follow him to a corner of the room for instructions. As Citta started to get up, he called out, "That don't mean you, Citta. Sit down."

Citta scowled and sat back down, wincing as he did so.

Nunzio, still unconscious, was given the necessary injections to keep him so while his collar bone was examined and found to be not just simply broken, but widely separated. Had he been conscious, the manipulation of the two ends of the broken bone would have returned him to unconscious very rapidly.

Outside, the Cong was advancing. The guards had begun to fire, and the others, according to Major's instructions were advancing in levels of three, each taking a key section of the camp surrounding the Quonset hut. The gunfire was not continuous, but it was becoming more frequent. One Vietcong was shot and his screams excited his comrades who began to fire willy nilly into where they were sure soldiers were hiding. In some cases they were right, and the numbers of casualties were growing rapidly. Both sides were losing fighters, but the enemy was not giving up. As they continued to approach the building, surrounding it as best they could with their remaining soldiers, the guards made heroic plays at eliminating the threat before they could get to it, dropping several of the seemingly growing crowd.

The doctor looked at the nurse as they did their best to keep their minds on the job in front of them, which was lucky for Nunzio, because a wrong move at that point might easily have paralyzed the limb. But the enemy was getting ever closer despite the valiant efforts of the Air Force and it seemed that it was only a matter of time before the deluge of darkness descended on the hospital.

Chapter Twenty-Five

Suddenly, a loud noise approached overhead, moving rapidly toward the camp. Its lights and urgency seemed to frighten the foot soldiers advancing, as if they had seen it before. They immediately ran for cover behind whatever they could find, even each other.

It was then that the tide of the battle was not only rapidly reversed, but virtually vanquished.

"Looks like Puff!" one soldier yelled to the man next to him, his spirits lifting considerably at the sight of the approaching aircraft, swooping low.

He was right. The major's SOS had been answered by one of the Air Force's most formidable defense weapons, the Douglas AC 130 Gunship, known to the men affectionately as *Puff the Magic*

Dragon. The plane was designed to maneuver its firepower in a seemingly continuous circular motion, taking out the enemy with awe-inspiring thoroughness with a new degree of ground support the Air Force was happy to get used to. Its accuracy was less ideal, but under the circumstances, the men on the ground were just happy to take cover and let it do its work.

As the pilot slowly circled the area, his gunners manning the multiple machine gun positions, the medical personnel inside breathed a sigh of relief. *Puff* retreated and returned to give the area another going over before sending radio word that the job was finished there.

The major gathered everyone inside the hut once again to take roll. Citta sat wistfully at the edge of his cot, watching the men assemble where he wanted to be. As he watched, his consternation turned to concern. Where was Mifsud?

"Major," he called from across the room, not one to exercise formality if unnecessary, "Where's Mifsud? Ain't he out there?"

"Where is Corporal Mifsud?" the major asked one of the scouts.

"Well, Sir, there are some casualties—"

"No!" screamed Citta. "He ain't hurt!"

"That's enough Citta," the major said, weary enough with the situation. "We'll get to the bottom of this. Just stay put."

The scout left and hunted with the other scouts, familiar with the area. Daybreak was coming soon and, in those situations, morning light was not the soldier's friend, often revealing personnel devastation not located during the dark hours of the night.

As Citta sat nervously fidgeting on his cot, Conway threw a box of bandages at him to get his attention. Citta turned sharply. "What'd you do that for?" he demanded.

"Look, if he's out there, they'll get him. If he's dead, he died in combat for his country. God's watchin' either way."

Nunzio twitched in his unconscious state, startling the nurse who was closing his wound. "Is he sedated enough?" she asked.

"Yeah, yeah, just hurry it up, nurse," the doctor said, eager for a cigarette.

Citta was still breathing hard when the scout returned. He approached the major and spoke quietly, his head down.

"Oh nuts!" the major yelled out without regard to his position or self-control. "Crap!"

Citta sat up, "What is it, Major?" he called.

The major looked at him and just shook his head before blowing out of the hut in haste.

Citta, too, then gave way to the grievous pain already cutting a deep cavern into his heart.

Corporal Mifsud was given a service right there on base before his body was flown to Honolulu and then on to Idlewild Airport in New York. Another plane would depart carrying Nunzio and the unsinkable Conway, along with seven other seriously wounded out of Red Beach Bay to the evac hospital in Fort Benning, Georgia. Citta would stay behind 'til the end of his tour three months later.

Conway's bed was next to Nunzio's in the cargo bay that formed their hospital floor. He was attached to a drainage tube as well as a saline drip; the drainage to relieve the fluids from the infection caused to his liver from the abuse and dehydration coinciding. "You gotta pick one or the other," the doctor had joked, "but you can't have both at the same time." The condition was serious and was causing a kind of jaundice that the doctors in Fort Benning were reputed to be able to treat. Conway joked that he hoped they get it fixed, as his yellow skin was clashing with his red beard.

Nunzio had been encased in a bandaging and plaster combination that the medics referred to as a *straight jacket*, to prevent his bones from movement and further wounding each other. They appeared to be knitting, but whether they were in the proper configuration was something the orthopedic surgeon at Benning would determine. If not, Nunzio shuddered to think of what would have to be done to repair it. His head wound was healing, but, like Citta, he had taken Mifsud's death hard. The guy had been such an inspiration, with all kinds of plans for once he got back home. He hadn't had a particular girl waiting for him, but he had decided he wanted to go the regular route—get a wife, a good job, and fill up a house with kids.

He wondered what the kids would have been like.

Nunzio looked over at Conway. "You gonna have kids?" he asked.

Conway was pensive. "Gee, I don't know."

"You like kids?"

"Oh yeah, love 'em. I just don't know. Maybe I'll go the other route."

Nunzio couldn't help but smile. The man had such an upbeat, lilting way of speaking. "The other route?"

"Well," Conway said, stroking his beard, "I'm considering the priesthood, ya know."

The statement hit Nunzio like a bucket of cold water. "Y'are?" he said, his mouth hanging open until he realized it and shut it. How could someone else be doing what he'd always been the one to be thinking about? He felt unjustifiably violated. Then stupid for feeling that way. Then confused about both feelings.

Conway bubbled on, seemingly oblivious to his response. "I've felt the calling for a long time, I have. It's a family tradition. I've got two cousins and an uncle, all priests. Two sisters who are Sisters, and one cloistered cousin!" he finished proudly.

"Wow."

"Yep. You and Mifsud—were you both from New York?"

"Uh, no, I'm from Philly. He was from Brooklyn." He paused. "He was quite a guy."

"He's in heaven."

Again, Nunzio was startled. "Huh?"

"Before the attack, he sat with me a while, and I told him about how God was with us all."

That's what I'm supposed to do, Nunzio thought again, irreverently envious.

"He was a Catholic, you know."

"I know," answered Nunzio. "So am I."

"Me, too. Anyway, when the priest came to visit us, I said 'take him, he needs Confession.' And Mifsud had Confession right in the room next door. He was in the state of Sanctifying Grace."

The hairs on Nunzio's arms and legs stood on end, the best he could tell under the plaster. How he envied Mifsud at that moment. How he envied Conway. How had he let himself get so far afield from his wishes, his dream, his calling?

"It was right after that he got blown off that roof, and then whatever happened."

"He said somethin' to us," Nunzio said then. As envious as he was of this optimistic Irishman, he wanted him to know that his mission had been complete. "He told us that you said God was with you either way, down here or in death."

For once, Conway said nothing. He nodded, a faint smile on his face. After a few moments, he choked out the words, "Thank you," and closed his eyes for a nap.

Nunzio suddenly felt tired as well, shut his eyes and immediately fell into a dream. Unlike his dark and scary boyhood dreams, and the ones he expected after the perils of War, it was a gentle, light, soft atmosphere that seemed to have the scent of lilac and gardenia, reminiscent of the gardens and fields in Virginia's Lexington Hall over summer. Yet the entire atmosphere was a cream-colored, satiny soft terrain, and he lay slightly inclined on thick, soothing quilts in the gentle clouds.

A man was there. Nunzio realized that the man was a priest whom at first, he couldn't see. Then, as he focused into view, Nunzio saw that he wore a white cassock and a gold and white chasuble that flowed and billowed like sails in the wind. Nunzio did not recognize him, yet he felt he knew him. He studied him as best he could, trying to understand that contradictory feeling he was having. The priest was equal to the atmosphere, gentle and easy to be around. His face was not visible, but as the short dream went on, he began to speak to Nunzio in a soothing and peaceful voice.

"Heaven is a place where all of our love is expressed in purity and without negativity," he said. "Our love is void of all imperfections. Only joy."

Nunzio was filled with an urge to ask, "Will you pray for me?"

But before he could ask, the priest nodded and said, "Yes, I will pray for you."

Later, when he woke up to the ministering of the flight nurse, the dream was still alive in his mind. He knew it had been a dream, but the priest seemed to be with him still. Nunzio looked over at Conway, still sleeping. The priest must already have prayed for him because he no longer felt the envy or indignation of before. Instead, looking at the enlightened Irishman, he felt that Conway was a true brother.

The doctors at Fort Benning determined that the field doc had properly set Nunzio's collar bone, and despite the rattling around it had done in transport, he was healing very well. His collar bone needed to be stabilized in a cast though, for quite a long recovery time. He was given strict instructions not to use the arm, or even to lift a piece of paper. "I'm telling you, there are guys who come through here and they never heal. They're in agony as they get older, all because they decided they knew best and disobeyed my orders," the gruff old military doctor said to him. "I'm telling you twelve weeks—that ain't so long when you consider you're a young soldier. But I'm cutting you off, Son. I'm afraid your military life is over. Once your tour's over in recoup, you're out."

The announcement was not one that gave Nunzio any grief. Aside from having lost over a year out of his life to the *preservation of democracy*, as the doctor had put it, he had become stronger and he felt a restless kind of urging forward to pick up where his life had left off. Try to find Carlo and maybe talk about what to do next, or at least write to him. He realized sadly then that his buddy would surely still be at sea.

When he departed the hospital at Fort Benning for four weeks in St. Rita's Hospital special unit in Philadelphia, he thanked Conway, and wished him well. "We gotta keep in touch, Conway," he said. It wasn't what he meant, but he didn't have the casual words to say *You've somehow managed to bring my spirit back and redirect my life*. But Conway caught a bit of it in his cheerful manner.

"Smooth sailin to ya then," he said, tipping his make-believe hat with his irresistible smile. "We'll meet again, my friend."

Nunzio backed away, his eyes still on Conway and the multiple contraptions serving to disinfect his battered, heroic body. “Yes,” his said, his throat tight. “Be sure of it.”

Chapter Twenty-Six

The shock of living again in the big house was enormous for Nunzio. His experience in Vietnam had left him grateful for little things, and a much deeper appreciation of loved ones, but there, in the big house with all of its adornments old and new, conveniences, and vast never-ending arrays of food, there was no love for him.

His mother did not display the very first indication of joy at seeing her young son returned alive, albeit seriously worse for the wear. The requirements for his care, including the visit of a nurse twice weekly to check the "straight jacket" and monitor the continued healing of his head wound, brought her open displeasure.

"She's not eating with us," she announced tersely when she was apprised of Nunzio's care requirements. "We're not running a charity here! She can do her job and then get out."

Nunzio showed no pain, but in reality, he had become distressingly vulnerable, and felt the wounds of her rejection deeply. He thought of the American lead back in DaNang who had died, leaving a wife and children behind, of Mifsud, who probably had a mother who would mourn his loss the rest of her life. He should have been one of them, switched places, provided them the life instead. There was no one there who would mourn him. Of that, he was certain.

"What do you think about all day?" the nurse asked one afternoon. "You trying to figure out your plans for what you're going to do next?" She was a small woman with a well-rounded figure, a happy smile and loads of puffy blonde hair worn in the popular beehive style.

"No, but I guess I should be," Nunzio answered, wincing as she removed the bandaging from his head. His hair had begun to grow in, making it a little harder to lift the bandages away cleanly.

"You're healing up very well," she said. "That was nasty I bet when it first hit!"

"Have you seen many returning soldiers and their wounds?" Nunzio asked.

"Not too many. The military hospitals usually keep them but as you know, they're starting to spill over and I may get a few more. But I've seen plenty of headwounds from other things. Looks like this one got you pretty good!"

"I was kind of blown into a wall that had things protruding from it, but at the same time, some shrapnel hit me, so it was just a mess. The collar bone hurt the worst though."

"Well, we'll keep you on your pain medicines as long as you need them," she said, unrolling the bandaging she would recover the stitching with.

Talking about the event brought back the first post-surgical experiences for Nunzio at the camp. Finding out Mifsud had been killed had hurt more than the wounds, was more frustrating and left him with his first inclination that it might better have been he who died.

"Do you ever wonder why one guy lives and one guy dies?" he asked suddenly.

The question startled the nurse, whose wisdom did not extend beyond the physical caring and nurturing of her patients. But she tried to respond positively. "It's all part of God's plan," she said, smiling sadly. "You never know when your time's coming."

Nunzio smiled. He had not been home long, but in that short time, he had found that an odd series of changes had come over a lot of the city. The young ladies were wearing shorter skirts and they seemed to be hanging on corners where before it had been only those particularly racy women in the company of the men who hung there. And all over, he saw irreverence and almost a disdain for God, His Church, and His Sacraments. At first, he hadn't noticed how prevalent it was, but after a few days of television and radio, it was clear to him that change was rolling in in large, darkly aromatic waves. The nurse's remarks, showing her steadfast faith was uplifting.

"Yes," he said. "Thanks."

Not long after that, when his head wound no longer required bandaging, Nunzio answered an urge to be inside the protective structure of the Church of the Sacred Heart. He draped one side of his coat around his wounded shoulder and put his hand through the sleeve of the other, checked his wallet for cash, and went to stand at the bus stop.

As he stood, people walked by singly and in groups, hurriedly heading East or West, speaking sometimes to each other, but never even noticing him. He thought back to how he and Carlo had made the short walk to Sacred Heart into almost a social event. Everybody in the neighborhood either knew them or knew who they were.

Maybe when I get closer to that part of the neighborhood, I'll see a familiar face, he thought. But after he'd taken the bus, alighted, and carried on a few blocks from the church, he saw only strangers. He began to panic, wondering suddenly if the Sacred Heart Church was even still there. He looked down the length of the block ahead and into the next. He didn't see the statue that had always been there at the top of the column on the corner. He picked up his pace and crossed to the next street. His shoulder was beginning to throb from the sudden, unfamiliar activity. But Nunzio could not slow down. A kind of panic had taken him over. *Where was the church? Where were the priests? Where was his. . . home?*

Just as the light flooding a room changes the unknown into known when a match is stricken, Nunzio spotted the missing statue. It was in the next block. It had always been in the next block. His breathing slowed as he clutched at his burning shoulder, slowing down to a walk, realizing he'd gotten the city blocks mixed up in his mind. Relief spread over him and suddenly, he could smell the hamburgers cooking at the stand down on 27th St. and the oil burning from the old jalopies so many of the city dwellers drove to work and back. He focused on the distant statue, feeling an enigmatic urge to run to it and embrace it.

Wouldn't that be a sight, he thought joyfully. I can see the local papers, *Returning vet mistakes statue for father.* He longed to share the joke with his buddy, Carlo. He had been unable to reach Carlo, and until that very day, he had not spent any time out of the house. He wondered where his old friend was then and how his carrier was faring in that Bay, wherever it was.

Unknowingly, he picked up the pace again, his thoughts once again bringing back the panic. What if Carlo had met the same fate as Mifsud? What if it was all too much for Carlo's pop and he had moved away from Philadelphia? But no, the phone had not been answered by a stranger. It simply had not been answered. No one was home. There was nothing to worry about. He shook it off.

This is a happy time, he told himself. I'll see Father Kelly and Monsignor French. We'll talk. It's only been a year, a little more, maybe. Even as he struggled to convince himself, he could feel a cloak of change descending over the area. The scents were familiar, but they were not the same, nor were the sounds, and certainly not the sights.

He reached the church, its beautiful statue of Christ Jesus up above and the richly colored stained-glass windows with the promise of everlasting peace within their refuge brought tears to his eyes. He could tell a Mass was going on, which was surprising at that time of day. It could be a wedding, or maybe a funeral, he thought. Then he spotted a black hearse out front and realized it would be a requiem for a parishioner.

That's good, he thought. It's been way too long since I've been to Mass in a bona fide church, and this one is the best in the world. But as he stepped inside, intending to nonchalantly find a spot in the back where he could remain unnoticed, he was stunned to see so very many clergy in attendance, and even a group of school children in Sacred Heart uniforms. It was then he saw that Father Kelly was there, but he was not offering the Mass himself. He was sitting in the sanctuary, next to several other priests. The Mass was being said by a bishop unfamiliar to Nunzio, although the man looked very Italian and had a modest Italian accent. He had just been incensed after chanting the gospel and was heading for the ambo to speak.

If he's officiating and Father Kelly is sitting there, where is Monsignor French, Nunzio wondered. There were so many priests and bishops that at first, Nunzio decided that Monsignor was mixed in with them and that he couldn't recognize him from the back. But as the stranger at the ambo began to speak, Nunzio soon understood the presence of so very many clergy, the flood of deeply fragrant flowers in the entry, and the fact that every one of the Sacred Heart altar boys was present. It was not a regular funeral. It was a special funeral, a funeral for a priest. And he would not see Monsignor French in the mourning cloud of priests and deacons. Because Monsignor French was dead.

Nunzio stood watching and listening but drifting between the words, not connecting them, yet holding them in his brain, like putting pennies in a piggy bank. It was Monsignor French. The funeral was for Monsignor French he told himself. Yet the reality of it bounced back off of him like a basketball gone astray and hitting the rim of the hoop. The American Lead died, Mifsud died, the other boys on the plane under those flags, they had died. But Monsignor French, he hadn't been in the war, and yet, he had also died. The world held Monsignor French and Father Kelly, and then just like that, it didn't.

In a lightning quick search, Nunzio's eyes shot to the spot where he had last seen Father Kelly. Finding him, he nodded repeatedly. Okay, okay, he reassured himself. He's still there. He's not dead. He drew in his breath involuntarily then and let it out. One of the ushers noticed and offered to find him a pew in the back where there were a few empty ones. He followed her, walking as if he were just getting off the plane in Fort Benning, his shoulders as erect as possible, face straight ahead.

He genuflected before entering the pew, and once he was down on one knee, he wanted to stay there. He looked ahead, all the way to the sanctuary, up above the richly adorned altar to the crucifix. Into the eyes of the Sacrificial Lamb he stared as his chest tightened, welling with the years of hard-hearted belligerence in persisting to hold onto his unjust anger.

He lowered his head, rising to enter the pew, as the easing of his soul began, the ancient cleansing with emotion, silent, humbling, and essential. "Sweet Jesus," he prayed in the privacy of his lonely place, "Forgive me."

Long after the solemn procession of priests and others followed the coffin of the beloved Monsignor French to the rear of the church and on to the cemetery, Nunzio remained in the church. For the first time in years, he was able to think clearly. He could once again connect his conscience to his mind, and he wanted Confession.

After a while, he heard the side door open. Looking up, he saw Father Kelly.

Father spotted Nunzio and smiled sadly.

It had not been that long since they had seen each other, but to Nunzio, Father Kelly could have aged ten years or more. His hair had bits of grey showing, and there were wrinkles below his slightly receding hairline. But he still had life in his eyes, and he welcomed Nunzio warmly with a handshake and then an embrace.

"I didn't know you were back," he said. "I would have called you. You know that."

"I know it," Nunzio said. "Today is the first day I've seen the outside of the house since I been back."

"That looks like a nasty wound," Father said, nodding toward Nunzio's shoulder.

"It's nothing," Nunzio said. "Father, I'd like to go to Confession."

"Come on," said Father Kelly.

After Confession, as the flood of Sanctifying Grace generated new life and courage into Nunzio's erstwhile beleaguered soul, he and Father Kelly sat at the table where they had sat so many times in the past, lingering after Mass. No doughnuts, but coffee, and the richness of a valued friendship grown stronger.

"I was so shocked when I got here, Father," Nunzio said. "Monsignor—I guess I'm just so cut off from everything."

"He wasn't sick long, Nunzio. Well, to be honest, he was probably sick a long time and just didn't want to burden anyone with it. When he found out what he had, he still kept it to himself until he could no longer do so. He was only bedridden two weeks. He was brave and Faithful to the end."

Nunzio was quiet, imagining the courage and strength the priest must have displayed as he suffered secretly. "He probably didn't want to be a bother to anyone."

"That's exactly right," said Father.

"I will pray for him, even though he probably don't need it!" Nunzio said, his voice rising at the end of the sentence.

"I understand your feeling that way, but I'm glad you'll pray for him anyway. It's harder for priests, you know. When a husband and father dies, there is a widow and children who pray for his soul. But a priest, he didn't have a family, his parents are most often deceased, and so the prayers are fewer, Masses even fewer."

Nunzio nodded. "There are so many sacrifices priests make."

"But so many benefits!" Father said, smiling happily again.

"I'd like to start serving Mass for you again," Nunzio said.

"Not with that wound you don't, Soldier," Father chuckled.

"As soon as I get this thing off, then," Nunzio said. "Meantime, I'll be here for Mass."

"Carlo said the same thing, but it's going to be a while—"

"Carlo!" Nunzio sat upright suddenly.

"Yes, Carlo's back, too. Didn't you know?"

"No."

"Well, I was over to see him. He's coming along—"

"Was he hit?"

"Yeah, I don't know the details, but he was on a transport that was hit, and they almost didn't get him. He ended up with some bad burns, and shrapnel—right about where you did! In the shoulder!"

Nunzio shook his head, exhaling hard. "I was just thinking about him and wondering how he was doing. And here he's been hit, too. I guess he's pending discharge then?"

"I think so, yes."

"I've gotta see him."

"I know he'd like that."

Later, when Nunzio got home that evening, he was startled to see a caterer's truck and several service people rolling up carpets, moving furniture, and carrying dishes into the house. A band had arrived and was setting up large columnar speakers, a drum set, and other instruments.

As he started up the stairs, his mother intercepted him. "Don't make any messes. Your brother's coming home tonight and we're having a party. So we're trying to keep the place looking nice."

The difference between where Nunzio had spent the afternoon and where he was at that moment was so stark, it hit him as ridiculous, almost as if he were in a comedy movie. The idea made him chuckle.

"I'm not kidding!" his mother said, misinterpreting his response. "Go on upstairs. You're going to have to get something in the kitchen tonight. There's no buffet."

It was at that moment, Nunzio knew that he would not be much longer in the big house.

That night, after heroic Louie arrived home unharmed and proud as a Prussian, a flood of young people, most of whom he didn't know, arrived to celebrate with him. As the party wore on, Nunzio watched from a distance as his stepfather, having had too many drinks, tried to impress some of the younger female guests with his strength in picking one of them up. Unable to sustain the action, he clumsily dropped her, at which point she shrieked, got up, and ran with her girlfriend out the door. Across the room, Nunzio caught sight of his mother's angry face. He wondered if there were to be another divorce in her future.

Humiliated, Fat Eddie turned and spotted Nunzio. “You’re going to work for me,” he said as if they had been discussing it all along, his voice sloshing with alcohol. “Don’t try to get out of it!” He pointed at Nunzio for emphasis.

No, thought Nunzio. I know who I’m going to be working for now, and it isn’t you.

Chapter Twenty-Seven

In a dream, the cunning snake, hiding within the ragged branches of a tree, swooped down on Fat Eddie and swallowed him whole. The serpent lowered his newly nourished body on the ground, licking its lips as the large figure of Fat Eddie struggled, arms and legs wildly kicking inside the belly of the beast.

Suddenly Nunzio awoke, sweating and breathing as if running for his life. Memories of the activities of the night before came at him like a flood of sewage across his chest. It was seven days since his brother's welcome home celebration. Louie had already re-settled into his daily occupation of sitting and gossiping with the secretary at Fat Eddie's dock office after his not-so-arduous military stint in France.

Somehow, he had managed to arrive with a medal pinned to his chest for a curious act of bravery performed in the line of duty well out of range of enemy fire, Paris being approximately 6,286 miles from Saigon. The honor did nothing to deter his appeal for the opposite sex, his already being the stepson of the wealthy don. But the sight of him and his secretary irked Fat Eddie, who spoke sharply to the girl any time he caught her near Louie's desk.

The day after the welcome home party for Louie, Fat Eddie had indeed followed up on his proclamation that Nunzio would work for him.

"You're not gonna take my money, eat my food, and not do your part!" he yelled when Nunzio protested. "You owe me!"

Nunzio detected just the slightest hint of desperation in the man's voice, as if he had the thought that Nunzio might somehow outwit him and leave him looking stupid in front of his mother and brother. But when he repeated the sentence, "You owe me," Nunzio realized he was referring to the bar fight where Carlo had been more or less rescued by his goons. Nunzio had never been sure if the clumsy man at the bar had been in on it, but having spent some time in the world since then, and seen the way a lot of crafty men work, he believed the entire situation had been set up. Maybe Fat Eddie meant to make his point again, similar to how he had done with Nick.

"There's not much I can do with this shoulder bandaged," he had said, turning to the monster. "That's all I meant."

"All right, but you can learn. You can come to the docks in the afternoons, learn how we do things and what you'll be doing when you start."

Fat Eddie's ego had taken a beating with Louie around, and he simply did not know how to accept it. With Nunzio down there, the girls would be moving from one DiAngelis to the other. Of that, he was certain. Louie might be a war hero and his stepson, but Nunzio had the looks and the brains.

"You come down 'round one o'clock. Got it?"

"Yeah, I got it." Nunzio had risked no additional conversation and headed out to the bus stop to catch a ride to the church in time for Mass. He had hoped to speak to Carlo on the phone, but because of the pressure from Fat Eddie, he'd decided to go directly there to visit him after Mass. He hoped Carlo wasn't suffering horribly. He'd seen burn victims and their pain was searing and seemingly interminable.

Sitting with the congregation at Sacred Heart made him all the more urgent to begin serving again. He thought of the classes Monsignor French had held for the altar boys. Monsignor had been so precise in describing their movements, but always with such good humor. He wondered how Father Kelly felt, alone in the rectory. Nevertheless, the Mass was enriching and brought him a degree of peace he knew he could find nowhere else.

On his way to Carlo's place, he remembered their years of traveling those same streets together. But now, he thought, will Carlo ever walk again? Is he mentally affected by the experience? He wouldn't be the first, that's for sure. He thought of the men that had come home when he had, specifically the one that seemed to repeat his recipe for water ice every hour on the hour. Would Carlo be like that. He shivered at the thought.

When he arrived, he saw that the door was open, and only the screen door was closed. He wanted to look in, but thought better of it, and tapped lightly on the door frame. At first, there was no response at all. He waited a short while and tried again. Tap, tap, tap. With each tap his anxiety grew, remembering the faces of the men on the medical transport. It didn't help that one of them had arrived at Fort Benning a DOA. But he had to stay, he had to see Carlo, even if things had changed irreparably. He would be strong for him through whatever hells his friend was navigating just then.

He knocked again and waited.

Then he heard a door slam and someone call out, "Coming! Gotta get off the john!"

Nunzio's jaw dropped.

The voice belonged to Carlo—the very Carlo he had said good-bye to on his way to Fort Dix. And he sounded exactly the same.

"Carlo?" he choked out.

"Nunz?"

Then Carlo came around the corner, leaning on a cane, wearing only a t-shirt and undershorts. "Nunz!" he repeated. "Gosh, I woulda dressed if I knew you were comin'!" He chuckled.

Slightly shaken by the suddenness of it all combined with his enormous relief, Nunzio could only smile broadly. "You look great!" he finally said. "I heard you got hit."

"I can *see* that you got hit," Carlo responded, opening the door. "We got twin shoulder wounds, but what's that you got on yours? Looks awful! Come on in."

Nunzio stepped in and shook hands with his buddy.

"You know I'd give you the hug of your life if I didn't think it would paralyze you in pain," he said laughing.

"You and me both! Hey, we do things, we do 'em right!" Carlo laughed. "Where'd you get yours? You wanna lemonade?"

"Yeah, thanks. The hooch got hit, sent us idiots who were on the roof in all different directions. I got sliced and diced on the way down."

"They say it was shrapnel in here," Carlo said, motioning toward his shoulder bandage, "but who knows? We were on a transport bringing supplies and out of nowhere comes this wild maverick firing and smoking. The pilot went right into the bay! But he got a couple of us on the way."

"Sounds like a Kamikaze wanna-be," Nunzio said, smiling. "Gosh it's great to see you! I was worried you'd be, you know, worse."

"My burns were pretty bad, Nunz, I ain't gonna lie to ya. Ooh! But the salt water—I was hanging on the edge of the transport for about 8 hours—had a positive effect, and it was cold water, so that helped, too. What didn't help was constantly looking behind me to make sure there wasn't a hungry shark. But I guess the action scared them away for the time because I got rescued without losing a piece of my rear quarters."

Nunzio burst out laughing. "You said that just like Monsignor French!" he said. "Rear quarters!"

Carlo nodded and smiled sadly. "I heard about him," he said. "We go out and get shot up and he's the one who dies." But his effort to make light of it fell flat. "I really wanted to be at the funeral Nunzio," he continued. "But pop wasn't around, and I couldn't have made it without help."

"No, of course you couldn't. I was only there by chance! It was a . . . horrible surprise."

They sat in silence.

"We'll meet him again," Carlo said.

"I'm sure of it."

They talked about their crews and where they had been, leaving out the details that soldiers do, but comparing their miles traveled, and irony of each having been hit around the same time.

"See that," Nunzio said, leaning forward to show Carlo the scar at the back of his head. "That's my best battle trophy."

"Oh yeah, look at that," said Carlo, squinting to see the line of the scar. "That must have been some head wound!"

"I think it was 37 stitches," Nunzio said. "Or twelve. I can't remember which." He tried to stifle his laughter as Carlo tried to figure out how to react to his friend's unsettling confusion.

"Oh shut up!" Carlo laughed. "I worried about that, you know."

"I worried you'd be an emotional disaster!" Nunzio said, openly laughing. "I guess that was a wasted effort!"

After a while, Nunzio felt he needed to go and see about things with Eddie. He had no intention of sticking around with him but he knew he'd have to spend a few days with the foul man before he found his escape route. But before that, he had to have the conversation with Carlo.

"Listen buddy," he had said, "there's some pressure mounting from that thug my mother married. He wants me to work for him—"

"Oh geeze, Nunz—"

"No, no, whatever I do it'll be very short term. But I don't know if you picked up on something a while back—in that awful bar fight after graduation—"

"Oh yeah, them guys. I knew who they were. I seen 'em talking to Bobby, what's his name, Bobby Skunk over there at the hangout. I guess I just didn't care at that point. Know what I mean?"

"No kiddin'. I didn't realize that. Well, they were there to make a point—a point to me, that is."

"Fat Eddie's guys?"

"Yep, rescue you, give me the bill."

"Oh Nunz—and I took the bait like a kindygarten guppy!"

"I don't care about that!" Nunzio said. "They'd have done something else if that hadn't worked. But now he's hinting that there could be more to that story. Another chapter, say."

"Okay, gotcha. So you gotta make it look like you're in or it's curtains for the cripple here."

"You ain't no cripple!"

"I am til these bandages come off. Look at that!" Carlo pointed to the heavy bandages on his left thigh and right calf and ankle.

"Well, these guys, I don't know. It's not like they have any kind of honor, you know."

"I know what you're saying. You gotta play along, or injured or not, they'll come after me. Well, don't worry too much about all that. Fat Eddie, I hear, has got trouble of his own."

Nunzio perked up. "Yeah? What'd ya hear?"

"Remember Cat O'Hearn? The guy who's friends with your dad?"

Nunzio cringed. He hadn't spent that first happy moment with his father since he'd been back. They'd exchanged letters, but both had kept it that way on purpose, preferring not to risk more strain on their relationship. "Yeah."

"Well he's a sergeant now, and a pretty powerful one since he knows so many of the other cops. He hates Fat Eddie, Nunzio. Really hates 'im. And it's causing problems with Fat Eddie's bosses, if you know what I mean. You know, Bruno, he don't like static with the cops."

"Your pop tell you that?"

"Yeah, he was having beers with one a' the beat cops who told him all about it."

Following that conversation, Nunzio felt some of the pressure ease, knowing that Eddie had problems of his own. Or did he? He might not even realize he was under scrutiny, he thought. The man seemed cunning but for someone capable of such scheming, he was also not very bright. What if he made another move against Carlo? Did he even know that it would have a backlash?

The answer to that would never be known.

The following week, after Nunzio had spent a few hours daily at the dock, watching the loads of Chilean, Argentinian, and Honduran vegetables come in, along with whatever else the crates included, he'd learned the procedure, the bookkeeping, the sales percentages, and the cash reporting, which was also a percentage. Fat Eddie was impressed.

"It ain't gonna be long before that thing is off your arm and you can do a little work around here," he said. "But tonight, I got another job for you. Good thing it's your left shoulder, 'cause you'll need your right hand for this one."

Nunzio wondered at his stepfather's lack of observation. During the entire week, he had carefully worked to write figures into Eddie's books, but with his right hand they were jagged and awkward. That was because Nunzio was left-handed.

But he ignored Fat Eddie's statement, sure that correcting him would go in one ear and out the other.

Later, the older man had pulled his car around for Nunzio to get in. When he did, he laid a revolver on the seat next to him. "You're gonna use that," he said.

Nunzio looked at Fat Eddie, and then at the gun.

"You know I got a daughter from before I met your mother," Fat Eddie said. "She don't like me, but I keep track a' her. She's going with somebody in the wrong bunch. I told him he'd better stop going over to her place, leaving in the bright morning light like some kind of dog on the run. But he don't listen."

Nunzio was shocked and secretly horrified. The man was a cheater, both against his mother and in his business, Nunzio knew all that. But he did not realize that he had sunk to the level of murder. He stayed calm.

"So I gotta let him know," Fat Eddie continued. "My daughter ain't a whore. And I won't have him treatin' her like one. I need you to get him. You're a soldier. You know how to do it."

Nunzio continued to ride in silence as Fat Eddie drove toward a relatively deserted road where the man worked at a gasoline station.

"Just do it and get back in the car," Fat Eddie said, certain that his orders were to be followed.

"I can't do that," Nunzio said, as Fat Eddie pulled into the station.

"What do you mean? You can, and you will!" Eddie was winding up for a wild bout of anger and threats until Nunzio shot a hole in his balloon.

Nunzio looked at him deadpan. "I'm left-handed, Eddie," he said. He left off the fact that whether he'd been left-handed, right-handed, or ambidextrous, he would never shoot a man in cold blood, no matter who requested the service.

"Left—what? Left-handed? Well, you never told me that! What do you mean, being left-handed! They don't allow that in Catholic school!"

Nunzio was amazed that the man who was imposing upon him to go and kill someone should at that moment bring up the stringencies of Catholic schools. He said nothing, but continued to stare at Fat Eddie, expecting him to angrily jerk the car around and speed off back home for an alternate plan.

Instead, he grabbed up the gun, stuck it in his belt, pulled his shirt out over it and exited the car. In seconds, he was at the entrance to the garage before Nunzio could even exit the car. The pumps at the station were deserted, but inside the garage, the repetitive sound of hammering could be heard of one trying to release a seized-up set of brakes. The hammering continued as Eddie entered the building from the side door. In the dark, Nunzio could not see when Eddie entered the garage. Maybe, he thought desperately and opened the door to get out, that idiot will just threaten the man, let him know he means business.

Inside, the hammering continued with growing ferocity as the hammer wielder grew frustrated with the task. Then, one particularly sharp hammer sounded, and anyone nearby would have felt relief for the fellow who must have finally released the brakes, since after that, there was no more hammering.

But they would have been deceived. Because with that final thunderous blast, the garage attendant received his last breath of life as his blood splattered across the windows of the old car, and covered the garage floor, shot with the bullet of the gun fired by Fat Eddie.

Chapter Twenty-Eight

As Nunzio lay there, slowly gaining a degree of calm, he recalled his conversation with Carlo. Eddie's latest act, and as far as Nunzio knew, his worst, would surely bring the ire of the organization down on him. The idea of having no gangster stepfather to contend with was appealing, but the stronger Nunzio inside knew that he had an obligation. If what Carlo said turned out to be true, and if Fat Eddie had let on to anybody his hatred for the man sleeping with his daughter, Fat Eddie would be dealt with in no time. He would be dead.

How could Nunzio concern himself with the man who'd just as soon order his father dead? And his best friend as well?

He rolled out of bed, intent on attending Mass, still unsure of whether he should call the police,

Father Kelly, or Carlo. For certain, all three of them would know before the end of the day. In fact, there was a good chance that at least the police and Carlo already knew.

Fat Eddie had gotten drunk after his evil deed, leaving him slobbering down the side of his pillow in a dead sleep when Nunzio left for church. The wind was howling as the fall seemed to be ushering in the winter a little early. Nunzio jumped onto the bus, watching out the window as the big house grew smaller with time.

At Sacred Heart, he inhaled the Mass as if taking fresh air into his soul. But at the same time, Our Lord's Presence urged him to accept that he had a role to play. He could not simply wait it out to see what happened. He had to act. But how?

"You look like you could use a friend," Father Kelly teased as Nunzio peered into the changing room. "Go and get the old man a cup," he said smiling to one of the young altar boys." Then he turned to Nunzio more seriously. "Everything okay? Is today the day you get your cast off?"

"I forgot about that. Yes, it is," Nunzio said before slumping into a chair. "Father, I need some advice."

"Come on," said Father Kelly. And to the young server, "Never mind about the cup, enjoy your doughnut!" And he led Nunzio over to the rectory. "I messed up before," he said, "I don't want to make the same mistake twice! Sit down, tell me what's going on."

While Father brewed fresh coffee and put some bread in for toast, Nunzio explained the evil that he assumed he had witnessed the night before.

"But you don't know for sure that that's what happened in there? Did you see it?"

"No, I didn't see it. But the gun had been fired. I could smell it. I have to assume it's what happened."

"But you were not party to it."

"No. I didn't know what he had in mind until we got there. Even when he left with the gun, I couldn't believe he would shoot the man. Maybe threaten him or something, but not shoot him. But that's not all, Father. Now I come to find out that Fat Eddie himself is in danger. And the same kind of danger that mechanic was in."

"Oh?"

"He's made some mistakes. You know how these guys play. And with this murder on his conscience—I guess I feel like I oughta be doin' something—if he gets whacked, Father, he'll go straight to hell."

Father Kelly sighed and set the coffee aside. "This is serious, Nunzio," he said. And together they knelt at the little prayer table in the rectory hall to ask for judgement and wisdom.

At the same time some miles away, Sgt. Cat O'Hearn stood over the lifeless body of the slain auto mechanic. "There's nothing here," he said to the detective on the case. "No marks, no prints, evidence of any kind. But I know who did this."

The detective was startled. "You *know?*"

"Well, Sir, I can make a pretty good guess."
"Who do you suspect?"
"The same guy who's been making it clear all over town that his daughter was being corrupted by some cheap mechanic in the area. Guy named Eddie Saco. They call him Fat Eddie."

Shortly afterward, in a little barber shop, where a sudden, unexpected influx of customers was occurring, Paffuto diFrancisco leaned against the back of Nick DiAngelis' chair as he worked on a customer he hadn't seen in years.
"O'Hearn's got your back," he said, "take my word for it. The word is out."
Nick squinted, unsure how much to believe of Paffuto's story that finally, Fat Eddie was about to face charges.
"I ain't saying he'll go to jail, you understand," said Paffuto.
Nick looked up sharply. "But you just said—"
"The cops don't have nothin', no proof, no nothin'. But there's other folks that don't need no proof," he said nodding for emphasis, raising his eyebrows. "Mmhmm."
Nick sighed. "Marón da mi," he said under his breath. "Okay, okay, Paff, lemme finish dis guy."
"Okay, Nick, just sayin', you know."
Nick nodded and raised a hand in resignation. "Okay."
But if Paffuto or O'Hearn, or even Nick had expected some big mob style explosion, they would be very disappointed.

In fact, when the word got out that customers were returning to Nick's barber shop, Fat Eddie himself came to confront Nick. In the intervening years since his message to Nick, landing him in the hospital, Fat Eddie had reiterated his feelings that men should avoid Nick's shop through occasional envoys in sport coats on surveillance. And the blatant reversal that had neighborhood folks talking, in which Nick's business had returned, was too much.

"I think we oughta have a conversation, a dialog," Fat Eddie said, pronouncing each syllable in the word *dialog* very distinctly.

His enunciation amused Nick, who smiled encouragingly from across the counter at him and said, "And did you just learn that word?"

While Fat Eddie wanted with all his might to take a swing at the wise-cracking barber, he simply held in his anger with plans to have his thugs take care of Nick. Unfortunately for Eddie, though, even then his thugs were generously sharing their boss's inclinations toward the murdered mechanic with police in exchange for being kept out of the situation.

They're always the last to know, Nick thought, watching Fat Eddie roll into his car.

Even without knowledge of his men's betrayal, when Eddie headed home that night, he was in a rage. As soon as he arrived, and well before he could make any telephone calls to order the hit on Nick, he demanded, "What are we having?"

"Fried chicken," said Della, as she headed for the kitchen, "with all the trimmings."

Eddie loved fried chicken but could tolerate only white meat, and for his part, trying to negotiate the wing was way too much work. Therefore, he was keen on the fried breasts. It was not fortunate for him that he had made his affinity for them so widely known. As soon as he bit into the very first one, his tooth hit a sharp piece of metal that had somehow wound up inside the piece of chicken. It pierced his rear molar and caused Eddie to scream in pain.

Della came running back into the dining room, while hurried footsteps from other parts of the house were ringing through the halls. He screamed at her, "What did you do? What did you put in that chicken?"

Della drew back, hands on hips, "Well, Mr. Eddie!" she said. "Are you accusin' me?"

"Call a dentist, get me a dentist!" he screamed.

Louie arrived and panicked at the sight of his buffer between the real world and personal luxury in such a state, quickly brought his car around and ushered Eddie inside. By then Eddie, although still in pain was calmer and regaining his dictatorial stance.

"Take me to Donati," he said. "Don't take me nowhere else. He's down Passyunk Avenue. Come on, step on it Louie!"

"Okay, okay," said Louie, nervously winding the car through the narrow streets. At rush hour, Philadelphia was no place to be in a rush, but he did his best.

"I only go to Donati. All of us guys go to him. We don't go nowhere else." Eddie repeated, as if trying to reassure himself.

"Yeah, okay," Louie said, wondering if there was something wrong with the man. He could see his easy paychecks and clusters of women fading already. "I'll get ya there in plenty of time," he said.

Donati had received a call earlier in the day, well before Eddie had needed to make use of him. It was a somber call, but one that Donati had been expecting. He'd heard about Fat Eddie's dealings and how the man had lost control. The Capo di tutti capi wasn't fond of folks in power who lost control. On top of that, Fat Eddie had made fun of Donati's son simply because he liked to tap dance. And because of Eddie's position, Donati could not defend the boy. That had been a source of slow burning frustration for several years. When the call came, it was not unwelcome.

"You can do 'dat, can't cha?" the anonymous voice asked him calmly. "Fill the tooth with, you know, somethin' special?"

"Yeah," said Donati. "No problem."

"He'll be there later today," said the voice. And then the phone went dead.

When Fat Eddie arrived, Louie was running interference for him, opening doors, keeping people away as the heavy man plodded straight ahead.

"Lemme sit down," Fat Eddie said to Donati as soon as they arrived.

"Come on back," Donati said, motioning Louie to take a seat in the waiting room. "What's the problem?"

"I bit into something. I don't know what the hell it is, but it's killing me."

"Okay, here, lean back in this chair, let me take a good look. I'm gonna give you something for the pain first."

"Thanks Doc, great," said Fat Eddie. It was the first time Donati could remember the man ever displaying the slightest bit of decorum.

Nevertheless, he enjoyed loading the large hypodermic needle and plunging it into his gum. A sedative coating around the poison would give the patient plenty of time to go home, probably slop down more dinner and go to bed before the inner layer were exposed. It would look like a massive heart attack. There'd be no investigation because the man was horse-sized, ate poorly, smoked heavily, and had a temper like a wild rhinoceros. In fact, folks would wonder how he lived as long as he had. No one would ever know what really killed him.

After the painkiller and the special treatment, Fat Eddie was ready for something to eat. Donati had told Fat Eddie that he'd gotten a chicken bone and that while it was sharp, he was lucky that he hadn't swallowed it because it would have choked him to death. He had warned him not to eat for eight hours, but Fat Eddie was not one for taking instructions.

"Don't gimme no more of that chicken," he said vehemently. "Lemme have meatballs and gravy. You got that ready don't you?"

"Yes, Mr. Eddie," said Della.

When Nunzio arrived, Della told him what had happened and that the dentist had been able to help him.

"So he's okay?" Nunzio asked, seeking reassurance. The strange occurrence, in his mind, could not be explained as a coincidence, not with all that Carlo had said.

"Oh yes, he's back to his nasty self again, ordering everyone around," Della said. "He act like I put something in the chicken when it first happened! At least he's over that now."

That must have been what Carlo was talking about, he thought. But it looks like they missed the target, whatever it was they used. Relieved, Nunzio decided to wait and talk to Eddie at work the following afternoon.

But before he could settle in for the night, Fat Eddie's lawyer showed up at the door with the news that he was wanted for questioning regarding some mysterious shooting the night before.

Nunzio listened near the stairway.

"Shooting?" said Fat Eddie, half-laughing, half-incredulous. "Me? What are they talking about?"

"I know it," his lawyer said. "It's ridiculous. They want to ask questions about the guy is all, did you know him, what kind of relationship did you have with him, that kind of thing."

"Well I don't want to go out to some police station this time of day. I had a dental emergency earlier and I'm wiped out."

"That's fine, that's fine," the lawyer said, nodding. "I already got them to agree to wait until tomorrow morning. I just wanted to prepare you. They wanna see you at nine o'clock."

"Nine o'clock," said Fat Eddie.

As the lawyer walked quickly back to his double-parked car he thought, the guy never even asked who got shot.

As Nunzio retreated to his bedroom, he felt a sense of relief. The man would be tied up the next morning and he'd be free to go straight to the doctor's from Mass where he'd have his cast removed and wear only a sling for a few days while his arm returned to full strength.

As most of the members in the big house slept that night, the snake in Nunzio's dream crept back down from the tree, capturing not only the bloated, bullying body of Fat Eddie, but his dark, hateful soul as well.

Chapter Twenty-Nine

Fat Eddie's funeral was attended by hundreds of people, most of whom were eager to find out who would succeed as the head of his family. He had two stepsons; which of them would take charge? The line of cars traveling to the cemetery was so long that traffic lights were held up for two whole cycles letting cars pass through so as not to interrupt the procession.

Louie and his mother attended as if they had known the man only slightly, taking their places at the front but without emotion and strangers to the procedures and ceremony, needing to be told what to do every step of the way. Nunzio remained behind, tortured by the conviction that the man's soul had been sentenced to everlasting damnation.

He had struggled in Confession, unable to relate his inability to redeem the man as some sort of sin. He simply could not find any manner in which his behavior had been sinful.

"But why then, Father," he had demanded, "do I feel wracked with guilt? So much guilt!"

"I suspect it's not guilt," Father Kelly had said. "I suspect it's the frustration of having lost an opportunity. Nunzio, you did nothing wrong. You had no idea he would have a heart attack."

"I know it. I know it."

But later, at the funeral, those conversations came back to Nunzio. The idea of making speeches, praying over his soul, happily now with God as one of the mourners had felt painfully empty. It was as if a space was being carved out in Nunzio's heart. He had not cared a lick for the man. He was vindictive and violent, selfish, and rotten to the core.

But then suddenly, with clarity, Nunzio realized that that was exactly why his death made him so unsettled.

The next day, as the numbers of phone calls increased, and Louie and his mother grew more and more uncomfortable, unable to determine how to move forward, Nunzio put on his newly acquired sling and jumped on a bus to Sacred Heart. He needed to talk to Father, he needed to see Carlo who would be there as promised, but most of all, he needed the Mass.

It was early and probably only the altar servers had arrived, for which Nunzio was grateful. He had hoped for a peaceful place, to pray for calm so that he could collect his thoughts and speak clearly when the time came.

He needed only to ask. Our Lord brought forth a sweet, gentle hush against the outside world as Nunzio knelt in the silence of the vast church. The incense was being prepared and began to perfume the air, hanging in clouds visible by the sunshine streaming in through the brilliantly colored upper windows. Nunzio leaned back, breathing it in as his eyes remained transfixed on the crucifix.

It was then that feeling overwhelmed him. He understood what God wanted of him, and the love pouring forth from God in its rich, blanketing warmth took away his breath. And it took away his frustration, leaving him charged with the love he had received and the knowledge of what his life was to become. He was urgent to get started, to waste not a single minute more.

Even before Mass started, he raced toward the Sacristy, his newly freed arm swinging in its sling. "Father!" he cried. "I was hurting because of that lost opportunity, you were right. I had failed to help that man, but because there are so many others, it's not too late."

"Nunz?" Carlo called from inside. "What's he sayin' Father?"

Father Kelly ushered the urgent Nunzio inside and closed the door, where the three of them sat huddled.

Nunzio and Carlo stared at each other, each waiting for the other to speak.

Finally Father Kelly, unable to hold back chuckled and said, "I think this is what you call a tie."

"Huh?" said Nunzio. "Are you—Carlo, what are you doing back here?"

"I ain't lookin' for doughnuts!" Carlo said, leaning against his cane.

"Well, I planned to talk to Father, you know, privately—"

"Well I can go," Carlo volunteered easily.

"No, no, I'm sayin' this is like a, I just had a, do you remember, Father, when you told us Number 10, I think it was, promises of the Sacred Heart?"

"Yes."

"The Sacred Heart gives the priest the power to touch even the most hardened hearts. That's when I decided for sure to become a priest."

"Yes," Father Kelly said. "I remember your expression when you read that."

"And I may have lost the opportunity with my stepfather, and we can still pray for his soul because we don't know for sure, but maybe there's hope for others like him, and my family, and so many."

"Yes."

Nunzio put his head down. "I'm so blessed," he said, suddenly quiet and peaceful. "I felt all the love, just now, in this church. I don't want to lose that."

There was a long silence, and then Carlo said, "That's what brought me here, too, Nunz. I just told Father almost the exact same thing."

"You want the seminary."

"Yeah."

Smiling, the two young men shook hands.
"We got a long way to go," Carlo said.
"I'm looking forward to every minute of it," Nunzio said.
"I'll be happy to be your formation advisor," Father Kelly said.
Just then, an altar boy came in carrying the incense burner. "Father? Are we still having Mass?" he asked.
"Oh!" said Father jumping up. "First things first!"

Nunzio and Carlo entered the seminary the following fall, affording the tuition through both their diligence and help from Carlo's father. Because of the proximity to Sacred Heart, they were able to stay in close contact with Father Kelly, who had indeed been assigned to serve as their formation advisor. The week before, however, the boys made one last journey past the garage project of Mr. Tucker and Mr. Finn to assess the men's progress. Mr. Tucker sat huddled in his coat, sipping away, and waved to the boys as if they were still in grade school, and the garage project behind him, to the great joy of Nunzio and Carlo, was still nothing but a big hole.

The End.

OTHER BOOKS BY CECE WHITTAKER

The Call to Serve, Book 1 in the Serve Series.

It was 1943 and things were heating up. Hearts broke everywhere as they prayed for the safety of their country. Friends Helen, Annie, Bernice & Joan struggled to hold onto devotion and service in a changing world. Would their loved ones survive the dark and destructive dangers of the War? When Helen's husband Harry and Annie's Sylvester go MIA at the same time, Joan and Bernice are determined to keep their dear friends from losing faith. As Christmas approaches, they are all possessed of a very special kind of hope. But will their prayers be answered? "You will want to read this story over again, just to enjoy the story and the characters." - V.E., Amazon Reviewer.

Love in the Victory Garden, Book 2 in the Serve Series.

June 1944. Joan Foster had no way of knowing when or if fate would reunite her with the maddeningly good-looking Sgt. Dick Thimble, the tall, soft spoken soldier from Washington, D.C. They had scarcely become engaged after knowing each other only weeks, when he had been called away.

The war takes a giant step closer when all of their men are suddenly deployed. Only Bernice's wild surprise is enough to take Annie's mind off Sylvester's MIA status. It's not until Helen comes up with a plan that Joan, Annie, Bernice, and she find the way to reunite them all in the Victory Garden.

Indivisible Hearts, A Christmas Story of Love & Devotion during World War II, Book 3 in the Serve Series.

In 1944, while waiting for the imminent arrival of her war weary fiancé Dick Thimble, Joan Foster is stricken to discover that he may not have survived. Learning nothing further, and with no recourse but to wait and pray, Joan and her friend, Annie, are distracted by the mysterious reappearance of previously pilfered Sacred artifacts. But when a blistering encounter with Gloria, Joan's seemingly ever-present challenger for Dick's affections, is followed by an explosion inside Annie's shop, Joan and friends see life's fragility. Just as it appears that the holidays will be one long lonely affair, good news causes a turnabout and a dazzlingly Joyful Christmas Celebration.

Angels in the Rough Book 4 in the Serve Series.

In a small town in New Jersey in 1944, Annie is set to have that life she has dreamed of for so long. But when Sly inexplicably exits and Joanie's fiancé does not even communicate with her, the girls are immersed in a continuing mystery.

A cozy chronicle of comic mishaps and the lighter side of post-war romance, Angels in the Rough combines the love and fun of friendship with romance--its challenges and its blissful rewards.

Love, Honor & the Cake, Book 5 in the Serve Series

By 1945, Annie diRosa was finally set to realize the future she had longed for; blissful union with heroic and handsome Captain Sly Bapini. While she and her three friends, Joan, Bernice, and Helen would always remain close, she chooses to symbolize their friendship in their shared creation of her wedding cake. To add to the happy occasion, Bernice organizes a choir out of the close friends (which she secretly hopes will provide music at the wedding) even while studying hard to pass her nursing exam.

Helen's husband Harry is on a two-day journey to deliver some cargo, but two days have come and gone while Helen attempts to take it in stride. Joan happily goes to work when scheduled, saving for her own future, and sharing many happy times with her fiancé, Dick Thimble.

All goes well, until an unexpected secret mission to rescue Harry summons Annie's handsome fiancé once again into harm's way. Sly's return is mysteriously delayed, and Annie, who knows nothing about the mission, begins to doubt their future together.

At home, trouble brews as well. When Joan's fiancé Dick takes pains to reveal a dangerous structure at the grocery where he works, his friend and boss Bob and he are buried inside when it suddenly collapses.

Will Dick and Bob survive amidst the gnarled wreckage and debris? Will Sly make it home in time to attend his own wedding? If Harry makes it home in one piece, will he survive Helen's response?

Beyond the Victory Garden Book 6 in the Serve Series

Will Bernice choose the love she has for God over the love she feels for Henry? In 1945, it's a tough decision to make, made tougher by the marriages of her friends. Now, with Laureen expecting a baby, Bernice's heart is deeply conflicted. Maybe, as Annie suggests, they have part-time nuns. Everything crystallizes when Gloria's seemingly eternal need for revenge takes her to the brink, driving her to consider life (only partially dressed) from the top of a 4-story building. Will Fireman Henry make it in time to change her mind? How will the whole incident affect Bernice's choice?

Follow the four women of Abbottsville in Book 6 of the Serve Series as they create their very special Mary's Garden, always in mutual love and respect for each other, and in service to God, transcending life Beyond the Victory Garden.

Glorious Christmas Book 7 in the Serve Series

In 2020, which I have affectionately dubbed "the Year of the Acorn," I think I obliterated a great deal of potential distress by creating a Christmas story for the girls in Abbottsville. Life overall was better for them than it had been, but what's happiness and utter joy if not preceded by nagging uncertainty?

Glorious Christmas brings home some of the feelings these characters suffer for their love of their fellow man, and of course their love for God. In Father Bertrand's case, his happiness is wholly dependent on the happiness or at least non-suffering, of his parishioners, his flock. When he is confronted with the very troubling story of a son missing, not just in action, but generally missing overseas, he endures the mother's pain. His prayer and actions do not cease until he has found what must be the workable solution, even if not happy news for all.

Another character with deep self-examination is Bernice, who struggles to understand the path she is meant to take. Her love for so many good things confounds her and leaves her craving a simpler life, or one with simpler instructions. She relies, as always, on her dear friends Joan, Annie, and Helen to help her see, and like Father Bertrand, seeks and finds peace in prayer.

I had a great deal of fun with Joan in this story, who grows quite a bit, too, with her dear friend Annie, at her side, and Helen to help keep her spirits high. And of course there is a mystery solved, albeit a light one, and some "cops & robbers" as Annie would call it, that turn out quite unexpectedly. I hope this journey into another, possibly more loving period in time, brings you some smiles, joy, and peace. Merry Christmas!

This story is suitable for readers of all ages.

Joyful Hearts Book 8 in the Serve Series

In ***Joyful Hearts***, our characters face very real physical dangers on a variety of fronts. The potential for tragedy is high but is met with their strength of character and as always senses of humor, which ultimately lead them to find the perfect resolutions.

When a tornado touches down in Abbottsville, the quick-thinking heroics of our wonderful former military, lawyer in the making, Dick Thimble proves very handy to have around!

Annie and Sly as well as Laureen and Bob may be experiencing an increase in their tax deduction status in Joyful Hearts, but not before all sorts of comic and sometimes touching potential disasters.

Saving Treasures Book 9 in the Serve Series

When Harry begins working with an old girlfriend, Helen keeps her cool. But not even Harry expects what comes next! In this cozy hybrid set in 1946, Helen, Joan, Annie, and

Bernice struggle to remain close through trying times. With Bernice and Annie having moved away, Joan becomes more dependent on Dick. But what will happen when he is offered a very lucrative position out of town? Will Helen's husband succumb to the vamping of Doris? Is Annie right when she thinks Doris is the new Gloria? And how does Bernice, newly Sister Mary Joseph, help them keep it all together? Read ***Saving Treasures*** for all this and much more!

Making the Grade Book 10 in the Serve Series
Joan Foster is hopelessly in love, and after three patient years of waiting, her wedding is gloriously within sight. There will be pink and white roses, bluebells, carnations, all the beautiful flora she's imagined for so long. Her dearest friends, Annie, Helen, Bernice, and Laureen make her beautiful veil, and make plans for a magnificent reception. But tragedy strikes when Bernice is suddenly stricken and hospitalized, Helen and Annie's husbands, Harry and Sly, disappear overseas, and Laureen's new baby falls perilously ill. With things already on a collision course, when her fiancé Dick comes up with a very practical suggestion, it is all too much for Joan. After all this time, is it curtains for Joan and Dick?

Thank you for your patronage!
If you enjoyed this book, please feel free to
drop me a note at my website,
www.CeceWhittakerStories.com,
or rate me on Amazon.

Yours sincerely,
Cece